# ONLY THE RIVER

ALSO BY ANNE RAEFF

*Winter Kept Us Warm*
*The Jungle Around Us*
*Clara Mondschein's Melancholia*

# ONLY
# THE
# RIVER

*A NOVEL*

ANNE RAEFF

Counterpoint
Berkeley, California

**ONLY THE RIVER**

Library of Congress Cataloging-in-Publication Data

Names: Raeff, Anne, 1959– author.

Title: Only the river : a novel / Anne Raeff.

Description: First hardcover edition. | Berkeley, California :
Counterpoint Press, 2020.

Identifiers: LCCN 2019030703 | ISBN 9781640093348 (hardcover)
| ISBN 9781640093355 (ebook)

Subjects: LCSH: Nicaragua—History—Revolution, 1979—Fiction.
| GSAFD: Historical fiction.

Classification: LCC PS3618.A36 O55 2020 | DDC 813/.6—dc23

LC record available at https://lccn.loc.gov/2019030703

*Jacket design by Donna Cheng*
*Book design by Olenka Burgess*

COUNTERPOINT

2560 Ninth Street, Suite 318

Berkeley, CA 94710

www.counterpointpress.com

Printed in the United States of America

Distributed by Publishers Group West

1 3 5 7 9 10 8 6 4 2

TO THE WORLD'S 25.9 MILLION REFUGEES

*A man takes his sadness down to the river and throws it in the river*
*But then he's still left*
*with the river. A man takes his sadness and throws it away*
*but then he's still left with his hands.*

—**RICHARD SIKEN,** *Crush*

# PART I

# CHAPTER 1

WHEN LILIANA CAME TO VISIT, OR RATHER WHEN SHE ARRIVED unannounced with her heartache and unhappiness, Pepa did not tell her there was something growing inside her, for she could not bear to add sorrow to sorrow. On the journey from San Francisco to New York, Liliana had eaten only raw carrots and nuts, and she did not sleep, except for a few hours here and there at rest areas. For the first few hours after she arrived, Liliana could not speak. When she tried to form words, nothing came out.

It was not until Pepa put on one of the old 78s from Nicaragua that she used to play for Liliana and William when they were sick and could not sleep that Liliana was finally able to tell her mother what happened, why she had abandoned everything, her students, her house that had been her and Irene's house—she could only whisper Irene's name. Pepa wanted to rage at Irene, who had been part of the family all these twenty years, who had spent an entire summer, not even a year after they got together, in New York helping Liliana and Pepa take care of Oskar when he was withering away from ALS. It was Irene who was strong enough to pick him up when he fell. It was Irene who had convinced him that he needed a wheelchair, Irene who bathed him, Irene to whom he dictated his last letters. The three of them lay on the floor together keeping vigil on that last night, listening to Oskar's dying breaths until the breaths finally stopped just before dawn. But she knew it wouldn't do any good to be angry. Anger was not what Liliana needed. Still, how could Irene have done it, left Liliana for a man, a hairy, wolfish-looking man? Liliana insisted on showing her a photograph of him on the computer, insisted on pointing out his many professional accomplishments, going through them all one by one despite Pepa's protestations. So, because she did not know how to comfort her, she prepared Liliana's favorite meal, *gallo pinto* and fried plantains, even though Liliana said that she didn't want to eat, that eating reminded her of Irene. "I have some cashews left in my bag," she said, but when Pepa brought the food to the table, Liliana ate, and Pepa ate, too, though she was not hungry, was rarely hungry anymore now that this thing was growing inside her.

At first she tried not to give it any attention, but Pepa could feel it taking root as she had felt each of her children taking root, staking their claim, and after a few months she accepted its presence, and it was as if it were a part of her like her heart and her liver, like her womb. Sometimes she almost forgot it was there, but then she would wake up in the night and she would have to lie completely still, breathing in and out until the pain subsided to just a dull aching. Sometimes she went a week, even two without pain. It shifted like a child shifts in the womb, taking the pressure off for a while.

In order to take her mind off this thing that was growing inside her, she threw herself into her work at her bookstore, La Librería Nuevo Mundo. Before, she had begun to consider cutting down on her hours, coming in later or leaving earlier, taking one of the slower days off. She was almost eighty-five, after all, and Humberto could manage fine without her, but then what would she do except worry, focus on every twinge of pain? And what would she tell Humberto? What would he tell the customers when they asked where she was? They would want to send her cards with earnest messages wishing her a speedy recovery. A recovery from what? Perhaps, if she just kept doing what she had always done, she sometimes allowed herself to think, it would disappear on its own, but she was always angry with herself after such thoughts, for hoping for miracles, for her weakness. Her parents would have chosen surgery, the precision of the scalpel. She dreamt that they were cutting her open, reaching in. Her mother held it in her hands like an offering for her to see. She awoke from these dreams neither shaken nor frightened, but determined to let it grow until there was no going back.

At some point she would have to do something. When it came to that, she would know. She always did. She was sure she didn't want doctors and tests and drugs, the long decline, the constant focus on hope, which was one of the reasons she sent Liliana to Nicaragua—by the time Liliana returned, it would be too late to do anything. What she had not expected was that once Liliana was in Nicaragua, Pepa awoke every morning expecting news, and this, she understood, was also a form of hope, a new hope that had been buried twenty-five years ago, buried in twelve-hour days so that there was no energy left to think of the photograph of her son, William, grinning, holding the machine gun, with the ammunition strip draped around his neck like a shawl. Pepa had given her daughter strict orders not to call and to email no more than once a week, just so she had a sense of where she was, and Liliana followed her instructions, though now Pepa wished she wouldn't. Of course she could tell her that she changed her mind, that she wanted to know the details of her journey, but she did not know what she feared more, that Liliana would learn the details of William's death or that she would find out nothing. Still, she was sure of one thing—it comforted her to imagine Liliana in Nicaragua. It was almost as if she were there, too, closer to William, and this made her feel stronger and the pain less frequent, though she knew it was just an illusion.

Pepa wondered where Liliana was now. The last email was just this: *On my way to Juigalpa. More later.* It was in the mountains outside Juigalpa, a Sandinista stronghold, where, twenty-five years ago in 1982, William died, though the time and place were never fully confirmed. All they knew was contained in a letter from a soldier named Carolina and in the report prepared by the American Embassy in Managua, though it very clearly stated that given what they called the rebellion, they could not fully corroborate the details of his death. After that report they heard nothing more until, a year after William's death, Carolina wrote again, informing them that the Sandinista government was erecting a mausoleum in Juigalpa in his honor. She wanted them to come for the memorial. "It would be an honor to have you," she wrote, but they could not bear to go. Months later they received the last communication from her—two photographs, one of the mausoleum and the other of the inscription: *William*, it said, no surname, only William, *héroe de la revolución*, and the date of his death: *28 de julio de 1982.*

When William went to Nicaragua to defend the revolution, they didn't hear from him for weeks at a time, so they forced themselves not to worry. Perhaps they should have worried more, but what good would that have done? The results would have been the same. What they should have done was not let him go, but how could they have stopped him? "We did not raise you to fight," Oskar told his son. Oskar knew better than to speak the names of his first son and daughter killed with his first wife in Birkenau. The Ghost Children, William called them once in a fit of rage. It was at dinner, and when William muttered those words—in no more than a whisper, barely audible, yet as clear and final as a gunshot—Oskar put down his knife and fork and got up without speaking, without looking at them, left Pepa there with William's anger, so she followed Oskar to the bedroom, and they lay on their bed in the dark and listened to Bach's unaccompanied cello suites over and over until morning. When they finally emerged from their bedroom, William and Liliana had already left for school. The table was cleared, the dishes washed, the coffee made, so they ate breakfast and got dressed and went to the bookstore as they always did.

When William left for Nicaragua, Pepa almost told Oskar about Guillermo. It was something she could give him, she thought, this piece of herself from long ago that she had not wanted to give up. She wanted to tell him what she had lost, so that he could understand that she loved him more than what she had lost, more than their son who had gone off to kill or die or both. But she said nothing. And then, when—in the summer of 1982 just months after William had stormed out of their lives—they received the letter from Carolina announcing his death, it was too late, for her confession would only have taken away from mourning William, who was dead.

Perhaps, she thought, she could have gone with Liliana to Nicaragua, but she had no way of knowing how fast this thing was growing, how quickly her decline would be, and she never liked being away from the bookstore, from home. She hadn't returned to Nicaragua since her arrival in New York in 1942, and she had only left Manhattan twice, first to visit her brother Karl in California and second when they went to Israel, Oskar's dream not hers, but she did not regret going, crying at the Wailing Wall, standing on the top of Masada, looking out at the desert. She never thought she would love the desert for its absence of water in the same way that she had loved the Río San Juan in El Castillo.

Going with Liliana to Nicaragua could have been a good way to begin handing over the store to Humberto, but there was no point rushing into things. It would be his soon enough. Though Liliana had grown up in La Librería Nuevo Mundo helping her parents, she never had shown any interest in shopkeeping, and Pepa didn't want to burden her with the store after she was gone. She and Humberto had already signed the papers. Pepa had planned on telling Liliana, but then after Irene left, Liliana got it into her head that she was going to abandon teaching, perhaps stay in New York, work in the bookstore. She said she was going to write poetry, but wallowing, Pepa knew, did not lead to poetry. It led, simply, to more wallowing, and this was another reason she sent her to Nicaragua, though she did not phrase it that way. "A trip will do you good" was how she put it.

Liliana was reluctant at first. "It's been too long. William died twenty-five years ago, we should have gone then, but . . ."

"But we didn't," Pepa said. She paused. "You will find out something, and you will go to El Castillo, to the river. That is where the poems are."

"And if I say no?"

"I thought that with the years my sorrow would shrivel up, but it has only grown," Pepa said. "I thought your father was right, that there was no reason to know anything more, that only his death mattered, but I realize now that the details of his death were part of his life. I need to know something, anything, Liliana. Otherwise, I can't be sure that he was ever even alive."

"Maybe you should go. You always said that before you . . . you always said you would go back someday, back to El Castillo and the river."

"I should have gone long ago when Carolina invited us to the convocation of the mausoleum, but I couldn't imagine listening to them making speeches in his honor, singing songs about heroes and revolution. My grief was still so full of anger, and then your father got sick and after he died, I had to turn away from all of it, all that dreadful sorrow, or I would not have been able to go on."

"We could go together," Liliana said, embracing Pepa, letting herself sink into her mother's warmth, willing herself not to cry because she knew that if she began to cry she would be crying not about William but about Irene, and that would be a form of betrayal, too.

"I can't," Pepa said. She got up from the sofa, walked to the window, and looked out at the rain, coming down harder now, it seemed, than just moments ago. She opened the window, lifted it up as high as it would go to let the sound of the rain fill the room. She breathed in deep. "I can't smell it," she said.

"I know," Liliana said, for this was one of Pepa's favorite topics—how the Hudson River had no smell and the rain in New York was hardly audible, unlike El Castillo.

"In El Castillo, you can smell the river in the bedsheets, and the sound of rain on the tin roof overpowers the human voice."

"I know," Liliana said again.

"Knowledge is not the same thing as experience," Pepa said as she always did when Liliana and William begged her to tell them about the river. "Take us there. Take us to El Castillo," they would say, and Pepa would begin as she did now.

"Close your eyes," Pepa said, switching to Spanish. "Can you hear the motor of the *lancha*?"

Liliana nodded. She could hear it now, the motor of the *lancha* getting closer and closer. Sometimes when she and William were lying on the floor in the living room, when the air was thick and still and there wasn't even the memory of a breeze coming off the Hudson, she was able to feel a warm rain falling on her, and she would open her mouth to let the water flow in.

"What are you doing?" William would ask.

"I'm drinking the rain," she would say.

"What does it taste like?"

"It tastes like mangoes. What are you doing?"

"I'm watching the monkeys."

"What are they doing?"

"Laughing."

"Shush," their mother would say. "If you talk too much it will all disappear."

"Put your hand in the river. It's warm. Can you smell it?" Pepa said now.

"Yes," Liliana nodded as she had done many times before as a child.

"Listen to the motor and the lapping of the water against the *lancha*. There on the right bank are some herons sunning themselves. Now you are coming around the bend. Soon you will see the Spanish fortress on top of the hill. It's so big the houses of the village look like toys in comparison. Look at the houses, all those colors. Ours is pink, but you can't see it from the river. Can you hear the falls? The *lancha* is approaching the dock now. There is Don Solano's shop and there is the church. Don't take your hand out of the river, not until you're there, not until the *lancha* has pulled into the dock and the driver cuts the motor. Sleep," she said. "You are safe now," Pepa whispered as she did when they were children. "Sleep."

# CHAPTER 2

Don Solano, the pharmacist who was not really a pharmacist, met them at the dock. He brought with him six men to carry their belongings, though there were only four suitcases, which, in addition to the medical reference books and family silverware, held mostly wool clothes from Vienna, which Pepa's parents had packed hoping that they would end up in Argentina or Uruguay, somewhere with snow and newspapers and electricity.

"We might as well be in the Amazon," Pepa's mother said when they arrived, not as a criticism but as a statement of fact. All around, along the banks of the river and in the trees, giant birds were watching them. High above on top of the hill, above the houses that clung to the river's shore, the ruins of the Spanish fortress loomed, dark and heavy yet comforting, and she felt as if it were speaking to her. *Come, my child. You are safe now*, it called.

When the launch was firmly tied to the dock, Don Solano helped them off the boat, though they were all capable of getting off by themselves. They had come a long way from Vienna without anyone helping them. But they did not want to appear ungracious, for they were indeed grateful that they were wanted here and needed, so they let Don Solano help them.

"*Bienvenidos a El Castillo*," he said, indicating the muddy path that led from the river up to the town, and the four of them, Pepa and her parents and her brother Karl, proceeded as if they had spent their whole lives walking on muddy paths. Don Solano and the six men with their four suitcases followed.

They emerged onto the only street of the town, which was really nothing more than a wider muddy path lined with colorful wooden houses on stilts. Don Solano pointed to his pharmacy, which was not really a pharmacy but a *pulpería*, a general store, where one could buy groceries and other basic necessities such as aspirin, a variety of salves and balms, and questionable medical potions.

When they first arrived in Managua four months earlier in October of 1938, they thought that *pulperías* were stores where one could buy *pulpo*. They had learned the word for octopus from the long list of basic vocabulary in the Spanish grammar and dictionary that they had studied on the transatlantic crossing from Europe to Panama. When Pepa learned that the *pulperías* sold nothing more exotic than cabbage and Vicks VapoRub, she was disappointed. She had liked the idea of octopus as a staple, of a powerful sea creature being the source of their daily nutrition, replacing schnitzel and potatoes and cucumber salad, food that had betrayed them, like everything else she had known.

In the few minutes it had taken to disembark and walk up the path to the main street, the sky had gone from blue to black, and now it began to rain. "Come," Don Solano said, and they all ran across the street to take shelter in the church. As soon as they were inside the rain broke loose, pounding down on the tin roof, drowning out Don Solano's voice so that even if they had understood more than the most rudimentary Spanish, they would not have been able to make out what he was saying.

"Sit," Don Solano said, so they sat down in the last pew. In front of them was Jesus, splayed out on the cross, eyes closed, head dropped to the side. Don Solano stopped talking. The rain continued to beat on the tin roof. A slight, warm breeze came through the door.

The trip from San Carlos had taken all day, and it seemed to Pepa that it both took months and went by in a matter of seconds, that the river was at once infinite and miniscule, the center of life and a footnote in history, and she wanted to go outside and stand in the rain, let the water flow over her as the river flowed over rocks.

When the rain stopped, they went back outside where the air was thick with steam and smelled of earth and wet wood. They continued on to the end of the main path and headed up the hill away from the river, past more houses, smaller and more primitive than the ones on the main street. Chickens and pigs wandered about. An unaccompanied horse went by. They came to the end of the path. "This is your house," Don Solano said. The horse that had passed them before stood in front of it, waiting. It stood still as they walked into the house, which, like all the others they had seen, was on stilts and made of wood with a red tin roof. The sun shone in through the cracks between the walls. But it was clean. The men had already left the suitcases in the center of the main room. The suitcases looked, Pepa thought, like abandoned children, clinging together, waiting for their parents to return to them. In the main room was a table with four chairs. In the second room were a double bed and two single beds with mosquito netting hanging from the ceiling.

"Come," Don Solano said, and they followed him to the back. "The kitchen," he said, pointing to a stack of wood, a stove, and a cement sink. "Food," he said, opening up a cabinet. Inside it were a flat of eggs, a few heads of cabbage, rice, and beans. On the sink were a half a dozen mangoes. "From the tree," Don Solano said, pointing to a tree in the yard. "Come," he said again, and they followed him outside. Next to the mango tree was the bathroom—a shack with a squat toilet and a red plastic bucket. Next to the shack was a basin, also red, and a faucet.

On the other side of the mango tree was another house. "*La clínica*," Don Solano said, smiling proudly. "*La clínica*," he said again, starting back toward the house.

"*La clínica*," Pepa's father repeated. "Let us take a look."

Don Solano watched them walk toward the clinic, his hands twitching at his side like the wings of a dying bird. Then he hurried to join them. The clinic was empty, devoid even of chairs or an examination table. In the corner by the door that led to the outside sink was a frog. Karl ran toward it, and it remained still, watching until the moment when Karl reached down to grab it. It jumped then and disappeared through the window.

Pepa's father's uncle, who had fled conscription at the beginning of World War I and ended up a wealthy businessman trading in bananas and rubber, had arranged the visas that got them out of Europe and to Managua, where they had stayed for three months as his guests while he was talking with important people on their behalf. When they first arrived, the uncle had wanted to make an investment in a private practice for her parents in the capital, but in Vienna her parents had been working on what they called "the war against polio" and so they were not interested in such a sinecure. If they were going to be in exile, they might as well fight a real battle, they said. They always referred to medicine as a battle, as if microbes and disease were forces of evil akin to Hitler and the Nazis. Yellow fever, the uncle said, was the biggest challenge. "Then we will go where the yellow fever is," Pepa's parents said, but it was not so simple.

They wanted to leave Managua immediately, but there were documents to be prepared and approved and signed, important people to be convinced. In order to get the approval for the project, military officers, colonels and generals, members of the government and their wives had to be invited and fed and kept happy with rum and cigars, and Pepa's parents had to drink rum with these guests and smile when the uncle proclaimed that with their help Nicaragua could be the first country in Latin America to eradicate yellow fever. "Imagine the honor," he said, "the glory," and they raised their glasses and toasted to a yellow fever–free Nicaragua.

In Vienna, Pepa's parents rose well before dawn, but at their uncle's house they often did not rise until lunchtime. Perhaps, Pepa thought, they were making up for all the lost hours of sleep accumulated over the years. Perhaps they could not bear to think about what they had left behind. In the afternoon when the sun was at its hottest, they also slept, so Pepa had to entertain herself and Karl on her own. They spent their days in their uncle's pool. Karl also chased lizards, but after a while he got so good at capturing them that it became boring, so they stuck to the pool. Three times a week a tutor came to give them Spanish lessons. The tutor was not a good teacher, and Pepa's parents gave up on him, saying that they preferred to study on their own, which Pepa never saw them doing. Perhaps, she thought, they studied in bed. Still, they insisted that she and Karl continue the classes, so they did, though most of the time they had no idea what the tutor was saying, and if they told him that they did not understand, he shook his head and called them imbeciles. Sometimes the tutor fell asleep during their lessons. In Managua it seemed that everyone was falling asleep or sleeping too late and that only she and Karl were interested enough in the world to stay awake.

Once the government agreed to the yellow fever project, Pepa's parents went to the Ministry of Health to sign documents and were asked to make a list of the supplies that they would need for the clinic. The official made it clear that they would only be able to supply the basics. "We are a poor country," he kept repeating. "Within reason, please." When they handed him the list, the official stamped it front and back and assured them that everything would be set up by the time they arrived in El Castillo.

Thus, despite their experiences in Managua, despite the red tape and the waiting and the long line of officials, they still expected the supplies to be delivered on time.

"Where are the supplies?" they asked now as they stood in the bare clinic. "They promised."

Don Solano laughed, patted Pepa's father on the back. "Welcome to Nicaragua," he said. "But do not worry. The supplies will come. We must have faith," and since there was nothing for them to do at the clinic, nothing to examine, no boxes to be opened or vials to be counted, they returned to the house, where they thanked Don Solano for his help and Don Solano shook each of their hands vigorously, saying "*bienvenidos*," many more times than necessary.

The day after their arrival, four patients, an old woman and her three grown daughters, came to the clinic. At first Pepa's parents tried to turn them away. They showed them the empty rooms and cabinets and said they were sorry, but the woman and her daughters would not leave, so her parents examined their eyes and ears, listened to their hearts, took their pulses. They recorded everything. The next day people brought chairs for the waiting room and a cot so that the patients could be examined properly, though her parents had to kneel on the floor in order to do so. On the third day, her parents lanced a boil the size of an orange that had grown in a young woman's armpit. Each day Pepa and Karl were sent to the *pulpería* to ask about the status of the supplies even though they all knew that Don Solano had no power whatsoever over the arrival of the shipment. Each day his answer was the same: "Soon."

On their sixteenth day in El Castillo, the supplies for the clinic finally arrived, after Pepa had already bought chickens from the market women, after she had learned to soak the beans before cooking them, after the neighbor's son showed her how to knock mangoes from the tree with a stick as high as their house and how to chop wood and refill the kerosene lamps, after she learned that they were not the only foreigners in El Castillo.

It was at the *pulpería* that she first met the Germans. The Germans did not usually stop at the *pulpería* since they had an arrangement with someone in San Carlos to bring them supplies once a week. The only time they came to town was to catch the *lancha* to San Carlos. What they did there no one knew, though Don Solano was sure there were women involved.

The day she met the Germans she and Karl were helping out at the *pulpería*, which is what they often did in the early days before the yellow fever outbreak, before Guillermo, before she befriended the Germans and began reading their books. It was a way to pass the time after the marketing and housework was done. It was good for their Spanish, and Don Solano always gave them coconut candy. When the Germans walked into the *pulpería*, Don Solano stood up and went to greet them at the door. "*Bienvenidos,*" he said, extending his hand, which they each shook with enthusiasm. They wore identical canvas rucksacks and were exactly the same height. One of them, the younger one, had a sinewy build like someone who would be good at climbing trees, Pepa thought, and the other had wide shoulders and thick thighs. Pepa was not good at judging the ages of adults, but they seemed younger than her parents though not too much younger. The men walked around the shop, touching things distractedly.

"Hello," Pepa said to them, annoyed that they had not greeted her and Karl as Don Solano's other customers always did.

"Hello," the younger one said, smiling.

"*¿Qué buscan los señores?*" Pepa said, as Don Solano had taught her to do.

"Nothing, really," the younger man replied. "We are waiting for the launch to San Carlos." He paused. "You are new to El Castillo?"

"Yes," Pepa said. "We have been here for only two weeks."

"I see," he said. He paused, took a step forward, and spoke in German. "Will you be staying for a long time?"

"It depends on the war," Pepa answered.

"Ah yes, the war," he said.

"And you?" Pepa asked.

"We are here to stay," the young man said. "Come visit us," he added before heading out the door. His companion followed, smiling at her and waving heartily, as if he would miss her when he was gone.

Don Solano was not able to tell her much about the Germans. They had built a big house at the edge of town, bigger, he said, than the church. They had ordered tiles from the capital, and the boats that brought the tiles had been so weighed down it was a miracle they didn't sink. Why they had come and why they stayed no one knew. In the town there were those who believed they had committed a terrible crime and those who believed they had been falsely accused of a terrible crime. Don Solano was in the first group. Innocent people do not flee, he said, which Pepa knew to be false, but she did not argue with Don Solano. She wondered whether the townspeople were already inventing tales about them, about what crimes her parents had committed on the other side of the world.

Pepa's parents were not as disturbed by the Germans' presence as she thought they would be, nor did they seem interested in why they were in El Castillo. "It's best not to have anything to do with them" was all they said. Still, despite her distrust of Germans, Pepa did not feel these men were dangerous. On the contrary, there was something soft about them, though they were muscular and broadshouldered and brown from the sun.

Pepa did not visit the Germans until weeks later, not because she was afraid to go against her parents' wishes but because there were other things that interested her more. Pepa had never paid much attention to animals in Vienna. She was not the sort of child who ran after dogs or pigeons or marveled at squirrels nibbling acorns in the park. Wild animals she knew about only from fairy tales. But in El Castillo human sounds were overpowered by the cacophony of insects and birds screeching and monkeys howling, and the constant rustling of trees, so she spent most of her time looking for the sources of these noises, keeping her eye out for parrots, which Don Solano said were almost in every tree, and watching for monkeys, but it was as if they were taunting her, and the harder she looked the more elusive they seemed to be. It wasn't until after the supplies came and Pepa had bought the chickens from the lady in the market and learned how to grab their eggs without getting pecked that the animals starting coming out of hiding, though she knew, of course, that it was she who was slowly learning to see her surroundings as they were, had always been long before she arrived.

Not long after the monkeys started coming right up to the house and peering in through the windows, yellow fever struck farther down the Río San Juan. "Don't forget to feed the chickens," her parents told her when they left for the jungle to take care of the yellow fever victims. As if she could forget such a thing. Wasn't she the one who took care of them, who collected the eggs, swept up the droppings, slit their throats with the scalpel her father had given her for this very purpose? If she forgot to feed the chickens, they would come pecking at the back door, would jump onto the kitchen windowsill and poke their beaks between the louvers. How could she possibly forget to feed the chickens?

They had been her idea, after all. Her parents had not approved at first. "What do we know about keeping chickens?" they said. They seemed already to have forgotten that in the beginning they had not known any of it. They had not known how to cook beans, had not known the taste of fried bananas or the Spanish word for rice, had not known how to hang mosquito netting or the sound of monkeys screaming in the night or that you had to bribe the health inspectors as well as hide the water cistern when they came around every so often looking for what they called "standing water."

"What do they expect us to do, live without water?" her father asked when the inspectors threatened to turn the cistern upside down. Of course he understood the danger of standing water. It was his job to eradicate malaria, after all, but one could not live without water.

Pepa smiled and spoke to the inspectors, using the few words of Spanish that she knew. "Please," she said, "can I offer you some coffee?" When she served them the coffee in the porcelain cups they had brought with them from Vienna, she set a few coins in each saucer. The inspectors thanked her profusely for the coffee, which they said was the best they'd ever had. They even bowed as they left, and Pepa's father smiled and bowed, also. After that, the inspectors were her responsibility too, like the chickens.

When her parents left for the jungle, they did not know how long they would be gone. Don Solano had offered to take in Pepa and Kurt while they were away, but they did not accept his offer. At fourteen, Pepa was old enough to handle the house, to watch after her brother.

"But won't they be afraid to stay in the house alone?" Don Solano asked. It was Sunday afternoon and, as they did every Sunday, they were dining with the pharmacist.

"They will not be afraid," Pepa's father said very sternly. "We will not be afraid again," he added. "Right?" he asked, turning to Pepa.

"I am not afraid," she replied.

"If they need anything, anything at all, I am here," Don Solano said.

On the evening of the first day of her parents' absence, Don Solano knocked on the door. She and Kurt were doing their lessons, their books spread out on the dining room table. Pepa prepared coffee and brought it to the table.

"Your parents are very brave to go to the jungle," he said.

"It is their duty as doctors to help people," Pepa told him.

"But it is very dangerous," Don Solano said.

"Life is dangerous," Pepa replied.

"I suppose it is," he said, laughing. "Well, promise you will let me know if you need something."

"I promise," Pepa said, but she could not imagine what she would possibly need from Don Solano besides the things he sold in the *pulpería*, which she could go and buy like everyone else.

Just before her parents left, they told her again not to go near the Germans. "What if we see them in town? Wouldn't it be impolite not to greet them?" Pepa asked.

"If you see them, turn and walk in the other direction," her mother instructed.

"That would still be impolite," Pepa said.

"It doesn't matter. Politeness is not always a virtue," her mother answered.

Pepa decided to call on the Germans two weeks after her parents left, on the morning of her fourteenth birthday, which went unmarked and uncelebrated except for this visit. She left Karl, who did not acknowledge her birthday and did not know how to keep secrets, with the neighbors and walked out to the house alone.

The Germans were standing in their doorway when Pepa

arrived, as if they had been expecting her. "Welcome," they said, showing her in.

"Thank you," Pepa said, holding out the bag of mangoes she brought for them.

The younger man took the bag from her and peered inside. "Ah, mangoes," he said.

The floors of the house, Pepa noticed, were made of the same rough wooden planks as theirs. Perhaps, she thought, the tiles had been used in the other rooms, or perhaps, and this was more likely, there had never been any tiles at all. Perhaps it was one of those things that Don Solano made up or imagined like the terrible crimes he believed they committed. But the house was, indeed, as big as the church, bigger perhaps, and actually consisted of two houses connected by a covered walkway, like an aboveground tunnel, she thought. They led her into the main room, which was simply furnished with a wooden sofa and three wooden armchairs. In the corner near the kitchen was a table with four chairs. Pepa had imagined that the house would be lavish like the apartments of her parents' friends in Vienna, with cushioned couches and oriental rugs, lamps made out of Chinese vases, but there were no curtains on the windows, no rugs, no paintings on the walls, for there was no room for paintings as all the walls were lined with bookshelves. The books were organized according to size, with the taller books on the bottom shelves and the smallest editions on the top ones. She wondered whether Don Solano knew about the books. Probably not, or he would have told her. The house had a sweet, familiar smell that she couldn't quite place. It was something from her life before they crossed the ocean.

The younger man handled the introductions, giving only their first names. Pepa wondered if this was because they did not want anyone to know their full names. "I am Georg and this is my friend Friedrich."

"Pepa," she said.

"Please, have a seat," Georg said, pointing to the armchairs. Pepa sat, and Friedrich sat in the chair next to hers. "I'll just be a moment," Georg said, and he left the room.

"So many books," Pepa said.

Friedrich smiled.

After that they waited in silence. Pepa concentrated on a lizard immobile on the wall across from her. Outside in the tree nearest the house there was a flutter of activity, and a leaf fell to the ground. "Monkeys," Pepa said, as if she had been living with monkeys her whole life.

Friedrich nodded. "Have you seen a jaguar yet?" he asked.

"Yes," Pepa lied.

"Were you afraid?"

"No. It heard me approaching and ran away. I only glimpsed it through the trees."

"It could have been something else."

"It had spots," Pepa said, and Friedrich smiled.

Georg came in carrying a tray, upon which were three clay mugs. "Please," he said, handing her a mug. She took the mug and held it up to her nose, breathing in deeply. Chocolate, of course. That was the smell. How could she have forgotten? "We grow the cacao ourselves," Georg said, setting the tray down.

Pepa took a sip.

"Is it sweet enough?" Georg asked.

She nodded.

"Pepa tells me that she has seen a jaguar," Friedrich said, setting his mug down on the floor beside him.

"But have you seen a sloth?" Georg asked.

"No, not yet," Pepa said.

"You have to go deep into the jungle to see them. We can take you sometime if you'd like," Friedrich said.

"I would like that." She wanted to tell them she had lied about the jaguar and that she was not in the habit of lying. She wanted to tell them she was to be trusted, that whatever their secret was, it was safe with her, but it was too late. She had already lied and they knew it.

"You have a lot of books," she said. "Did you have them shipped all the way from Germany?"

"Yes," Georg said. "It took six months."

"We only had four suitcases." She paused. "They took everything else."

"A terrible thing," Friedrich said. "A terrible thing. Did you bring any books with you at all?"

"We brought our school books and medical books. My parents are doctors."

"Yes, we know," Georg said. "Nothing else, not poetry even?"

"There wasn't room," Pepa said.

"Poetry takes up so little space," Georg said, getting up and walking to the bookshelf. He took down a volume from one of the top shelves. "Take this," he said, handing it to her. "When you are finished with it, I will lend you another. That way we are assured you will visit us again."

"Thank you," Pepa said. She opened it up. It smelled of rain.

"*The Odyssey*. You probably read it in school," Friedrich said.

"We read parts of it, but not the whole thing," Pepa said. "I don't remember much about it, though."

"Of course not. You can't remember someone's face or recognize it again if all you've seen is the nose or the mouth, even if all you've seen are the eyes. It will be different now that you have been on your own odyssey."

"I haven't read a real book since we left Vienna," she said, wondering why during those long months in Managua when her parents were sleeping she never thought of asking for a book. She was so fond of reading in Vienna and spent many a long winter afternoon curled up on the sofa with a book.

"And how long ago was that?" Georg asked.

"It will be six months next week," Pepa said.

"I would sooner die than go a day without reading," Friedrich said.

"When we were waiting for the books to arrive, we learned the six books we had brought with us by heart. Sometimes at night after dinner, we still practice reciting them so that we don't forget. It was such an undertaking that we don't want it to go to waste. It would be like losing six months of our lives," Georg said.

"Does that mean that everything that is forgotten is wasted?" Pepa asked.

"Perhaps," Friedrich said. "How can we know whether something even existed if there is no one to remember it?"

"We don't know the details about all the people who came before us, but we know they existed," Pepa said.

"But when you die, don't you want there to be something left so that people will remember you and what you have done?" Friedrich asked.

"When I am dead, I will not know whether I am remembered or forgotten. It will be as if I had never been born." Before they had to leave, when life was about nothing more than school excursions to the Vienna woods and sleep and lunch and dinner and snow, Pepa spent quite a bit of time thinking about her own mortality. In fact, at night when she was trying to fall asleep, she could not stop herself from imagining the moment of her death, when she would pass from consciousness to nonexistence, to nothingness, to oblivion. She tried to stop herself from thinking about it. She practiced adding large numbers in her head and she sang herself lullabies, but the negation of everything she had ever done or thought or dreamed always won out, and her heart would beat faster and she would not be able to fall asleep until dawn.

But when the real danger came, when they started taking people away and smashing store windows, she had important things to do like clean and cook and take care of Karl after her parents lost their jobs at the hospital and Herta had to be let go and her parents left for Frankfurt to get their passports and visas. Then she fell asleep as soon as she turned off the light and slept through the night without dreams.

"If you want to be remembered, what are you doing here, so far away in El Castillo?" she asked.

"Far away from what? From what is important, from war?" Friedrich said. "But we're not. You think you are a long way from all that, but you are just as close as you were before." He smiled, as if he had won a game of cards. "You didn't see that jaguar, did you?"

"No," Pepa said, looking down at *The Odyssey* in her lap.

Neither Georg nor Friedrich responded. Perhaps they were waiting for her to explain or apologize for lying, but she didn't feel that her lie required an apology, for they had told her nothing of themselves, and wasn't that another form of lying?

"It's getting late," Pepa said without looking up at them. The mosquitoes were already biting. She felt them lingering on her ankles and feet, but she didn't shoo them away. Maybe I will get malaria or yellow fever, she thought. "I have to get back to make dinner."

"Should we walk you home?" Georg asked.

"No, please, I know the way," Pepa said, setting *The Odyssey* on the floor next to her empty mug.

"You don't want to read the book?" Georg asked. He seemed terribly disappointed, as if he himself had written it.

"Of course, if it's still okay," Pepa said.

"Only if you want to," Georg said.

Pepa picked up the book and stood. "Thank you," she said.

Georg and Friedrich walked her to the door. "Thank you for the mangoes," they said.

As she walked down the path away from their house, she could feel them watching her from the doorway. "Good-bye," they called after her. She turned around and waved. They were holding hands.

When her parents returned from the jungle, their clothes caked in red mud, their breaths smelling of hunger, Pepa washed their clothes, stomping and rinsing them over and over again, the water flowing red like blood. Then she made a twelve-egg omelet, for the protein, and fed them mounds of rice and fried bananas. After the meal, which they ate dutifully and in silence, they slept for twenty-four hours straight.

Her parents began sleeping in the clinic. They had painted it a soothing blue like the eyes of an Alaskan husky, like winter. The house, they said, had a strange odor, something sweet that kept them up at night, gave them headaches. Pepa understood, however, that it was not about the smell. Rather, at night, when there was time to think, to remember their careers at the best hospital in Vienna, they needed not a soft mattress to lie upon or the sound of their children breathing in the next room but the certainty of steel instruments and the clean smell of alcohol. "We are just on the other side of the patio if you need us," her father said every night before they retired to the clinic, where they spent the evenings listening to the radio, waiting for scraps of news about the war.

"I am not afraid," Pepa said.

They were far from the dangers of Europe now, as far as one could be. At night they kept the louvers open just a crack, just enough to let the breeze in and keep the monkeys out. The monkeys were the only danger. They could destroy the house in a few minutes—pull all the dishes from the shelves, smash them on the cool tile floor, rip the sheets from the bed, urinate on the walls.

In the market, the cabbage woman did not even know there was a war on. "What are they fighting about?" she asked Pepa, and Pepa did not know how to answer her.

"They are fighting over Europe," she said, and the woman smiled.

"They will regret it in the end," the woman said. "They always do."

At night, after Kurt had gone to sleep, she lay in her dark room listening to the sounds of the night—insects, monkeys, the rain. She imagined her parents lying on the jungle floor burning up with fever, clutching at the red earth, gasping for breath. She made herself look into their wide-open dead eyes. She lay there perfectly still, arms at her side, palms up, her heart beating slowly as if she were asleep. She would never be afraid again. That is what she learned when her parents went to where the yellow fever was.

Pepa began going out at night. She walked all the way to the edge of town to where the jungle began. She walked into the jungle, pulling the branches apart as she went. Each time she went farther and farther, but always she found her way out. She could sense the path, sense which branches she had touched before, and, always, she found herself back out on the dirt path that led to the town and the river. When she had mastered the jungle and no longer thought about the possibility of getting lost in its rubbery shadows, she began spending her evenings, after she finished her lessons, on the church steps. On Friday and Saturday nights she went to the plaza where the *banda* played and people danced and she watched, counting the steps, counting the beats. Gradually she moved closer and closer to the dancers. Every night she came a little closer until she stood among the young women who were waiting to be asked to dance, and on the second night, a somber young man approached her. "I am Guillermo and you are the doctors' daughter, no?"

"Yes," she said, and he led her to where the people were dancing.

That first night they did not speak again until after the *banda* stopped playing. Pepa concentrated on the music and on Guillermo's hand pressed against her back. When the members of the *banda* had put away their instruments and the dancers had dispersed, Guillermo wanted to walk her home, but Pepa said that she liked walking by herself.

"You are not afraid?" he asked.

"Are you afraid?" she asked.

"No, of course not," he said.

"You see, there is nothing to be afraid of," she said, and she began walking away toward her house. That is how it started with Guillermo.

The next night Guillermo was waiting for her. "I thought you wouldn't come tonight," he said.

"Why did you think that?" she asked.

"I thought you were angry because I said that you might be afraid," he explained.

"That is no reason to be angry," Pepa said, and the music started, and Pepa took his hand and led him to where the other dancers were, and after the dancing was over they walked up the hill to the ruins of the Spanish fortress and looked out at the river. "Can you hear the rapids?" Guillermo asked, and Pepa nodded.

"Have you ever seen a jaguar?" Pepa asked.

"Only a dead one that my father had to shoot because it killed our pig."

"I thought they didn't come into settled areas."

"It was a long time ago, before they cleared the jungle and planted the rubber trees," Guillermo said. "I helped him skin it so he could sell the pelt. He went all the way to San Carlos to sell it."

"Who bought it?"

"I don't know, but with the money he made he bought another pig."

"And the body? What happened to it?" Pepa asked.

"We threw it into the river."

"I wonder whether the body made it all the way to the sea," Pepa said.

"It probably got hung up on some rocks or a fallen tree and was eaten by vultures."

"It could have made it," Pepa said. "I want to go deep enough into the jungle to see a jaguar."

"Only the Indians know how to see them now," Guillermo said.

"My parents went to where the Indians are."

"And did they see a jaguar?"

"No," Pepa said.

"You see?"

"You see what?"

"Only the Rama can see them."

"It's because they weren't looking. They were busy taking care of the sick. A year ago, when I first came to El Castillo, I couldn't see the parrots or the monkeys in the trees. I could hear birds rustling in the leaves, but when I looked up, I saw nothing but green, and then one day, I saw a parrot, a red and blue one, and then I saw that there were many of them, that the tree was full of parrots."

"Jaguars are different," Guillermo said.

"Do you really believe that, or are you just scared to go far into the jungle?"

"I am not scared," Guillermo said. "Come."

They walked then to the edge of the town, to where the jungle started, and Pepa led him into the thickness of the jungle. "Close your eyes," she said. "It is better to feel the way than to try to see," so he closed his eyes and took her hand. Around them was the sound of millions of insects. After a while they stopped, and the sound of the insects grew louder, like applause or water plunging onto rock. Guillermo kissed her and she was not afraid of his tongue and his hands on her body, and she wanted to stay with him all night, wanted to lie down on the wet earth, but he turned around and began walking back, pulling her behind him, and soon they were out on the road and the sound of the insects grew distant, and the trees no longer protected them from the stars. "Don't look up. The stars will blind you," Pepa said, and Guillermo laughed, but he did not look up.

# CHAPTER 3

**LILIANA ARRIVED IN JUIGALPA IN THE LATE AFTERNOON. SHE WAS** going to visit Granada or León first, make her way south slowly, but when she arrived at the bus station in Managua, there was the bus to Juigalpa, as if it had been waiting for her. It rained on and off for the entire trip, so they couldn't keep the windows open for long and the heat and lack of air made her queasy, but whenever she thought she was going to vomit, the rain stopped, and someone opened a window, and she felt better. When the bus finally let her off in Juigalpa, she asked someone to point her toward the center of town. She had not brought a guidebook with her. She and Irene always traveled with a guidebook. All the guidebooks, and there were many, were kept in chronological order on the top four shelves of the bookshelf in Irene's study. Sometimes on Friday evenings, they would drink wine and choose a guidebook and look through it together. They remembered every hotel room they had ever been in—the one in Beni Mellal where they had to remove the mattress and sleep on the springs because it was so hot, the one in Turkey during the blizzard with the red light bulbs where the heat and hot water were broken and with the bellhop that kept interrupting them when they were making love, coming to their door with tea, calling out, "Teacher Liliana, Doctor Irene, are you drinking tea?" and Liliana would have to get up and get dressed to take the tray and thank him, assure him that they were fine, that they did not need any more tea, but an hour later he would be back with more.

She walked uphill toward the center of town. The mountains were straight ahead, the mountains where William had died, the mountains that William must have seen when he walked up this same street and passed the plaza and the cathedral or stopped to sit on a bench to watch people go by. Had there been time for such things, for walking through town and sitting on benches? Had he been disappointed, as she was, by the cathedral, a cinderblock and cement monstrosity? Did he wonder what happened to the original colonial construction? Was it a fire or war or neglect or a little bit of each that had led to its final collapse? Perhaps he asked someone, an old lady? If he had, would she have known the answer or would she have made up a story just to make him happy? Pray for us, he had written in his last letter. In their family, they did not pray.

Liliana did not stop at the Hotel de los Arcángeles, though she was tempted. It was the sort of place where she and Irene would never have stayed when they were young, but in the last few years they had allowed themselves to splurge, to appreciate the comfort of freshly laundered sheets and clean tile floors and a fan whose blades were not covered in a thick layer of dust and did not hang precariously from the ceiling and spin with a furious clatter. She imagined a plate of fresh fruit for breakfast and good coffee, paintings of parrots and toucans above the bed, and, in the bathroom, a basketful of lotions and soaps. She imagined the birds singing in the courtyard in the morning. *Irene, Irene, Irene,* they would sing, and she would not be able to bear it.

She kept walking and came upon the Hotel Casa Country. It looked like exactly what she wanted, a hotel devoid of charm, utilitarian, neither aesthetically pleasing nor ugly. It was simply a building, a place with rooms and beds and bathrooms. The fan would be neither encrusted with dirt nor clean, neither firmly affixed nor hanging by a thread.

The woman at the front desk had lived in Miami for twenty years. "Why did you come back?" Liliana asked.

"That is the question," she said, but she was laughing.

She had a room that overlooked the street.

"Is it quiet?" Liliana asked.

"Of course," the woman said, "but I have one in the back if you prefer."

"No, the one overlooking the street is fine," Liliana said, though she knew it would not be quiet. Across the street was a bar.

"How long will you be staying?"

"I'm not sure," Liliana said, and the woman laughed in the same way that she had laughed before.

Liliana hung her clothes up in the armoire, took a shower, and, without drying herself off, lay naked under the fan. She thought she would read a little, let the sun set before venturing out for dinner, but she fell asleep and when she awoke there was just a hint of light left in the sky and she could hear laughter across the street outside the bar. Now, she thought, I will not be able to sleep again tonight.

She got dressed and stood at the window looking out onto the street below. There was a breeze and it was markedly cooler. She hadn't eaten anything since she left her mother's apartment the day before except for the pretzels they had given her on the flight to Miami, three power bars, and the sliced mango she bought from an old woman at the bus station in Managua. In the lobby she asked the woman what restaurant she recommended.

"Do you like beef?" she asked.

"Sure," Liliana said, though she could not remember the last time she had eaten beef.

"This is a beef town," the woman said. "Up there"—she pointed to the hill across the street—"in the park. The food there is good," she said. "Except the musicians are always there."

"I like music," Liliana said.

The woman shrugged.

Even though she was starving, she was restless after the long bus ride and the nap, so she ate another power bar to tide her over and set off to explore the town. She thought she would take a look at the cemetery she had seen from the bus, the cemetery where she supposed William's remains were buried. She liked cemeteries, always had. It was something that she and Irene had in common, this love of cemeteries, the overgrowth that covered those that were forgotten, the worn-out letters, the plastic flowers. But this cemetery was not like other cemeteries, and, no, she did not want to think about Irene, did not want to imagine Irene's hand squeezing hers as she read the inscription on William's grave. She stood at the edge of the main road, the new highway that just a few years ago, her seatmate on the bus had told her, had been a dirt road, and looked out at the hillside cemetery across the road, a jumble of pastel crosses and mausoleums, but she did not come any nearer. She wasn't ready yet.

When she entered the restaurant she was led to the table farthest away from where the guitarists and singers were sitting.

"What is good?" she asked the waiter.

"Everything," the waiter said, and she laughed and ordered a beer and asked to have a minute to peruse the menu, which included an entire page devoted to different preparations of bulls' testicles.

When the waiter returned with her beer she asked him which

of the testicle dishes he preferred, and he told her the grilled testicles were the best, so she ordered that and an avocado salad. "I'm famished," she said.

She took a sip of beer and leaned back in her chair, regretting that she had been seated so far away from the musicians. She saw now that all the other customers were seated near them, that she was the only one far away, separated from the life of the restaurant, and she was annoyed that the waiter had assumed she would not like to be near the music and the other customers, so when the waiter returned with her food she said, "The music is wonderful."

"They are here every night," he said, as if this were a burden he had to bear.

Liliana had never eaten bull's testicles before, though she was not opposed to eating things that other people considered disgusting. On the contrary, she and Irene had always sought such foods out. They had enjoyed pigs' ears in Spain, lamb trotters in Turkey, gizzards in Morocco, crickets in Mexico, but they'd never had the opportunity to try bulls' testicles.

The waiter stood off to the side, watching her take her first bite.

"*¿Le gusta?*" he asked, coming closer.

"*Sí, mucho,*" she said truthfully, and she ordered another beer.

Now that she was no longer starving, she turned her attention to the musicians. There were two guitarists, an old man wearing a cowboy hat and a man in his forties, his son perhaps, though they did not look like they were related. At their table were six other men of various ages. Some of them sang along during the chorus and the others just drank beer, and when a song was over they clapped and cheered and stood up and raised their bottles to the musicians, who bowed slightly without getting up and then began another song. The older man was singing alone now, the younger man taking the back seat, strumming softly. At first she thought she recognized the song from her mother's 78s. Every few bars she was sure the words would come to her, that she would remember them from the hot summer nights when they used to sit in the living room in the dark with the windows wide open, listening to the old records, waiting for a hint of breeze to come in off the Hudson River, waiting for that one moment of relief.

Before she finished her second beer, the waiter came to her table with another. "From the gentleman in the suit," he said, looking over toward the table with the musicians. The men at the table held up their beers and smiled at her, so she did the same and turned again to her dinner. Out of the corner of her eye she could see one of the men, not the one in the suit, coming toward her. "We would like you to join us," he said.

"Thank you," she said. "Perhaps when I finish my dinner." Before she could stop him, he gathered up her plate and beer. She realized as she followed him that she was not annoyed by his behavior, that, in fact, she was relieved, for she had not been looking forward to going back to her room, to lying awake listening to the noise from the bar across the street and the fan that was not quite rickety enough to come unhinged, but not a comfort either like the soft purring of the fan at the Hotel de los Arcángeles surely was. I will not think of Irene, she said to herself as the men made room for her to sit.

When they finished the song, the man in the suit took up the younger man's guitar and began playing "Yesterday." He sang, looking right into her eyes, and she helped him along with the words. "For you," he said in English when he finished.

"*Gracias por la cerveza*," she said.

"You speak Spanish?" he asked, disappointed.

"Yes," she said.

The man in the suit had lived in Florida, as had several of the other men at the table. "Have you lived in Florida?" Liliana asked the old guitarist.

"Never," he said.

"He has only four cows," the man in the suit said in English. "Only four cows, but he is a genius."

"Yes," Liliana said.

"Are we going to play music or talk?" the old guitarist said, starting another song. *"Pero ahora que ya sos libre, Nicaragüita, yo te quiero mucho más,"* he sang, and when he got to the chorus again, Liliana sang with him, quietly, mouthing the words.

"You believe in freedom?" the man in the suit asked.

"Do you?" Liliana asked.

"I used to," he said, "but now the ones who made us believe in it are rich, and all we have is this stupid song."

"You come here every night?"

He laughed as Liliana wiped the sauce from her plate with a tortilla and asked, "So, you like our local specialty?"

"I do," she said.

"That is what we are, a nation of castrated bulls. If you stay tomorrow you will see the bulls parading around the plaza with their black and red flags and life-size photos of Daniel, and the bulls will sing the praises of our dead revolutionary heroes. They'll all be there, and these two will sing 'Nicaragua, Nicaragüita,' and Daniel will throw a little money around and everyone will think he is a savior, and he and his Chinese cronies will build their canal or they will not build it, but he will get richer and richer nonetheless."

"Why did you come back, then?" Liliana asked.

"Because in Florida I was a cockroach, and I would still rather be a castrated bull than a cockroach," he said. He called the waiter over. "Bring a bottle," he said. "It's time to get serious."

The musicians were playing another song now, and the man stopped for a moment and listened. "Love," he said, "a nation of castrated bulls crooning about love."

"So what do you believe, then, if you do not believe in freedom or love?" Liliana asked.

"I believe in death," he said, pouring everyone at the table a shot of rum. "*Salud*," he said, holding his glass up.

"*Salud*," Liliana said, knocking it back all at once. "Death is not something to believe in or not believe in. It is simply a fact."

"True enough. Do you believe in God?"

"No," Liliana said.

"Good," he said. "We should dance now," he added, getting to his feet, tottering, then righting himself and pulling her up from her chair. "Enough of these sad songs," he called to the musicians. "Play us something we can dance to."

They did, and Liliana and the man in the suit danced. He pulled her close, and she followed the way her mother had taught her to do on winter evenings when she played the old records. He was kissing her neck now and she could feel him against her thigh, but she didn't stop him. He smelled good, like the outdoors and lemons. "What is your name?" she asked.

"Santiago," he said, "but they call me El Médico."

"You are a doctor?"

"A veterinarian," he said.

"I like animals," Liliana said. He pulled her closer, and she felt his breath on her neck.

She woke up with the first light of day, and just as she had every morning since Irene told her she was leaving, her first thought was of Irene—Irene's hand resting on the pillow, Irene coming out of the shower, Irene on the couch reading, Irene on the telephone, Irene. The fan was gyrating above her, spinning so fast that she was almost cold. Her pants she saw were neatly folded on a chair near the bed. Her sandals were waiting under the chair, but she

still was wearing her shirt, bra, and underwear. She reached for
the sheet that lay bunched up at the foot of the bed. The sheets
smelled of sweat, but she did not find it repulsive. She lay there
looking up at the fan. "Fall," she said out loud.

"Santiago," she called, surprised that she remembered his
name. "Where am I?"

"*Aquí*," he said.

"Where are you?" she asked.

"*Aquí*," he said, walking into the room and sitting down on the
bed, stroking her brow as her mother used to do when she was sick.
"Don't worry."

"Worry about what?"

"Nothing happened last night."

"Just the dancing?" she asked.

"Just the dancing."

She asked for water and he brought her water and she drank.
"I'm cold," she said.

"It is never cold here," he said, but he got up and turned off the
fan, and it was as if she had suddenly gone deaf.

"That's better," she said. Now that she was not cold, she could
feel that her head was pounding and her mouth was parched. "Can
I have some more water?" she asked.

Santiago brought her water and a plate of papaya. "I have coffee," he said, and she said that she would like some coffee, but that
made her think about Irene. It was always Irene who procured
coffee when they were traveling, Irene who went out in search of
a café at the crack of dawn to bring Liliana coffee before she went
out again for her run.

"Do you want sugar?" Santiago asked.

"No, thank you," Liliana said. The coffee was thick and rich
like soil. "It's good," she said.

"Thank you," Santiago said.

"What happened?" Liliana said.

"Nothing. We drank too much, and you came home with me, and we went to sleep."

"Thank you," Liliana said.

"Thank you for what?"

"For taking care of me," Liliana said.

"I have a sister like you."

"What do you mean like me?"

"You cried a lot. You don't remember?"

"No."

"Did Irene die?" he asked.

"No," Liliana said. She felt the hot air pushing down on her and the sweat trickling down between her breasts and thighs. "Maybe we should put the fan on again," she said, and Santiago got up and turned it on.

"Is that better?" he asked.

"Yes," she said, and she lay back on the bed again, closed her eyes, and listened to the sound of the fan turning and turning.

"So she left you?"

"Yes."

"And now you are here," he said.

"Now I am here," she said, and she began to cry.

"Come," Santiago said, and he pulled her toward him. She buried her face in his chest. "There is nothing worse than the pain of betrayal," he said. There was something soothing about the harshness of his words, about the reality of them. Once, when she was eight and William thirteen, they were running in Fort Tryon Park, and she tripped on a rock and fell on her face. William held her like Santiago was holding her now. "I know it hurts," William kept saying, and this acknowledgment of her pain rather than the usual adult assurances that she would be fine, that it was nothing more than a scratch, was a comfort.

"I can't imagine anything worse," she said, pulling out of his embrace.

"Not even death?"

"No. You know, I almost lost her once. At the time, I thought that there could be nothing worse than death, but." She paused, and Santiago took her hand. They sat on the bed, holding hands like an ancient couple. "I don't really want her to die," she said without turning to look at Santiago.

"I know," he said. "Tell me."

"It was when we were first together. We went on a trip to the Sahara to celebrate finishing her PhD, before she started her first real job in research at the University of New Mexico School of Medicine. It had always been a dream of hers, to cross the Sahara. We started in Morocco and were to end up in Burkina Faso, but that was the extent of our planning. The hepatitis started on the third day on the Niger. A terrible itching spread all over Irene's body, beginning at the neck and moving slowly downward and outward to her chest and stomach, thighs, arms, feet. She said it was like a ringing in the ears that she could not escape whether she lay completely still and concentrated on something else or paced up and down the crowded deck, stepping over people and bundles. This itching was the worst part, worse than the nausea and diarrhea, worse than the fevers that came quickly after the itching started. I had to hold her down, hold her hands behind her back to keep her from drawing blood.

"But once we got off the boat in Mopti, she felt better, so we thought it had been something she ate. We decided to spend a few days there to rest. She was well enough to walk around during the day, but at night the itching and fevers came back. I tried to get her to go to a clinic, but she was afraid that they would give her an injection with a dirty needle even though I promised I wouldn't let them. It was so stupid now that I look back on it, so dangerous. I don't know why I didn't notice the yellowness in her skin. I guess if you're not looking for it, you don't see it. She was still able to eat small amounts of food and she drank lots of Sprite to replenish her liquids, so we convinced ourselves that she was getting better and that she was well enough to start the final stage of our journey.

"When we boarded the bus for Ouagadougou, the itching had subsided, so Irene was able to sleep most of the way. She didn't collapse until we got off the bus. She fell to the ground as she tried to swing her backpack onto her shoulder. I remember screaming for help and people crowding around us. A man threw her over his shoulder and started running, so I ran after him to the hospital. For three days Irene was in and out of consciousness, so for three days I didn't sleep. I sat in a chair by her side day and night, holding her hand, just watching for changes, listening to her breathe. Whenever I felt like I was going to fall asleep, I got up and walked in circles around her bed until I felt awake enough to sit down. I used a bedpan rather than leave her. I was convinced that if I left the room, she would die. Finally, in the middle of the third night, I succumbed to sleep. I lay on the floor next to the bed and slept until one of the cats that roamed the ward jumped on me and I screamed, and the night nurse came and led me to a pallet of blankets on the floor in the corner of the nurse's station. When I awoke I couldn't get up. My entire body, even the roof of my mouth and underneath my fingernails, was itching, and I lay there, refusing to give in, clenching my fists so that I would not begin scratching—I was sure that if I gave in, if I started scratching, Irene would die. And I didn't give in, not until they told me Irene's fever had broken and that she would live. Then I unclenched my fists and I felt the burning leave my skin like thousands of insects retreating."

"You must have loved her very much," Santiago said.

"I always thought, we both did, that after our trip across the

Sahara, after beating death together, nothing could separate us. How could I have been so stupid? We were planning to walk from our house in San Francisco to Tierra del Fuego when we retired. We even bought maps and read books about Patagonia."

"How long had it been going on, before you found out?"

"Months. She wanted to tell me earlier, but then Guadalajara, our cat, got really sick, and she didn't want to make things worse, so she waited until she was gone to tell me, which meant that she ended up taking that away from me, too, because we couldn't even grieve for her together." Liliana began to cry again.

"It was a man?"

"How did you know?"

"I just did."

"They met at work. He's doing research on Sjögren's too."

"What's Sjögren's?"

"It's an autoimmune thing. Your body is overcome with an itching so bad that you feel like you're burning."

Santiago closed his eyes, put his hands on his knees, and breathed in deeply.

"What are you doing?"

"I'm trying to feel the burning."

"Can you?"

"No, but it must be terrible."


After Liliana finished the coffee and ate the papaya, after she showered and put on her clothes, she went with Santiago to check on a pig that had some kind of skin disease Santiago had never seen before, and she watched him talk to the pig and smear ointment on her rash. "She's a good pig," the pig's owner said, and Santiago patted the pig on the rump.

"The rash looks better," he said, but later, once they were back on the road heading for the next ranch, he told Liliana that this was not true. "There is no change," he said, and Liliana asked him why he had lied to the pig's owner.

"It was not a lie," he said. "It was an encouragement."

"Do you think it will live?"

"The sores are getting worse. Did you see the pus?"

"No."

"Tomorrow I will probably have to put her down."

"So soon?"

"There is no need for her to suffer. It will only get worse."

"So why did you tell the owner that she was getting better when all that is in store for her is more suffering?"

"Because he was not ready for the news."

"But how can he accept it if he thinks it's getting better? People only accept death when there is no other way."

"I suppose you're right. I should have told him, but sometimes with animals it's best not to think about it too much. Sometimes it's better to just be done with it."

They drove in silence. The road became rougher and the jostling and noise brought her headache back. She wondered if William once traveled this road, whether it was even more primitive then. She tried to imagine him in a jeep with other soldiers, singing a revolutionary song, his thoughts far away from those he had left behind. If he had received word of their father's illness, would he have returned? Was that why she and her mother did not write to him about the diagnosis? Was it that they were afraid he would not have come home?

"My father died of a terrible disease, ALS, do you know about it?"

"Yes."

"He wanted me to help him die, find a pill, something that would make it go more quickly. I read an article about how people were going to Mexico to buy the drug that veterinarians use to put down animals, and I showed it to him. I said that I would go to Mexico to get the drug. He seemed so rational when he asked me to help him, but then when I presented him with a plan, he broke down, started crying, so I didn't go to Mexico, and he had to go through the whole awful thing of not being able to move, not being able to swallow or breathe. I should have gone anyway. It's my biggest regret."

"Bigger than Irene?"

"That was not in my control," Liliana said.

"But she left."

"Yes."

"You didn't have any idea that she was not happy?"

"We were always together," Liliana said, but she did not cry. All she felt was the finality of it, and she thought of the pig suffering, her skin burning up, festering, without any idea that tomorrow it would all be over, that tomorrow Santiago would come with his injection and she would cease to exist.

They drove to the ranch of a man who went by the name of El Justo, where Santiago was going to examine a cow who had just given birth to twins—one male and one female. He explained as they drove that the female twin is usually infertile. "Something happens in the uterus. It is as if something seeps out from the male into the female and she takes on male traits. They act even more like bulls than the males, and when it comes time for breeding, they are useless," he said.

"And the bull? Does he act more like a cow?"

"No, the bull acts just like a normal bull," Santiago said.

"So what do they do with the female twins?" Liliana asked, though she already knew the answer.

"Usually they kill them when they're young, when they first show signs of being aggressive. If you don't wait too long, the meat is delicious, so tender."

They drove for a while in silence, but they didn't know each other well enough for it to be a comfortable silence, so after a while Liliana asked, "Do you have children?"

"Three. They live with their mother in Miami."

"Do you miss them?"

"I try to miss them, but I like this life. I am free now, like Nicaragua."

"But Nicaragua is not free."

"Exactly, but here we are all pretending to be free, so there are moments when I can forget that I'm not."

"Do they visit?"

"I go there mostly. They hate it here—no Internet, no video games, and they never remember to put the toilet paper in the wastepaper basket, so the toilet always gets backed up."

"And your wife?"

"She works hard, and she has a new husband who works hard. They are all better off without me."

"Why do they call him El Justo?" Liliana asked as they drove through the gate to his ranch.

"Something about the war. He was important."

"I wonder if my brother knew him."

"Your brother?"

"He was here during the war. He fought. He died here."

"So that explains things."

"Explains what?"

"I don't know," Santiago said. "Something."

Santiago pulled up to the gate, which was guarded by two young men, boys really, each wielding a semi-automatic weapon. The entire property was surrounded by a two-story electrified barbed wire fence. "Like the Berlin Wall," Santiago said. One of the guards walked over to the passenger side of the car and leaned in through the window.

"Who is she?" he asked Santiago. His breath smelled of cigarettes.

"A friend, an American. Her brother fought for us in the war," Santiago said.

The guard pulled away from the window and looked into Liliana's eyes. She did not avert her gaze or blink. He leaned in closer. "Boom," he said, but when Liliana still did not flinch, he smiled. "*Bienvenida*," he said.

"*Gracias*," she said, but she did not smile. She knew somehow that smiling was not what was required.

The guard motioned to the other to open the gate, and Santiago drove through, pulling up in front of El Justo's house, next to a shiny new SUV. The house was more like a castle than a house, complete with towers and a rampart upon which were posted four more guards. In front of the house stood El Justo, dressed in cowboy boots and jeans. He took one last drag from his cigarette, flicked it onto the ground. Despite the fact that he was dressed like a rancher, he did not look like a rancher or a war hero. He was portly but not in the way that a man who was strong and athletic in his youth is portly. He was small-boned, like a woman, and the fat was spread evenly on his body, not concentrated in the belly. His hands were small, chubby and smooth like a eunuch's, Liliana thought as they shook hands.

El Justo took them to see the twins. "She's a real fighter, this calf," El Justo said. "She was the first of the two to stand, and when her brother got up she rammed him, ran right into him as if she were the bull."

The twins were suckling, their mother standing stoically as they pulled and tugged, frantically it seemed to Liliana, as if they were starving. When they were satiated, Santiago examined the mother. Apparently the twins had come out easily and there had been no tearing, no blood. When he finished examining her, Santiago whispered something into the cow's ear and patted her on the rump, and that was it. El Justo insisted they have a glass of rum before they left. They followed him to the veranda, where a bottle and glasses were already waiting.

"Please," he said, motioning for them to sit down. He poured. "You are not afraid of rum, are you?" he asked Liliana.

"Of course not," she said, and he added another finger to her glass.

"*Salud*," El Justo said, and he took a sip the way one sips tea when it is still too hot to drink.

"*Salud*," Liliana said, downing hers all at once and setting the glass down on the table.

El Justo laughed. "You are an expert," he said, pouring her another.

"That's enough, thank you," Liliana said when the glass was about a quarter full, but he filled it to the top.

"Liliana's brother was here during the war," Santiago said. "Maybe you remember him?"

"There were lots of people here, lots of foreigners. I'm sure your paths didn't cross," Liliana said. She didn't trust El Justo. He was, she thought, the sort of man who would tell her what she wanted to hear and then laugh about how easily he had deceived her once she was gone.

"I know everyone, and I knew everyone," El Justo said.

"Are you going to kill her?" Liliana asked to change the conversation.

"Kill whom?" El Justo asked.

"The baby, the cow. Santiago said that is what is usually done."

"I never do what is usually done," El Justo said.

"So you will not kill her?" Liliana said.

"I did not say that," El Justo said. "Tell me about your brother."

"His name was Philip, Philip Muldoon," Liliana lied, using Irene's last name.

"Felipe, there were many Felipes, but not a foreigner by that name."

"Are you sure?" Santiago said.

"Of course I am sure," El Justo said. "Perhaps your brother was somewhere else?"

"He was here," Liliana said.

"You are not telling me the truth," El Justo said.

"Perhaps," Liliana said.

"I think you will like it here in Juigalpa," he said, smiling the kind of smile one uses when a child says something clever and funny.

"I think so too," Liliana said.

"More rum?"

"No, thank you," Liliana said. "It's too early in the day."

"You're right," he said. "Actually, I never drink before five. This was an exception. I didn't want you to think I was inhospitable. Next time you will stay for lunch, I hope. If I had known you were coming, I would have changed my plans, but now it is too late."

They shook hands formally.

"Let me know if you want me to take care of the calf," Santiago said.

"Of course," El Justo said.


On the way back into town, Liliana could tell that Santiago was waiting for her to ask him questions.

So Liliana asked, "Do you think he will let the calf live?"

"It depends on how aggressive she is," Santiago said.

"He could keep her separated from the others."

"Then she would be lonely," Santiago said.

"Perhaps she would like being alone."

"No one likes being alone," Santiago said.

Liliana rolled down the window, let the hot air in, and Santiago did not protest. He put in a CD, the Beatles. Liliana did not protest. William hated the Beatles. "Fucking fluff" was how he described their music, but perhaps fluff was what she needed now. Fluff and the hot wind in her face and the mountains and Santiago singing along to the fluff, looking over at her every once in a while.

"Why didn't you tell El Justo your brother's real name?" Santiago asked.

"How did you know?"

"Because it's true what he said. He knew everyone, so either you lied about his name or your brother was never here or you didn't even have a brother."

"My brother didn't like the Beatles," Liliana said.

Santiago turned off the music.

"That's not what I meant. You don't have to turn it off," Liliana said.

"There were six of us, all brothers," Santiago said, "so I understand about losing brothers. I was the only one who was too young to fight. The oldest died defending Managua. After the war he was declared a hero. There was a ceremony, and my parents and the other parents of the fallen were given plaques, and I, as the brother of a hero of the revolution, was sent to Cuba to study veterinary medicine, but as soon as I got back to Nicaragua I left for Miami. So much for the revolution."

"But you returned," Liliana said.

"That is only because I was not good at making money. If I had been, I would still be there, living in a big house, driving a fancy car. My kids would be in private school. I would be like my other brothers, the ones who didn't die. I would be like Daniel

Ortega. You know, I was thinking, if you are going to be staying here for a while, there's no reason to spend money on a hotel. I have plenty of room, too much room. I won't bother you. I am a man of honor," he said seriously.

"And what is that, a man of honor?" Liliana asked.

Santiago answered, still dead serious, though she had not meant it as a real question. "I will think of you as a sister."

They went to the hotel to settle the bill and get Liliana's bag. It was obvious that the woman at the desk did not think of Liliana as Santiago's sister. "He will take good care of you," she said.

Liliana thanked her. "Of course he will," she said.

"Do you invite all the foreign girls to come live with you?" Liliana asked, when they were back in the truck.

"Foreign girls don't usually pass through Juigalpa," he said. "There's nothing much to see here unless you know what you're looking for."

"So you would if they did?"

"But they don't, not alone in any case."

Liliana's room in Santiago's house was in the back and faced a small garden with fruit trees and a dozen or so chickens and ducks standing together in the shade of the avocado tree. The room itself contained only a single bed. In the corner there was a box full of toy trucks and cars. Despite her protests, Santiago had insisted on giving her the best fan in the house. He brought her a fresh towel that was stiff from drying outdoors and smelled vaguely of gasoline. He gave her the extra key.

For dinner Santiago prepared an avocado salad and eight eggs, four duck and four chicken, with tortillas. "It's hard to keep up with them," Santiago said, placing four eggs on her plate.

"I'm starving," she said, and she realized that this was true.

When they finished eating, they went again to listen to the musicians play. They played mostly the same songs they played the night before. After about an hour, a woman sat down at their table without greeting anyone, but they seemed to be expecting her, and Santiago ordered her a Toña.

When the waiter brought her beer, she thanked him, turned to Liliana, and smiled. "*Buenas noches*," she said.

"*Buenas noches*," Liliana said.

The woman sat completely still, her hands gripping her chair, as if she were focusing too hard on trying to control herself, as if she knew that if she let go she would break into an uncontrollable shaking. Only when the song was over did she take a sip of beer. "Another," she said, and the musicians nodded and began to play again.

When they finished the second song, the musicians took a break. The woman turned to Liliana. "Here," she said, handing Liliana a photograph. "I am Carolina."

It was William, of course, cigarette hanging from his lips, smiling, his arms around a young woman, who was not smiling. In the photograph one could see the muscles and veins in her forearms, and she stood legs apart, as if she were bracing herself for a sudden jolt.

"He hated smoking," Liliana said.

"War changes everything," Carolina said.

# CHAPTER 4

**WHEN HE WAS A BOY WILLIAM SHOWED NO INTEREST IN GUNS OR** swords. He liked baseball not football. For a while he was interested in birds and begged his parents to buy him a parrot. He collected acorns and chestnuts and did not complain about taking slow walks with his grandparents in Fort Tryon Park. He did not get angry when Liliana broke his toys or when his parents said that he could not have ice cream, but in the fourth grade he became a fighter. He punched a girl in the nose because she made fun of another student—a shy girl who held her pencil too hard and wore the same dress every day. Their father cried when he found out what William had done.

"But I was protecting her," William said.

A few months later he punched a neighborhood boy in the stomach, knocking the wind out of him, for throwing a rock at a stray cat. "This is our secret," he told Liliana after the boy ran away, William calling after him that the next time he would hit him even harder.

"You didn't have to hit him," Liliana said.

"I don't like it either, but sometimes it's the only way," William explained.

"You could have just told him to stop," Liliana said.

William laughed. "That's not the way the world works."

In middle school he got into a war of wills with his U.S. history teacher, who required the students to learn the Declaration of Independence backward, by heart. One by one they stood in front of the classroom to recite it while she smirked, waiting for them to make a mistake, at which point she told the student to sit down and flamboyantly recorded an F in her grade book. When it was William's turn, he walked to the front solemnly, bowed to the class, and proceeded to declaim. He made not a single mistake, and when he was finished he bowed again and instructed the class to follow him out the door. "That is the end of this futile exercise. We are leaving this dictatorship," he pronounced, but no one followed him. "Who's next?" the teacher asked as William slammed the door, shattering the glass.

The principal recommended a special school. At the school for troubled students, William learned to fix cars and build things. He liked building things. All his teachers said he was a model student, so polite, so helpful. They wondered what was wrong with him, but they liked having him there, a calming presence among all the wild boys who kicked and cursed and smashed things with the hammers that they were supposed to use for creating, not destroying. After a year without incident, their parents wanted William to go back to the regular school, but William refused. He had friends for the first time in his life. They called him in the middle of the night crying or raging or drunk. They showed up at their apartment in the dead of winter, coatless and hungry with black eyes. William invited them to stay for dinner, which they ate without speaking except to mutter *thank you*. These friends who slept in his bed while he slept on the floor stayed for as long as they needed to stay. They helped with the chores, and they always said please and thank you and did not smoke or drink in their home.

Their parents accepted these guests—William's boys, they called them—for how could they have turned them away given their own history? What would have become of their mother if she and her family had not found refuge on the river? And how different their father's life would have been if someone in L'viv had taken their father's first family in, hidden them from the Nazis, fed them soup and warm bread, then led them to a hiding place in the countryside. Think of your wife and your dead son and daughter, our dead brother and sister, William would have said, if their parents had protested, but they did not.

The apartment became William's realm. He took over the food shopping, cooking, and even the cleaning, enlisting his friends to help. Their parents were busy at the bookstore six days a week. When they added a café in the back, they stayed open later. Often they did not come home until after ten, but William always left food for them and always insisted that he and Liliana and whoever was living there ate dinner together. They ate with music blasting— William's favorite records, Jimi Hendrix, the Rolling Stones—so there wasn't much conversation, but there was something calming about eating without having to talk. And the boys were kind to Liliana. She was always welcome to join them in William's room, to sit on the floor while they listened to music. Sometimes it was so loud that she could feel it in her belly and it was difficult to separate the bass from the beating of her heart. They gave her gifts, things that they stole just for the fun of stealing like erasers and Matchbox cars and Elmer's glue. She kept their presents on the bookcase in her room next to her favorite books. Once her mother asked her about the Matchbox cars. "Since when do you like cars?" she said.

"I've always liked them," she replied, and her mother shrugged.

When Liliana first told Irene about William, it was not his death that struck her, but the fact that their parents had left Liliana alone with him and the troubled youths. "They could have hurt you," Irene said, wrapping her arms around her as if she still needed protection from them all those years later.

"I always felt safe with them, safe with William," Liliana replied.

"Today your parents would have been charged with negligence, leaving you alone with all those boys."

"Things were different then," Liliana said.

"Were they, or was it just that no one talked about it?"

"About what?" Liliana asked, though she knew, of course, what Irene meant.

"You were lucky," Irene said.

In his junior year of high school, William became a carpenter's apprentice. His teachers planned for him to go to college. They had all sorts of ideas about what he, their most gifted student, would study, what he would be. How about architecture? they suggested. But he wanted to work with his hands, feel the wood, smell it. Their parents would have preferred a different choice, but they did not protest. They understood that their objections would have no effect on his decision, and unlike most parents, they never had particular plans for their children's futures. They knew how unpredictable life was, knew that you could be walking in the park eating ice cream one day, or lying in bed at night listening to the rain, and the next day you could be running for your life or waiting in line at a train station.

William's first commission was a set of birch wood tables and chairs for the bookstore café. The tabletops were inlaid: La Librería Nuevo Mundo, they said. Their mother was worried that they were too beautiful, too delicate. "They will be ruined in no time," she said, but their customers seemed to understand that these were not ordinary chairs and tables, and they treated them as if their own sons had made them. "What beautiful tables," they said, running their fingers over the inlay. "They must be handmade."

"Yes," their parents said, but they did not say that their son had made them. They were not the kind of parents to brag about their children.

For Liliana's sixteenth birthday William made her a box in the shape of a caiman. The eyes were inlaid pearls, which made it look blind, and Liliana called it El Ciego. Inside the caiman she kept the poems she wrote. She kept El Ciego on the night table by her bed. If there were a fire, it would be the only thing she would take with her when she fled. She liked thinking of that, of escaping a fire, of all of them getting out alive with only the caiman and her poems. This fantasy of destruction made her feel brave and strong and strangely safe, like how she felt when she walked down the street with her brother and his friends.

William starting talking about joining the revolution when the Sandinistas declared victory in 1979, but in March of 1982, when the Contras began attacking in full force, William could talk of nothing else. He railed against the United States and Ronald Reagan like he had railed against the bullies of his childhood, and when there were reports that the Contras were operating out of Costa Rica along the Río San Juan, just across the border from El Castillo, William made up his mind. "I have to do something," he said.

"It's not your battle to fight," Oskar said.

"The battle for freedom is everyone's battle," William said.

"There is no such thing as freedom," their father said, putting an end to the conversation.

Liliana tried to talk him out of it. "They haven't slept since you told them you were going. Yesterday the downstairs neighbors complained, said they could hear them walking around all night long, and I thought you liked your job. I thought you were," she paused, knowing that William would scoff, but she said it anyway, "happy."

"I can't just sit here doing nothing, being happy."

"There are other things you can do."

"Like what, write to my congressman?" he said.

"There are protests."

"Protests," he said as if the word were a synonym for cowardice.

Liliana had gone with her mother to protests against U.S. involvement in El Salvador. The first one was after the nuns were killed. At the protest the organizers handed out buttons with photographs of the nuns. Her mother wore those buttons every day for over two years, until the day that William announced he was going to Nicaragua. At the time she imagined her mother ripping the buttons off her coat and throwing them in the garbage, but now she understood that her mother would never have done such a thing. She would have wrapped them each in tissue paper and put them in the box with the photographs from Vienna, or perhaps she gave them away to a customer, someone who came in looking for books about liberation theology or the poetry of Rubén Darío and Ernesto Cardenal. Her mother also took her to a memorial mass commemorating the assassination of Archbishop Óscar Romero at Riverside Church. "Don't tell your father or your grandparents about this. You know how they are about churches," her mother said when they were walking to the subway. It was something she cherished, this secret she had with her mother, and yet, ever since, whenever she stepped inside a church, she thought not of her mother but her father.

After William left, they did not hear from him for weeks, and during that time her parents did not talk about him, so Liliana did not speak of him either. She wondered if when they were alone together in their bed her parents held each other and cried, or if even there they did not speak of him, as they did not speak of her father's dead children.

Finally there was a letter. *I have been in the mountains. Pray for us.* There was a girl, too. *I love her,* he wrote. *Her name is Carolina.* Alone in her room Liliana tried to pray. She got down on her knees and faced the caiman. The caiman, she thought, was the closest thing to God that she knew. "Keep him safe," she whispered, but it felt like a betrayal, so she never did it again.

The next day the letter from Carolina was waiting in their mailbox when she came home from school. The letter contained just four lines, written at the top of the page in tiny letters—the first line directly beneath the date, the third below the second, and the signature, Carolina, under the third.

> *11 de agosto de 1982*
> *Fue su primera batalla.*
> *William está muerto.*
> *Carolina.*

He was twenty-four, three times as old as her father's eldest child when he died at Birkenau. Liliana was eighteen, three times older than her father's youngest. This mathematical calculation was the first thing that came to her mind when she finished reading the letter and she focused on the numbers, repeating them like a child practicing multiplication tables—three times eight is twenty four, three times six is eighteen—as she sat alone at the kitchen table with this letter, with all the blankness of it, until it was dark and she could no longer make out the words. Then she folded the letter, put it back in the envelope, and put the envelope in the bottom of the drawer where they kept the dishtowels, for she could not bear to have it sitting on the table in front of her. The worst of it was that, according to the date on the letter, he had been dead for at least seventeen days, and the thought that during those seventeen days she had woken up when the alarm rang and brushed her teeth and bathed and eaten and ridden the subway, and talked on the telephone as if nothing in the world had changed, as if he were not dead, made her think of all of the people who would never know of either William's life or death, and that made the blankness of the page, his absence, even greater.

When her parents came home from work, she did not take the letter out of the drawer. Instead, they prepared dinner together as they did every night. Her parents ate more than usual, for it had been a busy day at the bookstore, and they had not had time to eat lunch. She would tell them in the morning, she decided while she was washing the dishes. They deserved one last night of rest, of hope.

But once her parents had gone to bed and she was left alone with the finality of William's death, the burden of her knowledge became too heavy for her to carry on her own. She thought of going out, finding an all-night diner where she could sit among people who could not bear the loneliness of the night. Perhaps she would be able to cry there among strangers. Perhaps someone would ask her why she was crying, and she would tell them that her brother was dead, killed in his first battle, and maybe that person would offer her a cigarette and she would sit with that person and smoke cigarettes until her lungs were raw. But the letter with its blank spaces and tiny words would still be waiting, so she called her grandparents.

The phone rang twenty times before her grandmother answered. "Who is it?" she said, which was how she always answered the phone.

"William is dead," Liliana said.

"William," her grandmother said.

They arrived fifteen minutes later. Liliana watched them get out of the taxi from the window. Her grandfather was carrying his doctor's bag.

Liliana showed them the letter, and they read it out loud, whispered the words. Their Spanish, thick with German *r*'s, made the meaning irrefutable. They woke her parents. "What?" Liliana's father said when they turned on the light. "For god's sake, turn off the light," he said, and Liliana fled to her room. After a while her grandmother knocked on her door, and she came out, and they all sat together at the kitchen table without speaking until Liliana's father stood up, put his hand on his head, and said what he remembered of the Kaddish.

When her father sat down, her mother picked up the letter, folded it, and put it back into the envelope. "Perhaps if it was his first battle," she said. They waited for her to finish, but that was where she left it, with that "perhaps," and over the next weeks that "perhaps" took on the strength of truth, for it was the only truth that her parents could bear—the possibility that he had not had the chance to kill.

The next morning they sat in the kitchen together as her father called the U.S. Embassy in Managua. First he had to call the operator to get the proper codes. When he got a busy signal, he called the operator again, and she assured him that he had the right number, so he dialed again and still it was busy. Her mother tried to convince him to wait a while before calling back. "Perhaps there's something wrong with the lines," she said. "Everything is upside down there right now because of . . ." She could not utter the word "war." But her father couldn't wait. What was he to do in the meantime, listen to music, take a walk, eat? None of them were possibilities, so he kept dialing until he got an answer. He had to repeat everything several times because the connection was so bad, and every time he said William's name, Liliana felt as if she were being punched in the stomach.

A week passed and there was no word from the embassy, so her father called again, and they assured him that they were looking into things. It was not easy, they explained, to travel to Juigalpa because of the fighting there, but they had their contacts. They would be in touch as soon as they had more information. Her father hung up and then called right back, insisting on speaking with the ambassador, but he was unavailable. "When will he be available?" he asked, and they told him to call back the next day, so the next day he called back and the day after that, and finally when they had given up believing that they would actually get through to the ambassador, when calling the ambassador had become merely a way to pass the time, something to look forward to in the endless chain of hours that comprised each day, he answered.

Yes, William had been in Juigalpa. Yes, they had spoken to Carolina. They had taken her testimony, which they would send in an official report. The body, the ambassador said, has not been retrieved, cannot be retrieved until the fighting stops. Liliana's father explained all this still holding the receiver in his hand, and he kept talking even when the phone started to make that awful noise that says, *Hang up the phone now*, kept talking until the recorded voice came on commanding him to "Please hang up and dial again, please hang up and dial again," at which point Liliana took the receiver from her father and hung up the phone. That is when they all began to cry, and this crying was the closest they got to a funeral.

"It was his first battle," her mother said when the room began to get dark, and they realized that they had been crying for hours, when they knew they had to at least turn on the lights.

"Maybe we should go there," Liliana said, "to find out, to find . . ." She paused, and her parents shook their heads, willing her not to say the words, but she continued, "to find his body."

"The body is not important. The only thing that matters is that he is dead," her father said, and Liliana did not argue because when it came to death, her father always had the last word.

# CHAPTER 5

THE NIGHT AFTER THEIR FIRST TIME IN THE JUNGLE, GUILLERMO took Pepa out on the river. "I have something to show you," he said as they paddled through the rapids and down past where the Germans lived, past the rubber *finca*—owned by the president himself, though he had never set foot on his property—where Guillermo and his brothers worked. Working on the rubber *finca*, he made in three months what his father had made in his whole life. His brothers spent their money on trips to San Carlos, where they drank too much rum and bought fancy clothes and women, but he was saving his money. "When I have enough, I will build us a house," he said. She did not say that she would like to live in his house. She did not say anything at all, but this did not worry Guillermo.

He stood in the boat and shone his flashlight up and down the shore, sweeping it with the light. "There," he said, pointing. "Do you see it?"

"What?"

"The eyes," he said, focusing the light on the spot. "Don't you see them, the two orange dots of light over there? Come," he said.

She moved to where he was standing, and he pointed her toward the shore. "There."

She saw them then, two glowing lights staring at her. "Is it a crocodile?"

"Similar. It's a caiman," Guillermo said, steering the boat toward the light, keeping his eyes fixed on the spot. When he was almost at the shore, he cut the motor and pulled the boat to the bank with a pole. "There," he whispered, bending down, parting the plants so that she could see.

"I see it," she said.

"I can catch it," Guillermo said. "It's a baby."

"No," Pepa said, but he already had it in his hands. He held the caiman out for her to see. It was scared, his body stiff and immobile, the eyes dark now.

"You can touch it," Guillermo said.

"Let it go," Pepa said.

Guillermo threw the caiman back into the river and they watched it disappear into the grasses.

"I didn't hurt it," Guillermo said.

"I know," Pepa said, taking the flashlight from him and shining it as he had done along the riverbank, low where the ground met the water, pausing at certain spots and shaking the flashlight, calling to the caimans with light.

"There," Guillermo said. "You found one." And he pulled her close so he could feel her breath on his neck, and they watched the caiman watching them.

Don Solano said that when their war was over, the doctors and their children would return to where they had come from or go somewhere better, where there was money and gold, but Guillermo knew that Pepa would stay with him. Even if her parents and brother left, she would stay. He knew because of the way she touched him and because she was not afraid of the night. "You have to be realistic," Don Solano said, picking up a can of sardines, dusting it off with a rag. "What was I thinking when I bought these? Who wants canned fish when we have a whole river of them at our fingertips?" He laughed, setting the can down on the shelf again.

"I *am* a realist," Guillermo said.

"I am just watching out for you," Don Solano said.

"I know," Guillermo said. It would be cruel for Guillermo to remind him that it was Don Solano who was out of touch with reality, who clung to the fantasy that one day his wife would return, walk into the shop, and take up her place beside him behind the counter. It had been nearly ten years since she had left. Guillermo could not even remember what Don Solano's wife looked like, though he was one of the last ones who saw her as she slipped into the canoe at dawn, all dressed up as if she were going to church and not leaving her husband. Guillermo wondered whether sometimes late at night when no one else was around Don Solano comforted himself by imagining that she was dead, had died long ago of unhappiness in a squalid room in an isolated village. Or perhaps he no longer believed she would return or cared and it was just something he kept saying because that is what people expected him to say and if he stopped it would be as if the rains hadn't come and the river had gone dry and everything smelled of rotting fish.

"They don't want them or their people back in her country. They don't want them anywhere," Guillermo said, for though he had not known anything before, except that the war made the Americans hungry for rubber, he knew now. Pepa had told him about how they made it out on the last train, and about the old woman who was trampled to death in the rush to get on that train, and how people had stood on her body all the way to Amsterdam because there wasn't enough room to lift her up and throw her out. She told him about how cold it was on the train, and how her hands and feet were so numb that she couldn't even feel the rumbling beneath her. And to think that before Pepa he had not even imagined winter.

"What is the cold like?" Guillermo often asked, and he would close his eyes and sometimes, if he focused only on her words, he could feel it.

"You have to wear a coat and gloves or else everything goes numb, your hands and feet, your ears, and you can see your breath, like the mist that rises from the river after it rains. Sometimes even your teeth hurt," she said.

"Someday maybe you will take me to see the snow," he said.

"After the war it will be different," Don Solano said, but Guillermo knew things that Don Solano did not. He knew, for example, the difference between real and fake medicine, knew that what Don Solano sold in his store had no more curative powers than water. Some of it, Pepa said, might even be poison, not the kind of poison that killed you outright, but the kind that worked slowly, weakening the system, causing one's teeth to yellow and old age to set in early, sometimes even before the birth of one's first grandchild. Soon real medicine would come all the way from the United States, and Pepa's parents would vaccinate everyone in El Castillo against yellow fever. The villagers would be the first, and after that her parents would travel farther down the river to the Caribbean, and there would be no more yellow fever deaths. This was the real medicine.

Now that the Germans were teaching him how to read, he would be able to know even more. He told no one about the lessons, not even Pepa. Later, when he could read the Spanish books in the Germans' library, he would tell her and they would laugh about it, about how there was a time when he did not know how to read and she had not even suspected. She had, he imagined, never thought about whether he could read or not, for in her world reading was simply something that one did, like walking, just like he had not thought about not knowing how to read since for him the written word was as distant and unfamiliar as the snow. But then Pepa had taken him to the Germans, to their house full of books, and Friedrich read out loud in their strange language that he could not understand but that was beautiful in a hard, strong way like Pepa, and he felt that, even though he did not understand the words, he understood her more completely when they were with the Germans, for this was part of her and the place she had come from, this strange language, the books.

The first time he went to see the Germans without Pepa, he brought a bottle of rum, and the three of them drank together. They did not talk much as they drank, but they were not uncomfortable with the silence, and they kept drinking, and after half the bottle was finished, Guillermo asked Friedrich to read to him, but this time he read in Spanish, and though Guillermo didn't fully understand the poems that Friedrich read, they made him feel alone, and sad, but it was not the kind of sadness that made him want to cry. It was the kind of sadness that made him want to stay up all night listening to Friedrich read poems that he did not understand. "Will you teach me?" he asked when Friedrich put down the book to take another sip of rum.

"Teach you what?" Friedrich asked.

"To read," Guillermo said.

"We can begin tomorrow," Georg said.

They drank more and night fell and the jungle came alive. The crickets and frogs were calling out their own songs and everything was spinning and sounding, and Guillermo stood up and sang a song his father used to sing when he had drunk too much rum.

He slept that night at the Germans' house, and he awoke in the morning to the sound of the birds and the smell of fresh sheets, and he wanted to stay in bed listening to the birds, smelling the sheets, but he knew his parents would be worried, for he had never spent a night away from home and he had not told them where he was going. The Germans were still sleeping when he left their house that morning. The door to their bedroom was open, and before he left, Guillermo stood there watching them sleep, lying curled up against each other, naked underneath the mosquito netting, and he thought that soon he and Pepa would sleep in a real bed and in the morning when the birds woke them, there she would be.

Guillermo did not return to the Germans' house for over a week, for he was sure they had agreed to teach him in a fit of drunken enthusiasm and that when they awoke in the morning, they would regret it. He went to work on the rubber *finca* as usual, but the idea of learning to read would not leave him, and he began to see writing in the forms of the tapping slits on the rubber trees and in the veins of leaves and the shapes of clouds.

So he went again to the Germans. He went directly from work, his hands sticky from the sap of the rubber trees, his boots thick with mud. What if I can't learn? he thought as he raised his hand to knock on the door.

"We have been waiting for you," Georg said, letting him in.

"I did not want to disturb you," Guillermo said, his hands shoved deep into his pockets to keep them from trembling.

"If we are going to teach you, you must promise to come for your lessons. Otherwise it will be a waste of time," Friedrich said sternly, already taking on the demeanor of a teacher.

"I promise," Guillermo said.

It was Friedrich who gave the lessons, though at the end of each session, Georg was summoned and Guillermo was instructed to present what he had learned to Georg, who sat properly in his chair as if he were a parishioner, nodding in agreement, and slowly Guillermo grew more confident until one day he could hear his voice fill the room, and he laughed that he had been afraid of something as basic and beautiful as words.

At home after everyone had gone to bed, he practiced reading from a book that contained a poem about greenness and death, whispering the words into the night, copying first individual letters, then complete words, then passages into the leather-bound notebook that the Germans gave him. One evening, about a month into their lessons, Guillermo announced that he had a surprise, a gift for them. He turned off the lamp and waited until his eyes had adjusted to the darkness, until he could see their figures, sitting still, waiting:

> *Verde que te quiero verde.*
> *Verde viento.*
> *Verdes ramas.*
> *El barco sobre la mar*
> *y el caballo en la montaña . . .*

He felt them watching him, stiller than the moon.

When he finished reciting the poem, they asked him what he thought it meant.

"It's about death and what you think about just before it's right there in front of you, but when you already know you are going to die," Guillermo said.

"There is nothing more I can teach you," Friedrich said. "Now the books themselves will teach you what you need to know."

They sat for a while in the darkness, for none of them wanted to break the spell of the poem by lighting a lamp. Guillermo wondered whether the Germans were thinking of each other's deaths and whether they felt as he did about Pepa, that if she died, he would die too.

Finally Georg got up to light the lamp. "Wait," he said after it was lit. "Don't move," he added as he left the room.

Guillermo and Friedrich stayed exactly as they were, he standing, Friedrich sitting. Georg returned with a camera. "Recite the poem again," he said.

Guillermo began, *"Verde que te quiero verde."*

There was a flash of light and the room lit up for a moment and the camera clicked.

"Now you," he said as he turned toward Friedrich, and Friedrich smiled. Again the light and the sound of the camera. "Good," Georg said.

They led him to the hammock in the patio. "Fling your left arm over the side," Georg said. "Close your eyes."

Friedrich took Guillermo's right hand and placed it gently on his stomach. "There," he said. "That's perfect. Relax." Guillermo heard the shutter click again. He opened his eyes.

"One more," Georg said.

"With my eyes closed?"

"Yes, like you are sleeping," Georg said, and Guillermo wondered whether they knew he had watched them that morning after they drank all that rum.

They took him to their bedroom. They asked him to take off his clothes, to lie on the bed in the same way with one arm hanging off the side of the bed, the other on his stomach. "Close your eyes," they said again. Friedrich took his hand and set it on his genitals. "Think of Pepa," Friedrich said, and he thought of Pepa. He felt her softness on him and the crisp clean sheets like in the poem. Strange, he thought, how the poem had made its way into his life like Pepa and the Germans.

He felt like a jaguar resting, contemplating its own strength, and as he lay there listening to the camera clicking he could feel Georg and Friedrich's sadness, their desire for something that they knew they could not have, for which they did not dare ask, and it made him feel sad too, but in that sadness there was also strength.

When they finished taking photos, he dressed and they went back to the main room. "We must toast your success," Friedrich said, and Georg brought a bottle, and they drank. "To Guillermo," they said, and Guillermo raised his glass. "To my teachers," he said.

"We are going away for a while," Georg said.

Friedrich looked surprised, but then he nodded.

"We would like you to watch the house, feed the pig and chickens. You can sleep here if you like." Georg paused. "You and Pepa."

"How long will you be away?" he asked.

"That depends on what we find," Georg said.

"What are you looking for?" Guillermo asked.

"Many things and nothing," Georg said.

"That is not an answer," Guillermo said, and Georg and Friedrich laughed, but they did not say anything more about the purpose of their trip.

"We will leave you plenty of food to eat, enough for a month, and we'll pay you," Georg said.

"No," Guillermo said. "I did not pay you for the lessons."

"Very well," Friedrich said, "but if you change your mind . . ."

"I will not change my mind," Guillermo said.

Guillermo did not stay at the Germans' house. Instead he woke up early every day to tend to their animals before going to work at the rubber *finca* and passed by there in the evening on the way back into town. He checked inside to make sure that nothing was disturbed. They had left a note on the bed—*the sheets are clean*, it said—but he did not linger in the bedroom. He focused on the library, making his way slowly through the one shelf of Spanish books. What would he do when he finished them all? Read them again, he supposed, or he could memorize his favorites the way that Georg and Friedrich had done when all they had were those six books.

One night, however, when he was in the living room choosing a book to take home with him, he heard a sound from the back of the house. At first he ignored it. It was probably just a branch falling on the roof, he thought, but it grew louder and it sounded as if someone were trying to get in. Probably a monkey, Guillermo thought. Friedrich had told him to watch out for the monkeys. They were always waiting for an opportunity to get in. Once, two of them had jumped from the roof right as they were opening the door.

The monkeys had run through all the rooms, cackling and pulling books down from the shelves. Georg had to fire the rifle in order to get them out. He didn't aim to kill, though, Friedrich said when he showed Guillermo the bullet hole in the wall.

Guillermo walked past the bedroom, down the covered walkway that separated the first house from the second. He paused when he got to the door to the next house. The sound had stopped, but he did not turn back. The door opened into one large room. He walked in carefully, stopping and listening for movement, holding the kerosene lamp high so that its light filled the room, but there was nothing stirring, no scrambling, no scratching, just silence. Inside there was a long bare wooden table, a chair, a lantern, no books, but every inch of the walls was covered with photographs. Some were small like the snapshots that Don Solano had shown him of his wedding day. Others were the size of the tall books on the bottom shelves of the library. There were hundreds of pictures—flowers and birds and the veins of leaves close up, and butterflies, frogs, and caimans lounging on rocks, and fish lying dead on rocks. There was an entire wall of just fruit—papayas splayed open, their black seeds like eyes, bananas, mangoes half-eaten by birds, the pits still hanging from the tree. He was on the wall too, the only human: Guillermo in the hammock, Guillermo on the bed. His image was surrounded by photographs of hanging *oropéndola* nests and giant termite hives, and Guillermo did not know whether he wanted to tear the photographs of himself from the wall or whether he wanted them to stay there until long after he and the Germans were dead.

He looked at the photographs for a long time, holding the lantern up to the wall. Then he went back to the main house and brought all the lanterns so that he could see the photos from afar, one wall at a time, and each wall seemed like one giant image of motion and light and darkness. At some point it began to rain, and when it stopped the birds started screaming, and it was morning.

After discovering what was in the other house, Guillermo knew that he could not take Pepa to sleep with him in the Germans' bed, for he could not be there with her without showing her the room, yet he could not show her the room. He did not know how to explain it to her, how to tell her about the Germans' sadness, how to explain why he had agreed to take off his clothes and lie naked on their bed because he did not know why himself, though he did not regret it, did not regret having his image hanging on the wall with the nests and hives and all the living things that surrounded them.

Guillermo continued to take care of the Germans' house, but he did not return to the room with the photographs and stayed only long enough to feed the animals. On some days he did not even go into the house. He did not borrow any more books, and he did not know what was more of a temptation, the books or the photographs. At night he and Pepa floated downriver. The sounds of their lovemaking, Guillermo was sure, reached the houses along the river. Did people stop to listen and think, What strange new animal is that? Is it hurt? Once, as they came to the rapids, he stowed the paddles under the seats and let the canoe find its own way through. "Hold on," he said, and the boat thrashed like a trapped bird. "Again," Pepa said when they had made it through and were back in calm waters, but once was enough, he told her.

The Germans returned after twenty-three days. Guillermo helped them carry their gear from their boat to the house. They were thinner than before and even tanner. Friedrich's left arm was in a sling. He had tripped over a root in the dark. "You will have to go to the clinic to see the doctors," Guillermo said, but Friedrich was sure it wasn't broken. It would heal on its own, he said. They had been in the jungle north of the river and to the Caribbean side. They would have stayed away longer, but they had run out of film.

"It will all be gone, all of it, when they build the canal," Friedrich said.

"What canal?" Guillermo asked.

"Come," Friedrich said. He unfolded a map on the floor, and he showed Guillermo his river and El Castillo and the two oceans. "They will come with machines and dig deep into the riverbed, deepening it, and they will tear down this town and the other towns along the river, and the river will be twice as wide and twice as deep, and huge ships will sail on the river, and they will tear down the trees in the jungle and replace them with buildings taller than the tallest trees."

This is impossible, Guillermo thought. One cannot make a river bigger, just as one cannot make a rock grow or turn an ant into a canary. "They will bring machines with giant claws and they will destroy our houses, pluck them up, and throw them in a heap," Friedrich said.

"When will this happen?" Guillermo asked.

"When the war is over," Friedrich said, and his eyes filled with tears.

But, despite Friedrich's tears, for a moment, more than a moment, Guillermo thought, Wouldn't it be wonderful to see a city growing out of the jungle, to live high up in the sky in a house of stone like the house where Pepa lived before the war?

"That is why the doctors are here," Friedrich continued, wiping his eyes with his fingertips.

"The doctors?" Guillermo asked.

"Do you think they would send them to take care of you? Do you think they care about you?"

Guillermo shook his head, for he knew that the government did not care about him or anyone in El Castillo. But Pepa's parents were different. Pepa was different, he thought, though he said nothing.

"Have they sent the vaccine yet?" Friedrich asked.

"We were all inoculated last Sunday," Guillermo said.

"You see?" Friedrich said.

But he didn't see.

# CHAPTER 6

THE GOVERNMENT SENT SOLDIERS AND A SPECIAL PRIEST—A more important one than Padre Manuel, who came once a month to give mass, baptize babies, and perform marriages—to oversee the vaccination process. The soldiers spread through El Castillo, banging on doors with the butts of their rifles, calling the people to the church for mass, though it was not Sunday and Padre Manuel had celebrated mass just the week before. "Faster, faster," they yelled, pointing their rifles at them. The vaccines had come packed in ice from San Carlos, so there was no time for delays.

Once they were all in the church, Pepa and her parents and Karl sat in the last row. The soldiers stood behind them, guarding the doors so that no one would escape; they smelled of cigarettes and sweat and metal. When the congregation rose, Pepa and her family rose, and when they sat down they did the same. When the parishioners and the soldiers, carrying their guns, filed up to the front and opened their mouths like baby birds so that the priest could place the host on their tongues, Pepa and her family stayed seated.

After the members of the congregation had filed back and

kneeled down and bowed their heads, the priest spoke. "It is your duty to God and country to do as the doctors say," he said, and he called Pepa's parents to the altar. Her father carried with him his black leather doctor's bag, a gift from his parents when he graduated from medical school. At the altar, her father bowed to the people of El Castillo, and he spoke in his careful, simple Spanish about the new medicine that had come all the way from the United States, that would keep them safe from yellow fever forever. Then he called for Pepa and Karl, and they rose and walked down the aisle while everyone watched.

Her father opened his bag and set a clean white cloth on the altar. Then he set a dozen needles, which he had prepared already with the vaccine, on the cloth as well as a bottle of rubbing alcohol and a package of cotton balls. He held up the first needle like the priest had held up the wine. "Come," he said to Pepa, and she approached him. He cleaned a spot on her arm just below the shoulder with alcohol and injected the contents of the needle. She did not flinch, did not cry out, though her arm throbbed and burned. The parishioners gasped. "Did it hurt?" her father asked her.

"Not at all," Pepa said, smiling.

Pepa's mother was next, and then Pepa's mother inoculated her husband. Then it was Karl's turn, and he too did not flinch. They all stood still and strong, looking straight ahead at the people of El Castillo.

Don Solano followed and then the priest and the soldiers. Pepa's father spoke to the congregation again. "We will finish at the clinic; please come to the clinic."

The soldiers raised their guns. "To the clinic, everyone," they ordered, pushing the townspeople out of the pews with their rifles. They all filed out of the church, and everyone trotted toward the clinic with the soldiers on their heels. When they were just a block away from the clinic, a few of the boys who worked on the

rubber plantation with Guillermo tried to run, heading in the opposite direction of the clinic, but they didn't get far. The soldiers
were young too, and they cornered them before they were able to
make it to the jungle path. The soldiers made the boys walk with
their hands on their heads, and when they reached the line, they
ordered everyone to stop, and they pushed the boys down on the
ground. The boys tried to cover their heads, but the soldiers kept
screaming, "Hands on your heads, hands on your heads," as they
kicked them in their ribs and stomachs and faces.

Pepa's father ran to the boys. "That's enough," he said to the
soldiers.

The soldiers laughed and kicked harder.

"No!" her father cried out, but they kept kicking.

A man from the line pulled her father away. "Come, you are
only making it worse," he said, and Pepa's father allowed himself
to be led away.

When they arrived at the clinic, Pepa's parents washed and bandaged the wounds of the boys whom the soldiers had beaten while
those in the front of the line watched. No one spoke a word or even
coughed as they had done from time to time while the priest was
giving out communion. The soldiers did not interfere. After the
boys' wounds had been cleaned, Pepa led them to the chairs in the
lobby. Pepa's parents explained again that the vaccine was safe,
that it came from the United States and was created by the most
famous doctors in the world. "We would not hurt you. We are doctors," they said, and people looked at the ground. They explained
how the vaccine worked and that some of them might react to the
vaccine more strongly than others, that they might get a fever and
a headache. "If this happens, make sure to drink plenty of water
and to sleep as much as possible. And don't be afraid," they said.
"It will not last more than one day."

They asked for volunteers, and Guillermo came to the front of the line. He smiled when the needle went in, but Pepa could see that his lips were quivering like when they first used to dance together. It was Pepa's job to put on the bandage afterward and to explain to each patient again about the possibility of fever. Guillermo did not say a word, but he nodded, acknowledging the instructions. She wanted to grab him, hold him right there in front of everyone, but, of course, she did not.

Some of the villagers trembled and some were perfectly still. Some cried out when the needle went in, some closed their eyes, some looked up at the ceiling. Some crossed themselves before and some after and some before and after, but no one had to be dragged up to the vaccination table by the soldiers. The soldiers grew bored, slumping against the wall, looking out the window. They smoked. At one point, Pepa glanced in their direction, and one of them winked, and she stared back at him, looked him straight in the eyes until he turned away.

That night Pepa could not sleep. Her arm throbbed and her limbs ached and she could not keep warm, so she got up and found her winter coat in the suitcase that contained the things they no longer needed. She lay on her bed curled up in her winter coat until dawn, imagining all the people in El Castillo shivering and aching in their separate houses in their separate beds. "Do not be afraid," she said to them and to herself. "Tomorrow it will all be over."

She fell asleep, finally, and when she woke up it was still dark, and she thought she heard Karl crying. She wanted to go to him, but she could not find the strength to move. The next time she woke up it was morning, and she could smell coffee coming from the kitchen. At some time in the night she must have taken off her coat. It was lying on the floor next to her bed, and it seemed like an object from another time period whose purpose was now a mystery.

*

Afterward, the town talked about who had gotten sick and who had not. It became something that people asked one another when they met at the dance or the market. The ones who had not experienced any symptoms began to believe that they were stronger than the others, that they had passed a test the others had failed, while those who had developed fevers believed only they were truly immune from yellow fever. When Pepa overheard these types of discussions in the market or at the *pulpería*, she tried to explain that how they reacted to the vaccine had nothing to do with their strength or lack of strength. "We are all safe now," she said, and they nodded, but she knew they were not convinced.

When Pepa reported these conversations to her parents, they said, "People believe all sorts of silly things, but it doesn't matter what they believe. What matters is they will not get sick."

"It would have been better to explain it to them first. Then maybe the soldiers would not have been necessary," Pepa suggested.

"We had no choice. That is how they decided to handle it," her mother said, but Pepa knew that it was more complicated than that.

Three weeks after the vaccinations, when Pepa's parents were on their way to inoculate the people of Greytown—one hundred kilometers downriver where the Río San Juan empties into the Caribbean—and those who had not gotten sick were beginning to forget it had happened and those who had stopped talking about it, Don Solano's skin turned yellow. The yellowness came on gradually, and most of his customers did not even notice the change, but by the third day the whites of his eyes were the color of egg yolks, and his first customer of the day turned around and fled. Within minutes the entire town knew he was sick.

Pepa's parents had given it three weeks before they left for Greytown, though they were sure that after one week, two at the most, there would be no anomalies, but it was as if the fever waited until they were gone to strike. Because no one knew what to do, they banged on the clinic door. "We need the doctors," they called. Pepa opened the door, and they flooded in, pacing back and forth.

"The doctors are in Greytown," Pepa said, though they already knew that.

"We will all die," they said. "You must help us. Don Solano has the fever."

"You are safe," she tried to explain. "You have been vaccinated." But they did not believe her, so Pepa followed them to Don Solano's store, where they left her to enter by herself. "Go," they said as she hesitated before opening the door. She did not explain that she hesitated not because she was afraid but because she did not know what to do. Finally, she opened the door. The bell rang, announcing her arrival.

Don Solano was lying in the corner near the kerosene containers, shivering, curled up like a child. "Don Solano," Pepa said, "I am here," and he turned over and looked at her with his egg-yolk eyes.

Somehow she managed to help him from the floor and up the stairs to his room above the shop, where he fell into his bed. "I'm cold," he said, "so cold," so she wrapped him in towels and still he was shivering. She tried to get him to drink water, but he closed his lips tight, pushed the glass away. She sat down on the chair next to his bed and waited. A brown crust was forming in the corners of his mouth. After a while, she tried again to give him water, but he pushed the glass from her hand and it fell to the floor, though it did not break. He slept, then. The light in the room changed. She was thinking it would be dark soon when Don Solano jolted awake, his eyes popping open, staring at her with yellow confusion. She tried again to make him drink, but still he refused. It was then that she remembered the potions he sold in his store.

She chose three bottles, one for skin problems and two for pain, and, remembering her parents' warning about Don Solano's medicine, she emptied their contents from the back porch into the river below. She filled the bottles with water and brought them to Don Solano, who was still curled up in fetal position, moaning.

"Don Solano," she whispered. "I have brought your medicine."

He opened his eyes again and tried to get up, but he fell back onto the bed.

"Look," she said, bringing one of the bottles closer so he could see it.

He leaned forward to look at the bottle and smiled.

"Open your mouth," she said, and she held the bottle to his mouth. "Drink."

He took a sip and spit it immediately onto the floor.

"I know it tastes terrible, but it will make you better," Pepa said. "It is your only chance."

He drank then, taking the bottle into his hands, gulping down the water like a child.

Toward dusk Guillermo came with food. They took turns eating on the porch. "It's cooler outside," Pepa said, though the real reason for eating outside was that Don Solano's room was starting to smell of urine. Pepa and Guillermo cared for Don Solano together through the night, making sure he drank each time he awoke, but after dawn he did not wake up again, though he was still breathing, calmly now.

When it was time for him to go to the *finca*, Guillermo did not want to leave her, but she insisted that she could manage on her own. "He's quiet now," she said.

In the afternoon two of the women from the market came with food. They called to her from the street, and Pepa went down to let them in. "Do not be afraid," Pepa said, and they did not hesitate to enter and followed her through the store and up the stairs to Don Solano's room. The market women lifted Don Solano and removed the urine-soaked sheet and towels, took off his clothes and washed him everywhere, wrapped him in fresh sheets, and swaddled him like a baby so that he was still.

Before the arrival of the market women, Pepa had been so focused on listening to Don Solano breathe, on waiting for him to open his eyes so she could give him water, that she did not notice the silence. But now that she had help, she felt it. She went to the window and looked out at the main street of the town. There was no one, not even a horse wandering on its own as horses did in El Castillo.

"Where is everyone?" she asked.

"They are afraid," the women said.

"And why aren't you afraid?" Pepa asked.

"Why aren't you afraid?" they said.

That evening Guillermo did not return to the *pulpería*, and now she began to be afraid. She could feel it in her groin and in her breasts, like desire. The market ladies insisted she get some sleep. They pulled her out onto the porch and put her into the hammock. "Sleep," they said, giving the hammock a push. "Close your eyes." And she did.

In the middle of the night Pepa woke sure that Guillermo was sick, that his eyes were yellow, sure that everyone except her and the market women were lying shivering and aching in their beds, but she did not cry or call to the market women. In the morning the market women insisted she eat the *gallo pinto* and fried cheese that they had prepared in Don Solano's kitchen.

"How is Don Solano?" she asked.

"The same," they said.

"Did he drink?"

"We gave him more medicine," they said, holding up the bottle. "And we had to wash him again."

"You gave him this?" Pepa said, picking the empty bottle up from the table.

"It is the same kind that you gave him, the one with the flowers and the rainbow," they said.

"I should have told you that I used those bottles to give him water because he refused to drink from a glass. I thought that if he thought it was medicine . . ."

"But it is medicine," they said.

"Water is what he needs," Pepa explained, rising to fill the bottle with water. When she returned the market women were kneeling on either side of Don Solano's bed praying. They prayed until Don Solano woke up. "Come," they said to Pepa, "you can give him water now."

The next time that Don Solano awoke, he was able to sit up and the market women fed him a few teaspoons of mashed avocado. "Who is minding the store?" he asked.

"You must focus on getting better," they answered.

"What if people need batteries or run out of butane?"

"They will make do," the market women said.

That evening Don Solano was strong enough to sit on the porch and to eat two boiled eggs and a tortilla. He was noticeably less yellow, and Guillermo was still not there. Pepa and the market ladies sat with Don Solano, watching him eat, mopping the eggs up with the tortilla, looking out at the river. He ripped off a piece of tortilla and threw it into the water. "Look," he said, pointing to a fish leaping up out of the water for the tortilla. He broke off another piece, and another, and the fish kept jumping, and Don Solano could not stop laughing. Pepa wanted to laugh too, laugh about how he had not died, but she felt the tears coming, and she could not stop them.

The market women wrapped her in their arms, held her tight until she calmed down and was able to tell them that she had been worrying all this time about Guillermo. "You must go find him," the market women said.

Pepa ran down the stairs and into the deserted street. At the church she turned and headed up the hill toward Guillermo's house. A man on a horse was approaching. He pulled the horse to the other side of the street, giving her a wide berth. "*Buenas*," he said, crossing himself at the same time.

"*Buenas*," she said.

She began to run, and she felt that she was flying. It was as if all her weight had been made up of dread, and now the dread had left her.

She passed a woman with a baby, and the woman pulled the baby close to her and ran into the trees. "It's all right. We're safe," Pepa said, but the woman kept running.

When she reached Guillermo's house, his mother spoke to her from the window. "He has gone to get the doctors," Guillermo's mother said.

"But it's too far," Pepa said. "They will be back before he even gets there," she added, but his mother had closed the window.

She did not know what to do then now that she understood his absence meant that he was not dead. She tried to be angry at him for not telling her, but she couldn't feel the anger. All she felt was a tremendous sadness, thinking of him paddling alone on the river.

The first day Don Solano was back at work, only Pepa and Karl came in to buy rice and butane. He looked so alone standing behind the counter in his Sunday clothes, smiling when they came in as if this were just an ordinary day and he had not just almost died and his eyes were not still yellow, though they were surely not as yellow as they had been before.

He gave them both candy as if Pepa were just a child and not the person who saved his life, but she accepted it gratefully. "Stay a bit," Don Solano said as they were leaving. "I could use some help with these boxes." So they moved the boxes from one side of the store to the other.

"Give them time," Pepa said, as she turned to leave.

He started crying then, wiping his tears with his hand and drying them on his trousers, and Pepa could not leave him alone crying, so she adjusted the boxes that they had moved and Karl swept the floor, and when they were done, Don Solano stopped crying. "You must have things to do," he said.

"Yes," Pepa said.

Pepa was right. Slowly the townspeople returned to the *pulpería*, and Don Solano greeted them with a smile, and they gave him their money. He asked them about their children and they talked about when the rains would stop as they had before he was sick. They noted that the whites of his eyes were not as white as they had been before, and, indeed, they were not and never would be until the day Don Solano died.

After almost dying, Don Solano dedicated an entire wall of his store to various potions and salves and tinctures, and he recounted the story of his miraculous recovery to anyone who would listen. At first they sold well, better than before. Pepa suspected that this was due mostly to the guilt that his customers felt for having been too afraid to offer help. But after a while people got tired of feeling bad for Don Solano and for themselves, got tired of hearing him talk about how the medicine had felt like music flowing through his veins and how it had been as if God were singing to him, so the potions stayed on the shelf, collecting dust as they had before.

Of course, Pepa told Don Solano how she tricked him into drinking water by using the bottles, but he held fast to his faith in the potions.

"I didn't give you the medicine," Pepa said.

"But there must still have been some of it left in the bottle," he insisted.

"It was water," she reiterated. "Water is what you needed to keep your liver functioning, to help it fight the disease."

"But I could feel the difference between the water and the medicine," Don Solano said. "I could feel the medicine working."

Pepa gave up arguing with Don Solano. She let him believe that he was right, and she didn't hold it against him, this preference for belief over knowledge, for she understood that after his illness, he discovered that the people with whom he had grown up and lived with for his entire life, who had known his parents, had abandoned him. After he realized that the world was not as he thought it was, he needed to hang on to something, one thing that was as it had been. She tried to imagine what it would be like to go back to Vienna, to live among those who had abandoned them, turned on them, to greet them in the butcher shop and sit next to them on the trolley. She imagined that in order to be able to go back, she also would have to believe in things that were not true.

# CHAPTER 7

LILIANA AND CAROLINA WALKED THROUGH THE PARK PAST THE benches where young lovers were kissing and did not stop when they walked by, did not notice their presence.

"They have nowhere else to go," Carolina said sadly.

"At least they have each other," Liliana said.

"This is true. You are not married?"

"No," Liliana said.

"You have never been married?"

"Not exactly," Liliana said.

"I see," Carolina said, but she didn't see, or perhaps she did. What had William told her when they waited in the mountains, when they lay in each other's arms, their guns within reach, ready? Did he say anything about her at all? Did he tell Carolina about the time when Liliana was fourteen and he barged into her room looking for a record she had borrowed without his permission and found her kissing Angie Moreno? He didn't say a word, just grabbed the album and walked out, slamming the door. Afterward she avoided him for days, wouldn't even look at him until he finally told her that he wasn't angry about the record anymore. "In fact," he said, "you can borrow my records anytime." And that was all they ever said about it. If he had not gone to Nicaragua, he would have known Irene. Maybe he would have sensed something about her, a hint, perhaps, of her future betrayal. If he had not gone to Nicaragua, she could have told him about how she had fantasies of poking Irene's hairy lover's eyes out and kicking him in the ribs until they broke. William would have understood.

Liliana did not ask Carolina whether she was married, but Carolina answered her as if she had. "My husband died three years ago."

"I'm sorry," Liliana said.

"It is what happens," Carolina said. "My children are all in your country. It is also what happens."

They exited the park and turned left in the opposite direction of the hotel toward the mountains. The street got narrower and darker, turning from pavement to dirt. When they came to the end there were some steps. There were no street lamps to light the way. Some of the steps were loose. "Be careful," Carolina said every once in a while. Despite her plumpness, she took the stairs nimbly, jumping almost. Once Liliana stumbled, and Carolina caught her.

At the bottom of the stairs they continued walking on a narrow path. They came to a stream. Carolina crossed first, and then she watched to make sure that Liliana didn't fall. "You can make it," she said.

"Of course I can," Liliana said, trying not to be annoyed.

They arrived at a small wooden house. A dog ran to greet them, followed by a few scraggly chickens. "She won't bite," Carolina said.

"It's okay. I like dogs," Liliana said, petting the dog, letting it lick her hand.

Inside the house was pitch black. "Just a minute," Carolina said. Liliana heard her fumbling, the sound of a lighter, and then the lamp was lit and the room came into view. The only furniture was a plastic table and four plastic chairs. The walls were painted a violet blue that reminded Liliana of snow at dusk, like an igloo, Liliana thought, though she had never been in an igloo. In one corner there was a rifle. The air was still and hot. "Welcome," Carolina said. "I have prepared dinner. Please sit."

Liliana knew not to protest. "Thank you, can I help?" she asked.

"Sit," Carolina said again, so Liliana sat down.

Outside the dog was barking.

After a few minutes, Carolina returned carrying a tray with a plate of *gallo pinto*, a stack of warm tortillas wrapped in a cloth, a glass, and a jug of water. She set everything in front of Liliana. "Aren't you going to eat?" Liliana asked.

"I am not hungry," Carolina said.

Carolina stood up and went to the cupboard and took out a book, which she carried to the table in both hands as if it were heavy, though it was a thin volume. She set it down on the table. "This was his," she said, sitting down again.

It was Lorca. Of course it was Lorca, the same edition as hers, given to her on her thirteenth birthday as William's had been given to him. "*Verde que te quiero verde.*" It was the poem they recited instead of the Sabbath prayer every Friday night. When they were very young, her mother was the one who did the recitation, but when William turned six he took over, and after Liliana's sixth birthday they took turns, though for Passover, they recited it together, holding hands. "What exactly does it mean? What does it mean that he wants her green?" Liliana asked her mother when she began to understand that the poem was about death.

"What matters is not the meaning but that it is beautiful," her mother had said.

"What does it mean?" Carolina asked now.

"What did William say?"

"That death is beautiful, but that is only something young people say. I have my own thoughts." Carolina got up and returned the book to the cupboard.

The dog started barking again. Carolina opened the door and went outside, and Liliana could hear her speaking to it gently. "*Cálmate, que no pasa nada,*" she said, and after a while the dog stopped barking, and Carolina came inside and sat down again. "It's getting late. I will take you back now, and tomorrow I will take you to see his grave," she said.

"I can find my way," Liliana said.

Carolina laughed. "Come," she said.

The dog followed, but when they got to the stream it turned around and went home. "It doesn't like water," Carolina said. "Imagine, a dog who is afraid of water."

Carolina took her back to the restaurant, where the musicians were still playing, but they did not go inside. "I will meet you here at eight tomorrow morning." Just as she was turning to go back, she added, "You have met El Justo."

"Yes," Liliana said. "How did you know?"

Carolina smiled but did not answer. "What did he tell you about William?"

"I did not ask him about William."

"Do not believe anything he says," Carolina said, and she walked away.

Liliana stood at the entryway looking in at the musicians, and she tried to imagine William sitting with them, but she could only think of him as he was in that photograph, the cigarette dangling from his lips.

Finally Liliana went inside, and she stayed longer than she wanted to stay, sitting next to Santiago, drinking the beers that he bought for her, thinking each time the waiter brought a new one that all she wanted was sleep, but she did not want to be alone in

Santiago's house, lying in his son's bed in the room with the chest that contained the toy trucks and cars that Santiago's son did not play with.

It was after two when they stopped playing, and Santiago and Liliana stumbled home, arm in arm like sister and brother, she thought, though she had never walked arm in arm with William, never stumbled home with him. She would have liked that, to get drunk with William. She wondered what they would have talked about. Would they have reminisced about their childhoods, about the time he took her on the Staten Island Ferry and she threw up the whole way there and the whole way back? Would they have talked about love? They had never even drunk a toast together, not even at their last dinner before he left for Nicaragua. There was wine, but they did not toast. They ate, but she did not taste what they were eating, though their mother made William's favorite meal—roast chicken and marzipan cake for dessert. Perhaps William enjoyed his going-away dinner, but Liliana could hardly swallow, and their mother did not eat the cake. Their father was silent, and he did not speak William's name until they got the letter from Carolina. "William," he said, and then he was silent again.

She wished now, as she lay in Santiago's son's bed, that she knew a prayer, that she could lie there with the room spinning and the fan whirring and recite the Kaddish for her brother, but all she knew was poetry, "*Verde que te quiero verde*," she said, and then, "Irene, what have you done?"

Shortly after she fell asleep, she was awakened by dogs, a pack of them howling and barking. She tried covering her ears with the pillow, but she could still hear them in the distance. The room was spinning, and she felt as if she would suffocate or scream, but she did neither.

"Irene," she whispered. "Where are you?"

At some point the dogs stopped barking or she stopped caring that they were barking and she fell asleep, but she awoke again before dawn. If she wanted to escape, this was the time, she thought. She could walk down to the new highway that everyone was so proud of, take the first bus to Managua, be on a plane by evening. But then what would she tell her mother, that she was afraid of the details, that she was afraid to learn that he had killed? No, fear was never an option with her mother. How many times had she told them how she walked deep into the jungle at night, how she lay on the jungle floor and repeated over and over again, "I will never be afraid again," until her heart began to slow down and her muscles relaxed, how she stayed on the jungle floor, calm and unafraid, how she could feel the insects crawling over her, how she could hear rustling in the trees, how the monkeys screamed? No, there was no other choice but to meet Carolina.

When she arrived at the appointed meeting place at eight, Carolina was already waiting. They proceeded down the hill past the ugly cathedral. They crossed the new highway and walked up the path to the gate of the cemetery, which was locked, but Carolina had the key. They continued without speaking, Liliana following Carolina as she had the night before, though there was plenty of room for them to walk side by side.

"Here," Carolina said, and she stopped, pointing to a mausoleum painted black and red, the Sandinista colors. Carolina opened the padlock, bent down, and entered the mausoleum. Liliana did not follow her. "Come," Carolina called, but Liliana had never been inside a mausoleum before. Her father's grave was simple, a gravestone with no inscription, not even something in Hebrew. When they visited they brought stones, and she had forgotten to bring stones. "Come," Carolina said again, and so Liliana went inside. Carolina lit a candle and kneeled in front of an altar, upon which were a vase of plastic flowers and a gun—his gun? Liliana put her hand on the gun, kept it there for a moment. She had expected the metal to be cold because that is how she thought of metal, but it was hot like everything in Nicaragua. "You can pick it up," Carolina said, but she did not want to pick it up. She did not want to feel what he had felt when he held it. She did not want to think of him holding it, aiming, shooting—killing. She wanted to think of him that day on the ferry when he lifted her up over the rails so she could vomit into the water. She wanted to hear his voice in her ear, whispering, "Don't be afraid. I've got you." She wanted to feel safe.

"Why is there a cross?" Liliana asked in order to keep herself from crying. "I thought communists didn't believe in religion."

"We were not communists," Carolina said. "We were Sandinistas."

"Did William tell you what happened to our father's family? Did he tell you any of that?"

"He said that his father did not know how to fight."

A terrible smell was filling the tomb, a stink as familiar as spring and as fleeting as memory. It could not be William's body, dead and buried for twenty-five years.

"What is that smell?" Liliana asked, covering her nose with her hand.

"What smell?"

"How can you not smell it?" Liliana felt the contents of her gut rising to her mouth, and she leaned over and wretched right there in her brother's mausoleum, right there beside his gun and the stupid plastic flowers and the candle.

# CHAPTER 8

GUILLERMO KNEW THAT GREYTOWN WAS FAR AWAY, THOUGH HE did not know how far. He thought first of asking the Germans, for they would know, but he knew that they would stop him, say that there was no point, that it was too late to help Don Solano, so he left without telling anyone, taking with him only his fishing pole and rifle and a tarp to protect him from the rain. Perhaps, he thought, it was better not to know how far he would have to travel. Perhaps if he knew he would not believe he could make it.

Later when he returned, he could not say how long he had been away. He did not remember sleeping or eating, though he knew he must have done both, but he remembered clearly the moment he came to the end of the river and looked out at the waves of the Caribbean and the expanse of water before him, and thinking that seeing the sea was like being able to read books.

In town he asked a group of old men sitting in the park near the docks, already halfway through a bottle of rum though it was only eleven in the morning, if they knew where the doctors were staying. The doctors, they said, had come and gone the day before or the day before that. They could not remember.

"But I did not see them on the river," Guillermo said, and they laughed. The doctors had been flown in and out in the government plane.

"Has anyone gotten sick?" Guillermo asked.

"No, we have the vaccine now," they said, showing him the needle marks on their arms.

"In El Castillo a man is dying even though he had the shot," Guillermo said.

The men laughed again, exuberantly, to cover up their fear.

"Is it true they are going to build a canal?" Guillermo asked to change the subject because he felt his own fear welling up again, though he did not trust these men to know the truth about anything.

"That is what they say, but they have been talking about it ever since I can remember. The canal will make us rich; the canal will make us important," the oldest of the men said. "When I was a boy, steamships bigger than palaces used to sail up and down this river, and we used to watch them pass, my friends and I. We all believed that one day we would swim into the river and climb onto one of those ships. But now most of us are dead and nothing has changed except that the ships no longer sail on the river."

"Why didn't you go?" Guillermo asked.

The old man shrugged, coughed, and spat a wad of phlegm onto the ground. "Love," the old man said.

"You could have taken her with you," Guillermo said.

"Sometimes the ships stopped here, and the men disembarked, and they got drunk and destroyed the chairs and tables in the bars and in the morning the whores had black eyes and broken arms and bruises on their bellies. How could I have taken her to be among such men?"

"You could have protected her," Guillermo said.

The old man offered Guillermo a drink. He took a swig from the bottle, and the liquor burned his stomach. He could not remember the last time he had eaten.

"More," the old man said, and Guillermo drank again, feeling the rum find the emptiness of his gut.

When the sun was at its strongest, the bottle was empty, and the oldest man took Guillermo to his house at the edge of town and insisted Guillermo sleep in his bed. "No," Guillermo said, but the old man had already lain down on the floor.

"Sleep," the old man said.

"What happened to the girl?" Guillermo asked.

"She died in childbirth," he said.

"And the baby?"

"He lived three days longer than his mother."

"And after that?"

"Nothing," the old man said. "Nothing."

When Guillermo awoke it was dark, though he had no idea whether night had just begun or was about to end.

"Old man," he said, for he did not know his name, but the old man did not stir, so he remained in the old man's bed, waiting for daybreak, watching him sleep, thinking about, if he had to choose, would he choose Pepa or the ship, wondering whether love was just an excuse for cowardice. When dawn came, the old man was still sleeping, so he left him to his dreams and found his way back to the river.

After his journey, Guillermo found El Castillo was not as it was before, though on the outside nothing had really changed. Don Solano survived the fever despite the fact that the doctors were not there to help and only he and Pepa and the market women had come to his aid.

He lost his job on the *finca* because he left without asking for leave, though they would not have granted him leave anyway because there were more young men waiting to work on the *finca* than there were jobs. To fill the empty days, he spent more time with the Germans, accompanying them on their hikes in the jungle. He learned the Latin names of plants and trees and insects. They took more photographs of him—leaning naked against trees, facing forward and backward, close-ups of his thighs and belly. They spent more time in the jungle, and the rolls of film accumulated. At night he watched them develop the film, but they couldn't keep up—there were so many pictures. The Germans grew thinner, their faces gaunt from not eating, from staying up all night developing pictures. The chemicals burned away the outer layers of the skin on their hands, and they were covered with cuts and sores, but they would not stop, nor would they let Guillermo come anywhere near the chemicals. "Your hands are too beautiful," they said, and they took photographs of his hands.

In the evenings they drank rum and talked about what the Germans called "the unanswerable questions" and about the difference between courage and cowardice, weakness and strength. "We would have helped if we had known Don Solano was ill. Why didn't you tell us?" the Germans said, and Guillermo did not answer because he did not want to admit it had not occurred to him to ask for their help. Then he would have had to explain why, and he had no answer except that there was something about them that was not quite real to him. Instead, he recounted what he learned in Greytown about the steamships, and they told him about the thousands of men who traveled the river from the Atlantic to the Pacific on their way to California in the race to get gold. Gold fever, they called it.

"Like yellow fever," Guillermo said.

Friedrich laughed. "Yes, only much more deadly."

"You can die from gold?" Guillermo asked.

"You can die from wanting it," Friedrich said.

"You can die and kill from wanting it," Georg added.

"I cannot imagine wanting anything so much that I would die or kill for it," Guillermo said.

"That is because you have nothing," Georg said.

"But if tomorrow I woke up and I had everything, owned the rubber *finca* and cows and boats, I would still not die or kill to keep them," Guillermo argued.

"If you woke up tomorrow with all those things, you would no longer be you," Georg said.

"Who would I be?" Guillermo asked.

"That is impossible to know," Georg answered.

That was the way it was with the Germans. They talked like poems, and he could feel the truth in what they said, but when he tried to put into his own words what they were saying, he was left with nothing.

"During the gold fever there was a train in El Castillo," Friedrich continued. "Since the steamships could not navigate the rapids, the cargo from the steamships was unloaded on the far side of the rapids and transferred to a train, which would take it to the other side, where another steamship was waiting. It was the shortest railroad in the world."

"Where is the train now?" he asked the Germans.

"They took it away."

"Where did they take it?" Guillermo asked, but the Germans did not know. They only knew that it was not there anymore, that even the tracks had disappeared.

"I have never heard anyone talk of these things before," Guillermo said.

"You don't believe us?" the Germans asked.

"No, I believe you," Guillermo said, "but does that mean that everyone else is lying?"

"No, it means that they do not think it is important or that it has been forgotten," Friedrich said.

"Isn't that a form of lying?" Guillermo asked, and they agreed that it was.

# CHAPTER 9

"**Do you think the river can feel the rain?**" **Guillermo** asked the night that Pepa first knew something was growing inside her. They were out on the river, and it was raining, and they were lying naked on the floor of the canoe.

"The river cannot feel," Pepa said.

"How do you know?"

"Because it's not alive."

"I think it can feel," Guillermo said.

"Okay, let's pretend we are the river," Pepa said, closing her eyes. "What do you feel?"

"I feel the rain. Do you feel it?"

"I feel the fish swimming inside me," Pepa said, and that's when she knew.

"I feel them, too," Guillermo said, taking her hand. "And I feel the rocks."

"What do they feel like?"

"Like bones."

"Can you feel your bones?"

"Yes."

"What do they feel like?"

"Like rocks," Guillermo said.

"Can the rocks feel the river?"

"Yes," Guillermo said, and Pepa wanted more than anything to believe that the river could feel the rain and the rocks could feel the river and the river could feel them floating on top of it, letting the rain flow into their open mouths, but she didn't believe it, never would. She turned and pulled Guillermo close, kissed him softly on the lips. "I love you," she said.

During the time that the child was growing inside of her, she spent more and more time alone. Her parents were away almost all the time now, vaccinating the people of San Carlos and San Miguelito and the smaller hamlets along the river. So there were fewer chores, no clothes and towels to wash for the clinic, no instruments to sterilize. There was just Karl to take care of and the daily sweeping and the chickens and the garden to tend to. Guillermo was gone too, working on a coffee *finca* across the border in Costa Rica, so she spent most of her time reading. On Sundays she saw Guillermo. Once he brought her lipstick he bought from the traveling salesman who came to the *finca* on payday. When she opened the tube, it smelled of the past, of her mother when they lived in Vienna and she worked at the important hospital and her parents went out at night to the opera and to the theater, and she realized then that she did not know what her mother smelled like anymore. She went to her room to apply the lipstick, sucking her lips together as she remembered her mother doing. She stood looking in the mirror for a long time, trying to like the way she looked, telling herself that Guillermo had spent his precious money on this, on her. She closed her eyes and opened them again, and then she walked back to where Guillermo was waiting, sitting at the table. She approached, her eyes focused on a lizard on the wall behind him, her arms held fast against her sides. Guillermo did not say a word, but she kept staring at the lizard. If the lizard moves, I will look at him, she said to herself, but the lizard stayed put.

"Well?" she said without looking at him.

Guillermo kissed her hard on the lips. "It tastes like one of Don Solano's medicines," he said, wiping the red from his own lips, holding out his smeared fingers. Pepa took his fingers in her mouth, licking them clean, and he plunged his fingers deep into her throat and pushed her down onto the wooden floor, smearing the lipstick from her lips, wiping it on her belly and thighs. Afterward they lay on the wooden floor like wounded animals, Pepa thought, like dead monkeys.

They lay side by side on the floor until it began to get dark, and then they made love again, quietly, as if someone in the next room were listening. After Guillermo left, Pepa almost threw the lipstick in the garbage, but instead she put it in the pocket of her winter coat, the one that warmed her when she had the fever. She never wore lipstick again, not even when she was living once more where there was winter and movie theaters and elevators, but she always kept the tube in her coat pocket so that during the winter, when she was as far away from the river as she could be, she remembered.


Pepa's parents returned. Their work along the Río San Juan was done, and though the American embassy in Managua had made it clear there would be no visas until after the war, it seemed that someone, perhaps even the president, had pulled some strings. They were going to New York.

"We are leaving this place," her father said, making a chant of it, "We are leaving this place, leaving this place, leaving, leaving,

leaving," picking her up, twirling her around as if she were still the young girl she had been when they left Vienna four years ago. "How big you have grown," he said as if it had been years rather than weeks since he had last seen her, as if he had gone off to war and returned years later.

Pepa did not tell Guillermo about the visas. She let him make plans. He had money now. Soon he would have enough to start building their house.

"I want our house to be shaped like a triangle so that it is different from all the other houses in the town," Guillermo said.

"What if I want a circle?" she asked.

"Then it will be a circle," Guillermo said.

"What if I don't want to live in a house?"

"Where would we live if not in a house?" Guillermo asked.

"In the jungle," Pepa said, and Guillermo laughed.

Her parents left again, this time for Managua to take care of the paperwork for their visas, but they returned empty-handed, despondent. At the embassy, they made them wait for hours only to tell them there had been a glitch. "What kind of glitch?" her parents inquired, but the clerk shook his head. "It is impossible to know," he said.

Her parents called the uncle, and he called his important friends, who, in turn, called their important friends. "Leave it to me. You must be patient. When everything is ready, I will telegram," the uncle said, so Pepa's parents returned to El Castillo. They were so absorbed by their frustrations and the fear that they would never make it to New York, to what they considered their real lives, that they did not notice the change in Pepa, and Pepa did not tell them. It would have made things so much worse, and it would not be right to tell them before she told Guillermo, who was away more than he was home, making money for their house, for the baby he did not know existed.

Pepa was sick every morning, but by the time the sun came up, her parents were already with patients in the clinic, so she was able to keep this from them and they did not know that she put sugar on her eggs and could no longer stand the smell of bananas or fish. One afternoon she killed a chicken and ate it all herself. She buried the bones in the bushes behind the house. Only Karl noticed a chicken missing.

"It was sick, so I had to kill it," she told him.

"I thought it was behaving strangely," Karl said.

"Why didn't you tell me? It could have infected the other chickens. It's lucky I caught it in time," Pepa said.

"I forgot," Karl said.

"Well next time, don't forget," Pepa said.

She asked the women in the market what to do about the morning sickness, and they said it would go away once the baby was sure it had the strength to be part of this world, sure that it wanted to be part of the world.

"And what if it isn't strong? What if it's afraid?" Pepa asked.

"Then it will stop eating and die. If that happens, you will have cramps and it will come out of you in a stream of blood," they said.

"Thank you," Pepa said. "Please, do not tell anyone what I have told you."

"Does Guillermo know?"

"No," she said.

"You must tell him," they said.

"I will," she assured them. "Soon. Please, don't tell anyone."

"We won't," they promised.

There were times when she was sure that Guillermo knew, that he could feel the child growing inside her, feel its warmth in her belly and thighs. There were times, also, when she lost the sensation of its presence. This made her tremble with both relief and dread. It was during this time that she came as close as she ever had to praying. "What do I want?" she called out into the night, but only the monkeys answered, screeching as they always did about things that had nothing at all to do with her.

Finally word came from the uncle. The visas were ready. Her parents rejoiced, and Pepa dreamed that her sheets were soaked in blood. She awoke in the morning shaking and crying, covered in sweat, belly exposed, and her mother was there, standing in the doorway.

Her mother did not say a word. She did not ask who the father was. She did not demand to know why and how she had kept this a secret. She did not ask her whether she loved him, this boy, whoever he was. She leaned over and put her hand on Pepa's belly, holding it there. She left the room and returned with a stethoscope, and Pepa felt the coldness of it on her stomach, and she closed her eyes so she did not have to look at her.

"All right," her mother said, and she stood up and left Pepa there on her bed. Pepa waited, listening to her parents talking in the other room. All morning she waited for them to come to her room, to say something, but they did not. At noon, she smelled food cooking, but they did not bring her anything to eat or ask her whether she was hungry.

Night came and she rose and watched them from her doorway. They sat at the table, talking in low voices so that she could not hear. She would wait for them to go to bed so she could find Guillermo in Costa Rica. For hours she waited, and she grew tired, so she lay down on her bed to rest. At around midnight the talking stopped, but she did not hear them get up, didn't hear the chairs scraping on the floor, so she checked again. They were just sitting there looking at their hands, not talking. Pepa slept for a while, and when she awoke, she could hear them whispering again, though this time she could also hear her mother crying.

In the morning, her parents spoke to her from the doorway.

"Pepa," they called. How had she slept so long, so late? She always woke before dawn, when the roosters crowed. The chickens. She had forgotten the chickens. Her mother followed her out of the house onto the patio. "Where are you going?"

"To feed the chickens," Pepa said.

"I already did it," her mother said, putting her hand on her shoulder, leading her back into the house.

She thought about bolting then, running past her. She could go to the Germans. They would help her get to Costa Rica. Her parents would not run after her. It was not their way. But she didn't run. She went back to her room, to her bed. "We are all tired," her mother said from the doorway.

She lay on her bed, but she could not sleep. She put her hand on her stomach the way her mother had done, cupping it, feeling the tightness of it. She was so tired, more tired than she had been the night they left Vienna on the train that was so crowded that she fell asleep standing up, pressed up against the other refugees. She would rest now, simply rest. When she woke up, she would feel stronger. Then she would know what to do. Now was the time to sleep, to remember how she and Guillermo had danced like ships and lain down on the jungle floor.

# CHAPTER 10

**I**T WAS **D**ON **S**OLANO WHO TOLD **G**UILLERMO THAT **P**EPA WAS gone, that they had snuck off on the early *lancha* for San Carlos. He had not called to them or run down to the dock to say good-bye. "If they had wanted to say good-bye, they would have done so," he told Guillermo.

"I will find them," Guillermo said, but as he said it he knew that he would not, that he could not find them. The world was too big, the distances too far.

"She will come back someday," Don Solano said, but Guillermo knew that she would not. He knew that she would have found a way to stay behind with him if that was what she wanted.

Guillermo went back to the coffee *finca* in Costa Rica. He saved all the money he earned because there was nothing he needed except Pepa, who was gone. He took on extra shifts because there was nothing else but work. In the evenings when the other workers went to the nearby village to drink rum and walk with women, he stayed back in the barracks, reading poems from the book the Germans had given him, whispering them into the night.

On Sundays he did not return to El Castillo. There was nothing there now except the river, and he did not want to be reminded of the river and about his journey to the Caribbean and the steamships and the caimans whose eyes shone like stars in the night. He walked instead, walked for hours, cutting a path with his machete, and when he was tired, he walked back the way he came. "What are you looking for in the jungle?" the other workers asked him.

"Peace," he answered, and the men got the message and kept their distance.

Guillermo woke up one Sunday morning before dawn and realized that three months had passed since he visited El Castillo. Three months had gone by and he had no memory of living those months, though he knew that he had picked coffee beans and walked and eaten and slept and worked again, and he supposed that he had longed for Pepa, supposed that this ache had always been with him, even in sleep. Yet he did not remember any of it. And the pain of losing her hit him with an even greater force than when he first learned from Don Solano that she was gone. So he went to the village with the other men and he drank too much and paid a woman three times what she asked for, and she did not thank him, or let him sleep in her bed until morning, even though he paid her three times what she asked for, even though he had nowhere else to go. There were men waiting outside in the hall. "I cannot turn them away," she said.

"I will pay you five times more," Guillermo said.

"If I turn them away tonight, they will find someone else, and then I will be left with no one."

He passed the men waiting patiently outside her door. "*Adiós, amigo,*" they called after him. "Be careful," they said, laughing as he stumbled into the wall.

Outside the night air was heavy and hot, the stars hidden behind the clouds, though it was not raining yet. He started walking back toward the *finca*. He felt as if he had been walking for days without sleeping, without food, though he was not hungry. His foot caught on a root in the path and he fell, and after that he could not get up, so he lay there, and the rain started, and it beat down on him, and he fell asleep. In the morning his clothes were thick with mud.

When he arrived back at the barracks the men were already at work. Since he did not want to explain himself to the boss, standing there covered in mud, did not want to beg for his job just so the boss could tell him that he never wanted to see him again, he returned to the barracks, where he took his time washing up, pouring buckets of water over himself, letting the water touch him where Pepa had touched him, feeling her in the water. When he was clean and dressed, he packed his few belongings and went to where he had buried the tin that held the money he was saving. He wanted to rip the bills into tiny pieces, leave them useless on the wet ground, but he knew he would regret it as he regretted his night in San Carlos with the woman, so he put the money in his pocket and headed home.

When he got to El Castillo, he stood on the banks of the river for a long time. A few paces away was a pig, and it watched him watching the river, grunting. It was as if it were goading him, saying, what are you going to do, just stand there in the mud like me watching this river that never changes, breathing in the smell of your own feces, waiting to be slaughtered? "No," he said out loud, and he turned away from the river and began walking toward his parents' house to say good-bye.

His mother was so happy to see him, and she cried and told him how much she missed him. Because of this, because he knew he was leaving, that night it was impossible to sleep in his own bed in the house where he had grown up. The night was so long, and the thought of lying in his bed waiting for the sun to come up filled him with dread and with longing for Pepa, who was far away living a life that he could not even imagine, so he got up, put on his clothes, walked out of his house and into the night. He thought he would walk to the river, sit on the banks and listen to it flowing, but instead he found himself on the path to the Germans' house.

They welcomed him as they always did, brought out the rum and mangoes, and the Lorca, and the camera, of course the camera. "We missed you," they said, and Guillermo said that he missed them, too. Friedrich made fried plantains and they ate the plantains and drank more rum, and when they were full, they went outside and walked into the jungle, and they took photographs of Guillermo, the flash setting the jungle on fire, and Guillermo could feel that Pepa was there, watching him, touching him. He could feel her on him as he lay on the ground.

Afterward, he fell asleep as soon as his head hit the pillow, and he would have slept soundly until morning if Georg had not come into his room, had not lain down beside him, pushed his tongue into his mouth. But that is what he did, and Guillermo did not stop him. He welcomed the taste of him, the hardness of Georg's body, the power of it. Like the river flowing to the sea, it could not be stopped. They slept then, Georg's arm around him, and when they woke with the first light of dawn, Friedrich was standing in the doorway. "Why?" he whispered, "Why?" and Guillermo wanted to get out of the bed, go to Friedrich, take his hand and lead him to the bed so that the three of them could sleep with their arms around each other and their legs entwined like the roots of a tree, like vines.

Guillermo went home, back to his parents' house. "Where have you been?" his father asked.

"Nowhere," Guillermo said, and he crawled into his bed and slept, and when he woke up it was noon.

His mother killed a chicken, and she fed him chicken soup and tortillas and plantains, and he ate the whole chicken because she insisted she was not hungry, that he should eat it all himself. After eating he was full and tired, so he slept again until dusk, when he woke with a start, though there had been nothing to disturb his sleep. His mother was waiting with more food, and his father offered him beer and rum, but his stomach was still heavy from the chicken and from sleeping all afternoon, and because he didn't know what to do, he ran.

Guillermo stayed away from El Castillo for two years. There was nothing in particular that made him return, no longing for home, no specific sadness. Perhaps he was tired of moving around, and in the two years since he left the river he had not found any place or anyone in any place that made him want to stay. Granted, he had not gone farther than the Panama Canal, which turned out to be a big disappointment. He had imagined a city growing out of the river and ships the size of mountains. He thought he would find work on one of those ships that would take him far away, but the ships already had their crews and they just passed through quietly, leaving him behind. Yet he stayed, working on the sidelines, watching the ships pass, saving money. He was good at that, saving money. He thought perhaps that when he had enough money he would buy a ticket on one of the ships, but in the end, that is not what he did, for he understood that he preferred imagining all the places he could go, dreaming about them and about the day that he would knock on Pepa's door, and she would answer it and say his name, say I knew you would find me.

Though he had felt no longing to return, the first sight of the river brought tears to his eyes, and this sudden flow of emotion both surprised and embarrassed him. "I don't want to see it," he said out loud, quoting Lorca. "*¡Que no quiero verlo!*" But he did not look away. Instead, he confronted it straight on—the white herons drying their wings on its shore, the trees standing guard, the rocks—and he felt an urge to fling himself into the river, to let it carry him away so that he would never again have to think or cry or work or sleep. "I give up," he said, but he did not jump.

The day that Guillermo returned, El Castillo was unusually hot, and the vendors who waited for the *lanchas* to arrive barely had the energy to advertise their wares. Instead of calling out what they had to offer, making a song of it as they usually did, they simply stood there, holding heavy baskets of tortillas and cheese, fruit and candies. It was as if the town had gone mute.

Two days earlier Don Solano had collapsed in his store. His customers had carried him upstairs to his bed, and the market women watched over him again, fed him broth and avocadoes. Don Solano did not speak a word to them and so they thought he had lost the ability to speak, but when Guillermo came to see him he said, "I knew you would come."

Guillermo sat down on the bed and took Don Solano's hand. "Of course," he said, though he had not been summoned.

"I have no one," Don Solano said.

"I am here," Guillermo said.

"I will be dead soon and then all this will be yours," Don Solano said. "Open that drawer," he said, barely able to lift his arm to point.

Guillermo opened the drawer. Inside was the photograph of Don Solano and his wife on their wedding day. "Underneath the photo. Read it," Don Solano said. "It's all yours now."

Though Guillermo knew it was a gift, it sounded to him like a curse, so instead of accepting the offer, he squeezed Don Solano's hand. "Sleep, Don Solano," he said, and Don Solano closed his eyes and never woke up.

The day after Don Solano's funeral, Guillermo invited everyone in the town to a feast. Tables were set up in the plaza in front of the church and the *banda* played and there was plenty of rum. The townspeople drank toasts to Don Solano and to his store and to his remedies. The sun was already hot when the last revelers stumbled home. Guillermo stayed until the end. Though he did not drink too much or dance, it was pleasant being there, with the people of the town, with the music playing and the river flowing by, and he understood that perhaps Don Solano had not been unhappy after all, that perhaps he had found pleasure simply in being where he was.

The Germans did not come to Don Solano's funeral. They disappeared shortly after Guillermo two years earlier, the townspeople said. "What has become of their house?" Guillermo asked, and they warned him not to go near it. "There is something evil there," they told him, and he laughed. "There is no such thing as evil," he said, and they laughed.

Still, after the party he went to the Germans' house. It was as it was when he had last seen it, but there was a stillness surrounding the place that had not existed before, even in the dead of the afternoon when the jungle slept. He opened the door. The smell of feces overwhelmed him, so he shut it quickly and prepared himself to confront what he would find inside. He put his hand over his nose and mouth, held his breath, and opened the door again. Books were everywhere, strewn all over the floor, their pages scattered about. The chairs were overturned, as was the table. He slipped on a smashed papaya and fell. On the piano sat a monkey, smirking. There were more of them, perched on the shelves where the books had once been, watching him. He stood up slowly, trying not to make an abrupt movement, keeping his eyes on the monkeys. He took a step backward; one of the monkeys jumped from the bookshelf onto the piano keys. *Pling*, another *pling*, and when Guillermo stepped farther into the living room, the monkey jumped down, screeching, calling to the others, who came, an entire platoon of them lunging toward him, and he crouched on the floor, covering his head, waiting for the attack, but when he finally had the courage to look up, they were gone, even the piano player.

It was a year before the smell of the monkeys was completely gone, though he had washed and scrubbed the walls and floors and burned everything—the furniture (all of it except the sofa, which he stripped and repainted); the rugs; the books, of course; the photographs, even the ones that the monkeys had not defecated on. He thought of keeping one photo as a memento. One day, perhaps, there would be someone to tell about the Germans and he could show that person the photograph, but he couldn't decide which one to pick, so they all went into the fire.

On the day he woke up and could no longer smell the monkeys, he knew that this was where he would always live, and he imagined the years that lay ahead of him stretching out as long as the river. He invited his parents to live in the back wing where the photographs had been, but they refused to step inside the house. No one in El Castillo would, not even the priest, who claimed that at night the sounds of the Germans' unnatural acts could still be heard even after they were gone.

"What unnatural acts?" Guillermo asked, though he knew precisely what the priest meant. "They were in love with nature, with the jungle, the birds, the insects even. Is it unnatural to love nature?"

"One cannot love nature and defy it at the same time," the priest said.

"This is true," Guillermo said, and the priest thought Guillermo finally understood, but that was not it at all.

"The noise, thank God, stopped when you arrived," the priest said, crossing himself.

Guillermo did not tell him that what they had heard were only monkeys.

"We are happy to have you back," the priest said, putting his hand on Guillermo's shoulder.

But I am not me anymore. *Pero ya no soy yo*, Guillermo thought.

The first time Marta came to El Castillo, a year after he had salvaged the Germans' house, she came into the *pulpería* with her heavy sacks filled with what she called *artículos de lujo*. She dumped the contents of one bag on the floor—plastic dolls, brushes, key chains that said *¡Qué viva Nicaragua!*, toy trucks, belts and party shoes and dresses. "Take a look," she said. Guillermo picked up a pair of white patent leather shoes.

"Very nice," he said, though he had no opinion whatsoever about shoes.

She took a can of sardines off the shelf, dusted it off. "How long have you had this?" she asked.

"A while," Guillermo said.

"I guarantee you will sell every last item from these two bags by the time I return."

"And when will you return?" he asked.

"In less than a week. In five days," she said, leaving the dusty can of sardines on the counter.

Guillermo dedicated a section in the store to clothing and the other *artículos de lujo*, and the people of El Castillo agreed that the products at his *pulpería* were just as good as what they could buy in San Carlos, and they were cheaper, too, for Marta always gave him a good price. "People are more comfortable spending a little bit of money often than a lot of money at once," Marta told him, and he found she was right, and he found, also, that at the end of every month, after all the bills were paid, after he had stocked up on staples, he had money left over, a good bit of money.

About a year after Marta first appeared in El Castillo with her *artículos de lujo*, she made Guillermo an offer. "It's a lonely life traveling up and down the river, carrying these heavy sacks and sleeping in a different bed every night, and I'm tired of the hard seats of the *palangas*. I like El Castillo, and I like you," she said, looking him right in the eye. "We could be a team," she said. "I am sure you are lonely too."

"Who will go to Granada to buy the goods if you stay here?" Guillermo asked.

"I will go a few times a year to keep up with the newest fashion and will arrange for my cousin to have things shipped to us."

"And what about the other towns?" Guillermo asked.

"They will come here, to El Castillo, to buy what they need," she said. "It's perfect."

At first she stayed above the store, but she did not sleep well there because of the sound of the rapids. It was like the sound of a pounding rain that she knew would never stop, so Guillermo invited her to stay with him. At first she occupied the back part of the house. Guillermo wanted to give her his room in the front, but she did not want to be an imposition, so Guillermo made her a bed and a chest to put her clothes in and she slept in the back room where the photographs had been.

In the evenings, after they closed the store, they prepared dinner together and they talked about business while they ate. After dinner, Marta did the bookkeeping. She set up a proper system for keeping accounts and chastised him for having been so inattentive to the details of his business, and he thanked her for taking such good care of everything, though, truth be told, he could not imagine that his inaccuracies could ever have led to chaos. Still, he was glad to be rid of the responsibility of keeping the accounts. He had never been interested in the adding up and subtracting of things.

At first Guillermo thought he would miss his privacy, that he would sleep with the door closed, hoping she would stick to her wing of the house, but he found that he enjoyed their routine—the going over of the day, the planning for the future, and the righting of the books—and after their work was done they lingered at the kitchen table, drinking rum, though never more than just one glass. She liked his stories, too, but she never asked questions, did not try to learn more about him than he was willing to tell. Eventually Guillermo told her about the Germans, how they taught him to read and that they disappeared and the people of the town let their house be taken over by monkeys, but that was all he told her. That was enough.

About Marta he knew very little. She was from Granada and had attended the convent school there. The nuns were kind, she said, and she thought for a while she would join them, but when she prayed she never felt the presence of God. "Have you ever felt it?" she asked Guillermo.

"No," Guillermo said, and that was something else they had in common.

After she decided not to become a nun, she had a suitor for a while. He was from a good family, a better one than hers, and her parents were terribly excited about the engagement, but she felt about him the same way she felt about God—nothing—until one day when they were walking through the plaza and a street dog started following them. When he wouldn't go away, Mario, her betrothed, kicked the dog so hard it went flying. "After that I hated him," she said.

He wanted for a fleeting moment to put his hand on her shoulder, to comfort her, though she did not look as if she needed comforting. She was as she always was, sturdy and tall. Beautiful, he thought, not for the first time, but this time it was not just an observation. "Well," Marta said, getting up. "We have a lot of work to do in the morning."

"Yes we do," Guillermo said.

That night he did not sleep. He thought of Marta kneeling on the stone floor in the chapel trying to feel the presence of God, and he got out of bed and knelt on the wooden floor, closed his eyes and imagined her lying in her bed naked, the sheets thrown off. "Click," he said, holding his hand up to his eyes like a camera. "Click."

He got up, then, and walked to her room. The door was open, and he could hear her breathing. I shouldn't wake her, he thought, and he turned to go back to his room.

"Come," she whispered, and he lay down beside her on the narrow bed that was like the beds that nuns slept in.

"What if they come back?" Marta asked in the morning when they awoke together in the narrow nun's bed.

"The monkeys?"

"No, the Germans."

"They aren't coming back," Guillermo said, and he felt like a traitor.

In the beginning Guillermo was sure Marta would not stay for long, that she, like Don Solano's wife, would get tired of the routine and the endless flow of the river. Even after they had their first child, he believed she would leave. But after their second child, he understood that she was not going anywhere, and he was relieved finally to know that this would be his life.

# CHAPTER 11

THE GERMANS LEFT IN THE MIDDLE OF THE NIGHT. THEY HAD lanterns, but they did not need them. They knew the way, knew every rock in the rapids. If they capsized in the rapids, that would have been their fate, and they accepted that, to die in the river, but they did not capsize. After the rapids there was no danger. There was just the river flowing steadily to the sea. They did not know where they were going except that they were leaving, their refuge, their house with their books, the photographs, the mangoes. They did not speak of any of these things just as they did not speak of those they had left behind in Germany where the war raged, and in the middle of the night they turned toward each other and made love with fury like soldiers on the night before a battle, like enemies. In the morning they did not speak of the night, and their life together was filled with the unspoken.

"Remember when we believed that all we needed was each other?" Friedrich said one night after they had made love.

"I remember," Georg said.

"What do we want?" Friedrich asked.

Georg did not answer, so they kept paddling, Friedrich at the stern and Georg at the bow, and the birds woke up and they swooped into the river after fish and the sun rose and it was hot again. It rained, and they let the rain fall on them, and they kept paddling, and it stopped raining, and the sun came out again, and it was hot until it set, and then it was dark and the cicadas started singing, and they did not need to speak, which was a relief for both of them, though it had been words that once brought them together so long ago, so far away they could not be sure any of it had happened, that they existed before they met, before they came across the ocean to the river. And now they did not know whether they would exist once they were no longer together.

In the afternoon of the third day when the sun was at its strongest they arrived in Greytown. There they took two separate rooms at the only hotel and bathed and slept in their separate rooms in their separate beds. In the morning they ate breakfast together on the veranda overlooking the river. It was still cool and they almost believed this was a new beginning, but then the sun grew stronger and the air heavy and the smell of garbage wafted up from the river.

"The river is different here," Georg said.

"We can still go back," Friedrich said.

"I suppose we could," Georg said, but they did not.

They spent the next seven days sleeping in their separate rooms, eating together at the table on the patio overlooking the river. When they were not sleeping they drank in the hope that at the end of the night, they would stumble up the stairs and into the same room, the same bed, but every night they went to their own rooms, yet in the morning they did not have the strength to part. Neither had the strength to say, *I will go east or west or north or south and you will go another way, and that will be the end of it,* so they asked the woman who owned the hotel to bring them another bottle of rum and they began to drink. They were known in the town already; *los borrachos* they were called, though the town had many drunks of its own. "Where are you from?" the other drinkers asked them. Every time they were asked, they answered differently, and each answer was accepted as if it were the truth, for they all knew that it did not matter where they were from, just that they were there. No one asked them where they were going even though they knew they were going somewhere because no one except those who were born in Greytown ever stayed in Greytown.

On the eighth day they had enough of waking up with sour stomachs and dry mouths, with headaches that did not go away until they began to drink again. "We are not destined to be drunks," Friedrich said at breakfast.

"What is our destiny?" Georg asked.

"We have no destiny," Friedrich said.

They walked together to where the river met the sea, watched the foaming waves brown from the silt of the river.

"We have come to the end of the world," Georg said.

They removed their clothes and took photographs of each other. They threw the camera into the water. They waded into the river, lay on their backs, and let the river carry them. They closed their eyes so that they could not see each other drowning.

# PART II

# CHAPTER 12

THEIR FIRST WINTER IN NEW YORK, THE HUDSON RIVER FROZE over, and Pepa and her parents walked to New Jersey on the river, slipping and sliding their way across. "We should have bought ice skates," Pepa said, but her parents said they didn't remember how to skate.

"I remember," Pepa said, and her parents laughed, sure that they knew better, that skating wasn't something one remembered. It wasn't part of a person like a language or food or the taste of cold, which is what they breathed in as they walked from New York to New Jersey and back again across the frozen river thinking, we are home now. We are far away from monkeys and yellow fever and chickens. We are where the snow falls and the river freezes over and taxis speed up and down paved streets and stop at traffic lights, and one can buy heavy cream and tickets to see *Don Giovanni*.

Pepa thought she would learn to love the winter, to exalt in the snow and the cold wind that blew from the river, as she had learned to love the hot rain and the call of howler monkeys in the night. But winter just made her feel more distant from herself and she did not know what she was feeling, whether it was sadness or nothingness. Still, she forced herself to plunge into winter, walking until she could no longer feel her fingers and toes and then drinking a cup of hot coffee in a diner, sitting in the back, watching people come in and out, wondering where they had come from and where they would go after they walked out into the biting cold. She thought at first that the winter might help her focus on the future, not on what she had lost. She thought that the cold wind on her face would wipe away the memory of Guillermo's warm breath, that snow would cover the damp dark earth upon which they had lain, that she would come to love the blurry vowels and harsh consonants of English. Throughout that first winter she concentrated on learning English, staying up late memorizing as many new words as possible, practicing her pronunciation in front of the mirror, making sure not to let her tongue touch her teeth for the harsh *d* as in *dog*, leaving her tongue hanging in the middle of her mouth, useless, as she repeated *the rotten red raspberry, the rotten red raspberry*. Weekends, armed with a dictionary, she spent in the library, reading the *World Book Encyclopedia*. At first it took hours to read just one paragraph, and even then she was never sure if she completely understood what she had read, whether, for example, mother penguins did try to steal other penguins' babies if their own baby died and that all the other penguins joined together to protect the living babies from these grieving and selfish mothers. The kidnapping sounded right, like something mothers would do, and yet at the same time she could not imagine it, taking from someone else what had been wrenched from you.

　　She felt at home in the warm library with the smell of books and the sound of pages being turned. She liked thinking of everyone around her learning things they did not know, reading the same words she was reading but in a different order so that they were all far away from each other despite the fact they sat at the same long tables and were warmed by the same sputtering radiators. In their apartment the radiators were always blasting so that even on the coldest days when the river was frozen over, they kept the windows wide open and walked around in their shirtsleeves and bare feet. But when Pepa was home alone, she closed the windows, letting the heat and humidity from the radiators accumulate. Then she would lie naked on the floor of her bedroom and try to feel Guillermo inside her, but all she felt was that terrible dull pulling. She saw her mother at the sink in the clinic washing her hands, while she lay on the cold operating table with nothing left inside her. She tried to feel angry, wanted to rage at her parents for ripping her child from her womb, but all she felt was exhaustion. It was as if she had swum the entire length of the Río San Juan from San Carlos to the sea without stopping, so she closed her eyes and fell asleep to the sound of water running and more scrubbing and whispering. In New York as she lay on the floor, she tried again to feel anger, but, always, weariness overtook her, and she fell asleep on the living room floor, and when her parents came home, they kneeled down and woke her. "What are you doing sleeping on the floor?" they asked, and she did not answer.

She thought she would like school, thought she yearned for it, but she was not accustomed to the confines of the classroom, to sitting still. Her life had been one of activity and purpose, and now all she did was sit and listen until the bell rang and she was expected to rush to another room where she would again sit and listen. At first she told herself this restlessness was due to her inability to understand English, and she was sure that once she understood what the teachers were saying, she would feel differently, but though the list of words she knew in English was growing and she was able to read the encyclopedia with greater ease and confidence, she could not find a way to put English words together in speech, to utter anything more than the most basic pleasantries or requests. She had been sure that English would come to her the way Spanish had, in a dream almost, so that she would wake up one morning and there it would be and she would understand everything and could speak to anyone, but the words did not come, so she sat quietly in the back of classrooms waiting for something to change.

For the most part, except for Mr. Hoppe, the history teacher who had studied German in college, her teachers ignored her. Since she was used to taking care of herself and figuring things out on her own, this did not bother her at all even though she got Ds on most of her assignments, which her teachers handed back to her with their eyes averted. She always received these returned papers with a smile and a thank-you so as not to make them uncomfortable or to lead them to think they should be more helpful. The students also ignored her, even the others from Europe, even the girl with the number tattooed on her arm who survived the worst of it. To be fair, they tried to include her in the beginning, but she was not used to the company of girls and didn't know how to talk about the things they talked about. She didn't know the songs they knew, hadn't seen the movies they had seen, didn't care about clothes, so she preferred to spend the lunch period in the library. Of course she knew that she could learn all these things. She could read the fashion magazines, listen to the radio, go to the movies, but she was afraid that if she took those steps she would no longer be who she was and that everything she had known before would also cease to exist.

At home she had no chickens to tend to, and Karl, who was learning English faster than all of them, did his homework on his own and spent his free time playing out in the street with the neighbor boys. Her parents passed the medical boards on the first try. They set up a clinic in a Puerto Rican neighborhood in the Bronx, but though her father still worked long hours and on Saturdays and Sundays, her mother barely worked at the clinic, helping him out only a few afternoons a week. Pepa would have preferred to take care of things as she had always done, but her mother seemed to like being at home. At first she tried to include Pepa in her home-making efforts, but Pepa said she didn't have time for cooking and cleaning now, so her mother let her keep her distance, which, Pepa imagined, probably made it easier for her, too. On Fridays her mother baked for the Sabbath, and on Friday night they lit candles and prayed, which they had never done before, either in El Castillo or in Vienna.

At school she continued to sit in the back of classrooms. Except for in Mr. Hoppe's class, she stopped doing homework. She handed back tests completely blank, and her teachers handed them back to her with notes that said, *See me*, but she never did. She left her books in her locker at the end of the day and walked home from school unencumbered. Sometimes she ran. Spring arrived and with it the rain, and in the rain she could smell what she had lost, Guillermo's body encircling her and the chickens and fried bananas and the wet earth beneath her. One morning, when she came to the gates of the school, she did not go in. The next morning she did not go in either, and the third morning she did not even make it to the gates.

She thought someone would call her parents or send a letter. She imagined her parents bringing her back to the school and her going obediently, just as she had done when she climbed up onto the table at the clinic while her parents watched, unsmiling. But there were no calls. It was as if she had never been there at all, and that is when she knew she would never let anyone decide her fate again.

Every morning she left the apartment with Karl, dropping him off at school. Usually he met up with friends on the way, and they ran ahead talking in English, chasing each other so that by the time she reached his school he was already out of sight. After this one unnecessary responsibility, the day was hers, but there was nothing to do, no food to buy or prepare, no floors to clean or water to bring in from the cisterns. The long day stretched out before her. The first few days of her freedom, she went to the library, for it was the only place she knew besides the apartment and the school and the stores on Dyckman Street. But the library had become a prison, too, and the articles in the encyclopedia seemed now to be even more difficult to decipher, the unfamiliar words jeering from their glossy pages.

She moved from indoors to outdoors, spending the long days in Central Park, walking and sitting on benches. Once as she was walking around the lake, she heard a couple ahead of her speaking Spanish, and she followed them, keeping her distance, listening to them, trying to imagine what they looked like. She could tell by their voices and clothes that they were not young, probably her parents' age. The man wore a hat and a summer suit, though it was not quite summer yet. The woman wore a tight lavender suit and a fur stole. She imagined the fox's head resting dead underneath her chin.

They were not speaking loudly enough for her to catch more than isolated words, but she hung on to those words, repeated them softly to herself: "*Su hermana, una lástima, tal vez, el hotel.*" What had happened to the sister?

They exited the park on Fifth Avenue. At the light, they stopped and the man lit a cigarette. The light changed and they crossed the street, and Pepa followed. They walked into the Sherry-Netherland hotel, and Pepa followed. They retrieved their key from the desk clerk. The man put his arm around the woman's shoulder. They pressed the button on the elevator and waited. The elevator opened and they stepped onto it, turning around to face the doors, looking out blankly as people on elevators do. "Twenty-three," the elevator man said as he pulled the gate shut. Pepa moved closer to the elevator. "*Adiós,*" Pepa said. The woman and man looked at each other, puzzled, but the doors were closing, and then they were gone.

As she walked back through the park to the subway she wondered whether they talked about her once they were back in their room, once the man had taken off his jacket, loosened his tie, once the stole was hanging over the back of a chair. Perhaps they stood at the window looking down on Fifth Avenue or out at the park. "Who was that girl?" the woman might have asked.

"No idea," the man would say, taking her hand.

But the woman wouldn't be convinced, and she would pull her hand away and walk over to the bar, pour a drink.

"Don't be ridiculous," the man would say, and the woman would start crying, and the man would get annoyed and grab his jacket and hat and walk out. He would slam the door, and the woman would be left inside crying.

Or maybe it would go like this: "Who was that girl?" the woman would ask.

"What girl?" the man would say.

"The one who called to us; didn't you see her?"

"No," the man would say.

"She looked familiar," the woman would say.

"Hm," the man would say.

There were so many possible stories, but she wasn't really part of any of them. She was just the girl outside the elevator.


A few days later she walked into the offices of the *Aufbau*, the newspaper that served the German-speaking Jewish community. "I am looking for work," she said to the receptionist in German.

The receptionist picked up the phone and dialed without answering Pepa. "There's a girl here looking for work," she said. "Sit," she told Pepa after she hung up.

Pepa sat. In the distance she could hear the sound of typewriters. It sounded like rain on the tin roof, and she felt less nervous about walking in unannounced. After a while an older woman appeared from the back.

"So you're looking for work?" she asked without introducing herself.

"Yes," Pepa said.

"Can you type?"

"Yes," Pepa said. This was not exactly true, but she had spent many an afternoon sitting with Don Felipe, El Castillo's letter writer. Don Felipe had traveled from town to town with his typewriter, plying his trade, before he arrived one day in El Castillo burning up with fever. Don Solano's parents took him in and nursed him back to health, and when he was well again, he found that he no longer had any desire to travel. So he stayed, and every afternoon from one to eight, except on Sundays, Don Felipe could be found in the plaza with his faded sign: *Don Felipe's Letter Writing Services. The best in town.* They were, of course, the only such services to be had in El Castillo.

Now as she followed the woman to the office, she wondered why she had never asked Don Felipe to teach her how to type. She supposed it was because she felt that she was the one helping him.

The woman led her to a back room and introduced her to her secretary. "This is, what's your name?"

"Pepa."

"Give her the usual test," she said, and she walked away.

The secretary, Frau Lowenstein, handed her the latest edition of the *Aufbau.* "Type this," she said, pointing to an article on the front page. Pepa sat down and held her fingers over Frau Lowenstein's typewriter, tapping the keys without pressing down on them, warming up. "Ready?" Mrs. Lowenstein asked.

Pepa nodded.

"Go," she said.

Pepa began typing, making sure to use all her fingers the way Don Felipe had done.

"Stop," Frau Lowenstein said after she had typed only one line. Frau Lowenstein pulled the paper out of the typewriter, looked at it, picked up the telephone, pressed a button. "Frau Herzman, she can't type," she said. She nodded. "Frau Herzman wants to talk to you," she said to Pepa.

Pepa knocked on Frau Herzman's door even though it was open. "You don't have to knock if the door's open," Frau Herzman said. Pepa walked into the office and stood in front of Frau Herzman's desk. "Why did you tell me that you know how to type?" Frau Herzman asked. She smelled like the Germans' house, of chocolate.

"I learn fast," Pepa said.

"Why didn't you say that rather than lying? Lying is not at all becoming."

"I am not in the habit of lying," Pepa said. "I've never had an interview before. We just came here, from Nicaragua, my brother and I."

"And your parents?"

Pepa looked down at her hands. "They died from yellow fever. They were doctors," she said, and she understood that she was completely on her own now, and something shifted inside her, not a filling of the void, but an opening up, a relief. "So you and your brother came here alone?"

"We have a sponsor, but we want to get our own apartment. We're very independent."

They did have a sponsor, from HIAS, the organization that helped refugees. Their sponsor was a doctor who lived in a big apartment overlooking the park. They went there once a couple weeks after they arrived. A maid wearing a uniform opened the door and led them to the sitting room, where the walls were covered with African masks and shields. Pepa wanted to look at them up close, but she knew her parents would forbid it, so she sat down. They waited for almost an hour. Finally the doctor came into the room, and they all jumped up to shake his hand. The doctor did not speak German, and after the initial pleasantries they did not know what to say, so they smiled at what the doctor said, though they did not understand much of it at all.

"Come," Frau Herzman said, getting up, so Pepa followed her through the main room, where the typists were, to the back. Frau Herzman took out a key and opened a closet door. It was piled to the ceiling with boxes. "This will be your job," she said.

"What should I do with them?" Pepa asked, but Frau Herzman left her there without another word and headed back toward her office.

Pepa counted the boxes first, slipping into the crevices between them. There were twenty-seven. She lifted down the one easiest to reach. It wasn't heavy, so she carried it out of the closet to the light to examine its contents. Inside were unopened letters, not packed in bundles or arranged in any way but just tossed in. All the letters were addressed to *Aufbau: Gesucht Wird (looking for)*. The stamps were from all over the world—South Africa, Australia, Canada, Poland, Bolivia—and from all over the United States. There was even one from Alaska.

Pepa sat on the floor next to the box and reached inside, feeling around among the envelopes as if she were choosing a number for the lottery. The letter she pulled out was postmarked Chicago and written in German. *Gesucht wird, my brother, Herman Weissman. Last seen on June 24, 1941, in Krakow. Former address . . . His brother, Fritz Weissman, Chicago, Illinois* (and then the address and phone number). Pepa opened all the letters in the box, read every one, smoothed them out and set them aside with the envelope in which they were sent. When she had finished with the first box, she went to the nearby desk of a young man and asked for paper clips.

The man gave her a box of paper clips. "Are you okay?" he asked her.

"Of course I'm okay," Pepa said.

"If you need anything more, just ask," he said.

She clipped the envelopes and letters together and set them carefully back into the box. At five o'clock, when Pepa was on box number six, the young man told her that it was time to go home.

"I just want to finish this box," she said.

"We all leave exactly at five," he said. "Let me help you put these away."

"I can manage," Pepa said, but he helped her anyway, putting the boxes back into the closet.

For seven days she arrived at the office promptly at nine and proceeded directly to the closet, where she worked until five, stopping at noon for her lunch hour as she had been instructed by Frau Herzman's secretary. No one came to check on her or to tell her what to do, so she continued reading and clipping the letters to the envelopes. Toward the end of her seventh day, Pepa called for Frau Herzman to meet her at the closet so she could show her the order she had made. "I have finished reading them."

"All of them?" Frau Herzman asked.

"Yes."

"Were there any matches?" she asked. "Anyone looking for each other?"

"No," Pepa said. "But that doesn't mean there is no one out there waiting to be found."

"Oskar was in charge of them first," Frau Herzman said, pointing to the man who had given her the paper clips. "Actually the whole thing was his idea." She leaned in closer and whispered, even though the door was closed and no one could hear them. "He lost his wife and children, you know. For the first year after the war we ran every *Gesucht Wird* letter we received, but we got not one single response. It seemed as if every day we were getting twice as many letters as the day before, and so he had to start choosing and that was just too much for Oskar, especially when people started calling, asking why we didn't publish theirs, so we had to stop printing them altogether and eventually people stopped calling, but we couldn't throw them away, so they're still there, weighing on us."

"We could print one long list of all the names along with their birthdates and last known addresses. If we printed five hundred at a time, we could do it in five issues. I could type them up."

"But you can't type."

"I can type, just not fast."

"You'll make mistakes."

"No," Pepa said. "I will be careful."

"And what about the new letters, the ones that keep arriving?"

"We can start a list of new names, and after we finish the old names, we can run one hundred names from the old lists along with the new names each week. We can rotate."

They set up a desk for Pepa in the main room across the aisle from Oskar. They gave her a file cabinet and she filed the letters alphabetically. She learned to type. After the first list was published she waited eagerly for responses, but there were none, not after a week, not after two weeks, or three. The same was true for the other lists and for the new names and the repeated lists and names that they continued to print every week, so she stopped waiting, though she kept typing up the lists dutifully, whispering the names as she typed as if somehow the lost relatives would hear them, feel her calling to them from the darkness of their graves.

Once the *Gesucht Wird* names were organized, there was plenty of time for her to do more, so she became Oskar's assistant and was given an official title: Assistant to the Advertising Manager. At first her job consisted of doing the things that Oskar did not like to do such as calling up customers who were behind on their payments and going every Tuesday to see Herr Grau, the old man who owned Grau's Jewelry on Broadway and insisted on checking the proofs for his ad himself even when there were no changes.

"Things can change without our noticing, without our doing anything to make them change," he always said, which, she supposed, was true.

"What do you do with the money you earn?" Herr Grau asked her one afternoon after he had finished running his thick fingers over each line of his ad.

"I save it," Pepa said.

"Where?" he asked.

"I have a bank account," she said. Another lie. She had tried to open an account, but the clerk told her that since she was only seventeen, she was not old enough to have one on her own. So she hid the money in different places, underneath her underwear in the dresser, in her books, not under the mattress, of course. She knew that would be the first place a thief would look.

Eventually she started carrying the money around with her when she went out. She sewed a belted pouch and wore it on her belly, but the money grew, and she was afraid that someone would notice, so she went to a different bank, but they told her the same thing: "Your parents can open one for you."

"My parents are dead," she said, and they said they were sorry but the rules were the rules, and she was angry that she had wasted this lie at the bank, where the rules were so clear-cut, so easy.

"And what if it happens again?" Herr Grau continued. "Then your money will be stuck in a bank, and they won't let you take it out." Herr Grau closed his eyes as if suddenly a bright light had been shined on them. Then, just as abruptly, he opened them again. "Poof, and it will all be gone," he said, and he broke into laughter, and his laughter grew stronger and morphed into a violent coughing. "We will never be out of danger. You will never be out of danger. You must always be prepared to flee," he said between coughs. He paused, catching his breath. "I have only one lung. I had an infection when I was a child. I slept for months, couldn't keep my eyes open. What I would give now to be able to sleep."

He rolled up his sleeve, thrusting his arm in her face so she could see the gold cuff, like a piece of armor that covered his entire forearm. He rolled up his other sleeve and said, "Look." He splayed his ringed fingers. "All diamonds," he said. "I can make you one too." He held his arm up in the air. "I have them on my legs too."

"Thank you," Pepa said. "I don't think I have enough money yet."

"You have to start small, keep adding to it so when it's time to run, you will be prepared."

"I will think about it," she said.


The next time Pepa called on Herr Grau she convinced him to buy a half-page ad for Valentine's Day. No one had asked her to get Herr Grau to buy a bigger ad. Herr Grau was always complaining about how bad business was, how he barely made enough money to pay the rent.

"People know where to find me," Herr Grau said when she suggested the larger ad.

"Then why do you advertise at all?" Pepa had asked.

"I suppose I could waste my money on worse things," he said.

"You could offer a Valentine's Day discount if they show you the ad," Pepa suggested.

"That's ridiculous. Why would I want to sell for less when it's Valentine's Day and I know they're going to buy anyway?"

"So they keep coming back to your store when they need a gift for their daughter's birthday or a new watch. That's what the market ladies do. The first time you buy from them, they give you a great deal, and then they start charging you a little bit more each time, but they chat more too, tell you that one of the cows died or that their daughter is pregnant. They ask how your family is doing, get you to tell them things. After that you won't bargain so hard and they will get top price for everything they sell you."

"Market ladies? What do they have to do with jewelry?" Herr Grau said.

"It doesn't matter what you're selling. The principle is always the same," Pepa said.

"What does a young girl like you know about business?"

"I'll just add the line about Valentine's Day, then?" she said.

"Yes," he said.

"Very well," she said, getting up and walking toward the door. Just as she reached it, he said, as she knew he would, "Wait, maybe I could offer 10 percent."

On Wednesdays she and Oskar went with the editors down to Spring Street to oversee the printers. Oskar was more relaxed there than at the office. It was hot from all the machines, so he left his jacket on a chair, loosened his tie, rolled up his sleeves. He laughed at the printers' jokes, which Pepa mostly didn't understand, but she could tell that they were harmless. She liked the printers. They called her *bambina* and showed her how the machines worked, how to set the words, letter by letter. She admired their patience. After the paper came off the press, it was Oskar's job to proofread all the advertising, including the list of names in the *Gesucht Wird* column, and the classifieds and obituaries. Oskar read every word out loud to her, and she checked it on the freshly printed sheets that the Italian printers brought them. They smelled of hot ink and water, like earth mixing with rain, and it reminded her of El Castillo. When they were at the printers they ordered in lunch, and Pepa and Oskar always got the fried egg sandwich. It came with pickles. The printers had an espresso machine, and they made espresso for everyone, and they all drank espresso together after lunch before they went back to typesetting and proofreading.

It was one Wednesday after leaving the printers' that Oskar took her to walk across the Brooklyn Bridge. "The Brooklyn Bridge is the most beautiful thing in New York," he said. They stood in the middle of the bridge with the cars rushing below them, looking through the spider's web of cables up at the sky and the clouds. "The day they opened the bridge there was a stampede," Oskar said. "Someone cried out that it was collapsing, and everyone started running, and they trampled each other. I don't know how many people died, but it was a lot."

"But it wasn't collapsing at all?"

"No," Oskar said, and they looked up again through the cables to the sky.

They walked to the other side, to Brooklyn, where they stopped at a diner and ate pie and drank coffee. On the way back to Manhattan, Pepa told Oskar about Herr Grau and his golden armor.

"I will have to get you a golden bow and arrow to go with it," Oskar said, and she smiled, but she didn't dare laugh, not at Herr Grau who had only one lung and could not sleep and was weighed down by all that gold.

"It must be so heavy," she said, thinking of him lying in bed with the burden of his wealth, and the pouch with her savings pressing firmly on her belly no longer felt like a reassurance. At that moment she felt like ripping it away from her body and flinging it in the river, but she was not foolish, so she breathed in deeply. She smelled the river, and before her the buildings rose up like the trees in the jungle and underneath them the cars sped by, shaking the bridge like millions upon millions of insects, and she said, "The city is so bright that you can't even see the stars."

"But it's still beautiful," Oskar said, and she agreed.

The next day when she arrived at work there was a match. Someone's brother in Poland was still alive. "I am Fritz Licht from Vienna. My brother is Hershel," it said in English. Enclosed was a sealed envelope addressed to Hershel Licht. She brought the letter to Oskar, and he took it from her and held it in his hands.

"Finally," he whispered, and he handed the letter back. "You'd better tell Frau Herzman."

She could see his shoulders shaking, so she put her hand on his shoulder, left it there without speaking. He did not recoil, and he did not stop crying. All around them was the sound of typewriters. She stood like that with him for a long time, until he spoke. "You must tell Frau Herzman," he said again.

Frau Herzman's lunch, a thick pastrami sandwich, was spread out before her. There was mustard on her cheek. She took the letter from Pepa, grabbing it as if Pepa had been trying to keep it from her even though Pepa was holding it out for her to take.

"A match," she said. "Finally a match. We must call the brother immediately. Do you have his information?"

Of course Pepa had the information. Frau Herzman made the call. The editors and Oskar and the secretaries and Pepa, all of them crowded into her office, watched her dial. "Yes," she said, "yes, your brother wrote. He's alive."

After that they all thought there would be more responses, but that would remain the only one even after the war was over. Although there were no more matches, the paper was full of advertising largely due to Pepa's boldness. She got the Greek-owned coffee shop to place a regular quarter-inch ad. No one had thought to go outside their circle, but the old Jews spent most of their days in the Greek coffee shop, drinking watered-down coffee, eating the breakfast and lunch specials. She got an ad from Bloomingdale's and Macy's. Why not? Didn't Jews shop there? Macy's took out a full-page ad for the high holidays. You can't show up for atonement in an old dress or suit. Because of Pepa's advertising campaign, they added eight pages to the newspaper. Pepa's money-belt pouch grew thicker. Soon it would be impossible to conceal.

She and Oskar spent more time together. On the weekends they went to double features. In the darkness of the movie theater, they held hands, but once they were outside again they did not. Still, the feeling of his hand in hers stayed with her like the stories in the movies they watched. Sometimes after they sat next to each other through two good movies, she felt she was ready for more than watching people who did not even exist reveal themselves to her on the screen. But she wasn't sure, not like she had been with Guillermo, when neither of them had anyone before and did not think about the gravity of what they were doing. So she waited for Oskar to make up his mind since she could not, though she knew that his memories were so much more insurmountable than hers. She worried that when the decision was finally made, that when she was finally with Oskar, she would be pulled away from him, back to the jungle floor and to the smell of rain on dark dirt and the strains of the *banda* playing in the distance and the salt taste of Guillermo's skin and of course the river.

But "life must go on," as Frau Herzman always said whenever there was an insignificant problem like they forgot to put the pickle on her sandwich. Pepa and Oskar used the expression too, mocking her and the lives they led now that they were safe, now that there was no more danger. "Life must go on," they said when they missed the train. "Life must go on," they said when the printers couldn't make any more changes and had to let the newspaper go with a mistake. "Life must go on," they said when it rained and they didn't have an umbrella. Perhaps they thought if they said it enough Oskar would allow himself to accept the truth of Frau Herzman's dictum, but the thing was, he did accept the truth of it. "I wish I could hate all this," he told her one night when they were walking again on the Brooklyn Bridge. "I wish I could scoff at the beauty of this bridge, and the genius of its creators. I wish I hated the moon and the sun and birds or that I could let myself go crazy and run through the streets howling and cursing at everyone who was walking across this bridge or eating dinner or whistling a tune while my wife and children were being killed. I wish that I wanted revenge, but I don't. My problem isn't that I can't go on. It's that I want to go on."

Pepa looked at the city before them, then up again at the spidery cables, through them to the sky and the few stars that could outshine the city lights. She thought of the sky in El Castillo, so bright with stars that you could almost not see the black between them. "It's a different kind of beauty," she said.

"Different from what?"

"Different from El Castillo."

"Would you go back to live there if you could?" Oskar asked.

"No," she said.

"Why not?"

"Because this is my life now," she said.

Oskar boarded in the apartment of an elderly Russian man. Though he was neither ancient nor physically incapacitated, he went out only once a week, on Tuesdays, when his niece came to take him to lunch, and this he did more out of a sense of duty than for his own pleasure. The Russian man had played the bassoon for the Radio City orchestra, but his lungs were no longer strong enough to play music, so he spent his days listening to records or reading. Oskar did the grocery shopping and cooking in exchange for rent, but they ate alone in their separate rooms, as the Russian was not interested in conversation. Once a week a cleaning woman came. All this had been made very clear to Oskar right from the start, and Oskar accepted the arrangement since he believed at the time that he wanted solitude.

It was in the Russian's apartment that Pepa and Oskar made

love for the first time. It was a Tuesday, a nice day, not as hot and humid as it had been for the past weeks, and they had been walking, as they often did after they ate their sandwiches, in Riverside Park. Oskar lived just a few blocks from the *Aufbau* offices on West End Avenue, and he had pointed out his building to her before. "That's my window up there, the one with the purple curtains," he said. "Mr. Erlich likes purple."

On this cool summer day with a hint of autumn in the air, they turned on Eighty-Ninth Street toward West End Avenue. "Do you want to see the apartment?" Oskar asked. Later he insisted that he had not planned it out, as Pepa was sure he had.

The apartment was dark, the purple curtains drawn. It smelled of books and something sour. "It's the yogurt," Oskar explained, though Pepa had not mentioned anything about the smell. "Mr. Erlich makes his own." Pepa went to the window and pulled open the curtain.

"There," she said. "That's better."

Oskar joined her at the window, and they looked out for a while in silence. "From my room you can see the Hudson," Oskar said, and Pepa took his hand, and he led her to his room. "Look," he said, pulling open the curtains.

"Look at me," Pepa said, and he turned toward her.

They did not undress that first time, didn't take it slowly, and when they were finished they were embarrassed by their own urgency, so they lay on their backs looking up at the ceiling without talking until Oskar jumped up and said, "We're going to be late," which they were, arriving back at work at 1:07, out of breath, sweating even though it was a cool day. Frau Herzman looked up from her papers and then at her watch as they passed her office, but she didn't say a word.

That night at dinner, Pepa could smell Oskar on her as she ate the roast chicken her mother had prepared. She was sure they could all smell him too, but they wouldn't be able to imagine what it was, and this made her laugh.

"What's so funny?" Karl asked.

"Nothing," Pepa said. "I was just thinking."

"Thinking about what?"

"Nothing," she said, for she knew that she could not tell them any of it. She hadn't even told them about her job. As far as they knew she was still in school, though they never asked her about it and she did not make up lies to cover her tracks.

That night she didn't take her usual shower so she could lie in bed with Oskar's smell still on her and think of him in his bed that faced the purple curtains and the window that looked out onto the Hudson River. Yet, the first thing she thought of when she awoke in the morning was Guillermo, and she wondered what Oskar had awakened to, whether he had dreamed of his wife and children waiting patiently in line to be taken away from him forever, and she thought, this is another thing we have in common.

The next time they made love, they planned for it, waiting until night when Oskar was sure the Russian bassoonist was sleeping, so that they could take their time. When they were too tired to go on, in the darkest moment of the night, Pepa showed Oskar her money pouch and the thick wad of bills that it contained. "Help me get a bank account," she said.

Oskar didn't understand. "You just have to take it to a bank. They will give you the forms to fill in. It's easy."

"I'm not twenty-three," Pepa said. Twenty-three is what she had told everyone, and no one had questioned it.

Oskar tilted his head, raised his hands palms-up to the air. He still didn't understand.

"I'm seventeen."

"Seventeen?" Oskar said.

"Seventeen," she said again.

"You should have told me."

"I'm sorry," she said, but she wasn't really sorry because what difference did it make whether she was seventeen or twenty-three except that she couldn't open up her own bank account? "Will you help me with the bank account?"

"What about your sponsors?"

"What sponsors?" Pepa asked.

"Frau Herzman told me that you and your brother are orphans, that you live with sponsors."

"So you asked her about me?"

"She told all of us. She wanted to help you."

"She did help me. You all helped me," Pepa said, fingering the bills from her money pouch, feeling their crispness.

"What else don't I know?" Oskar asked.

"What don't I know about you except about your wife and children? There is so much that we still have to learn about each other."

"I don't have any secrets," Oskar said. "That is how it is when you are the victim of history." Pepa knew then that this was her last chance to run, to flee the life she was going to live. "Come closer," she said, pulling Oskar toward her again, and she felt his breath on her breast and then his tongue, and she closed her eyes, and she did not think of Guillermo.

They got married at city hall on a Monday morning a year to the day after Pepa started working at the *Aufbau*. Frau Herzman was their witness. After the papers were signed, they returned to the *Aufbau* offices for a simple reception of cake and champagne, and the employees of the *Aufbau* toasted the newlyweds and presented them with a set of dishes and twelve glasses from Macy's.

It was only after they decided to get married that Pepa finally told Oskar her parents were not dead. The night after she told him, she announced to her parents that she had not been going to school, that she had been working and met Oskar, and that they were going to be married. They already had an apartment. It was small but had a view of the Hudson. "We wish you well," her mother said.

"Yes," her father said.

She brought Oskar to Friday-night dinner. Her mother prepared her Viennese specialties, and her father wore his best suit. Her parents and Oskar talked about music and agreed that Bach was a greater composer than Mozart. "His music achieves the perfect balance between intellect and emotion," Oskar said.

After Oskar went home, Pepa did not ask her parents what they thought of him, and they did not make any comments except to say that they were happy he loved music, and they wished her well again and gave her an envelope with money, which she did not open until she was alone. "To help you get started," they said, and she thanked them.

If it had not been for Oskar, Pepa would have kept her parents at a greater distance, would, perhaps, have stopped seeing them altogether. Maybe that would have been easier for all of them, but that would not have been fair to Oskar, who had lost more than she had lost, who had lost everyone. Still, it was Oskar who kept the past from intruding, who, in accordance with Frau Herzman's dictum, kept them moving forward into their new lives. He initiated the custom of having Sabbath dinner as a family every week. One week Oskar and Pepa hosted and the next they would go to her parents' place.

Two years after they got married, the war was finally over, and it was Oskar who insisted that now was the time, when everyone was focused on rebuilding, on the future, to make her dream of opening a Spanish bookstore a reality. Even when the banks refused to lend them the money to start the bookstore, Oskar found a way. He went to see Herr Grau, the jeweler who advertised in *Aufbau*.

"Do you have any competitors for this Spanish bookstore?" Herr Grau had asked, raising his arms into the air as if he were a conductor calling his orchestra to attention.

"It will be the first one," Oskar explained.

Herr Grau brought his arms down and rested them gently on the table. They made only the faintest knocking sound that would have gone unnoticed by anyone who did not know about the gold armbands. "My father opened the first vacuum cleaner store in Frankfurt. 'Who needs a machine when we have servants,' everyone said, but five years later he had an empire with stores all over Germany." He paused. "All gone now, of course, but we should not dwell on such things."

"So you agree?"

"I did not say that," Herr Grau said.

"But you did not say no either," Oskar said.

"I did not," Herr Grau replied. He took a pad and a stub of a pencil out of his back pocket and began to write, leaning over so that Oskar could not see what was on the page. When he was finished, he tore the page off and handed it to Oskar. "These are my terms."

Although the numbers were barely legible, Oskar went through them all carefully. "Can I borrow that pencil and paper?" he asked after he reviewed the calculation.

Herr Grau smiled, pushing the pad and pencil across the table.

Oskar checked all the calculations twice to make sure that there were no tricks involved in the offer. When he finished, he said, "I accept."

"Never miss a payment," Herr Grau said as he walked Oskar to the door.

"We won't," Oskar said, and they never did.

It took them twelve years, until 1957, to pay the money back to Herr Grau. On the day they sent him the last check, Oskar and Pepa went out to dinner, something they had not done since they had opened the store. It was summer, so when they came out of the restaurant it was still light out and hot. "Let's go dancing," Pepa said.

"Where?" Oskar asked, for they had never gone dancing before.

"We can look in the yellow pages," Pepa said.

"I have a better idea," Oskar said, taking her hand.

"Where are we going?" Pepa asked.

"You will see," Oskar said, and they walked together holding hands without talking, running sometimes, slowing down when they were out of breath, then running again all the way to the Brooklyn Bridge. In the middle of the bridge, Oskar stopped. "Here," he said, and he took her in his arms and Pepa began to sing, *"De la sierra morena, cielito lindo, vienen bajando,"* and they danced to the songs the *banda* had played until they were too tired to take another step, so they lay down in the middle of the Brooklyn Bridge, and they could feel the bridge vibrating beneath them. When they rose again it began to rain, and Pepa could feel the change, and that change was William.

# CHAPTER 13

CAROLINA CROUCHED DOWN BESIDE LILIANA AND HELD HER HAND
while she wretched again and again until there was nothing left and
she was too tired to stand, so she lay down on the earth that was
the floor of her brother's tomb. The ground was damp and smelled
like wood, like the caiman William made for her that she had left
behind with Irene, Irene who had betrayed her. The caiman and
the Lorca, of course, were the first things she packed, but just when
she was about to leave, she decided to put the caiman back in its
place on the bookshelf in her study so that when Irene returned to
deal with what was left of their lives together, she would see the caiman and be reminded of her betrayal. She regretted this vindictive
act now, for it did not make her feel any better at all.

Liliana did not remember walking out of the tomb or walking
behind Carolina back down the hill to the road to the plaza, but
there she was all of a sudden, sitting on a bench in the plaza sipping
a Coke through a straw. "Aren't you thirsty?" she asked.

"I don't like soda," Carolina said.

"I don't either," Liliana said.

"And the smell? Is it gone?"

"I think so," Liliana said, though she felt as if it could come back even stronger, like music at a party that stops for a few moments and then resumes with even greater intensity.

"We must go now, if you are feeling strong enough."

"I'm fine," Liliana said, taking the last sip of soda and standing.

"Do you know how to ride a horse?"

"Yes," Liliana said, though this was not exactly the truth. She had ridden a horse only once before in Wyoming in the Grand Tetons. She and Irene had hired a guide, but they soon regretted it, regretted having to follow someone else's lead. By the end of the day they were stiff and tired. It was, they agreed, not much different than sitting on a bus all day, so as soon as they got back they took a hike even though it was already dusk and they had no food or water with them and had only the light of a thin sliver of moon to guide them. Irene fell, and Liliana lifted her up. Toward the end, Liliana fell too, and Irene lifted her up, and they laughed about how dark the path was and that they might have taken a wrong turn, but they were fine.

They returned to Carolina's house, and there were two horses waiting, already saddled up and packed.

"Where are we going?" Liliana asked.

"You will see," Carolina said, helping Liliana onto her horse. She could have managed herself, but the horse was nervous, so Carolina whispered in its ear and patted it as Liliana settled into the saddle. Carolina swung onto her horse easily and led the way, back to the stream and the road down which they had come, but this time, rather than turning toward town, they went in the other direction, toward the mountains. They rode in single file. It was hot, and Liliana was hungry and thirsty and the slow pace and heat made her sleepy; she was afraid she would fall asleep and slip off her horse and Carolina would not hear her fall.

After about an hour, they stopped at a stream just long enough for the horses to drink. Then they continued their ascent. It was cooler now. They were high up and the air smelled of rain. The clouds turned gray and suddenly the rain came down hard on them, but the horses kept going. They came to a meadow and crossed the meadow. On the other side there was no longer a path, but the horses seemed to know the way. Carolina turned around and said, "We are almost there."

They stopped finally at what Carolina called the camp, though it did not look as if anyone had ever camped there. There was no fire pit, no trash. It was just a patch of dirt among the trees. They set up the tent in the rain and then they sat in the tent and listened to the rain falling, waiting for it to stop. Carolina said it might rain until morning, but eventually it stopped, and the sky was so thick with stars it seemed as if there was more light than darkness. They made a fire and ate the food Carolina had packed, and they drank from a bottle of rum, just enough to make them tired and warm.

"There are jaguars in these mountains," Carolina said.

"Have you ever seen one?"

Carolina nodded.

"My mother saw one, just once," Liliana said. "The chickens woke her up in the middle of the night, flapping around and squawking. She thought it was monkeys, so she went out into the yard to shoo them away, but the chickens were completely still, frozen, and then she saw it, creeping across the yard, its eyes shining."

"What did she do?"

"Nothing. She didn't move, and it stopped and stared at her. They stared at each other for a long time, until she got up the nerve to back into the house."

"They don't usually come into town," Carolina said. "Did she find the tracks in the morning?"

"I don't know. I never asked her."

"Do you believe this?"

"Why would she make something like that up?" Liliana asked.

"Because that is what children want to hear. They want to hear about how brave their parents are, about how they stared into the eyes of a jaguar and did not run."

"My parents told us exactly what children do not want to hear. There was no heroism in it. That is why I know they did not lie. Did William tell you about our father?"

"He did not talk about his family."

"Not at all?"

"There was so little time for talking."

"And you don't know my mother. Just a couple years ago, just before she was about to close up, she owns a bookstore in New York, a man came in and held her at gunpoint. He told her to empty the till, and she just stared at him like she stared at that jaguar. That's what she told me. She stared at him without moving, and he started screaming, saying that he would blow her head off, but she just kept staring, and the guy started trembling. 'You're fucking crazy, lady,' he said, and then he ran out of the store."

"People are different. You can smell their fear, but you can't tell what a jaguar is thinking. That is what makes them so dangerous."

"Do you lie to your children?"

"I don't lie, but there are many things I do not tell them. Perhaps if they would ask, I would tell them more, but perhaps not."

"Did you tell them about William?"

"They didn't like to hear about the war. It frightened them."

"Even when they were older?"

"Especially when they were older," Carolina said.

"Do you think we might see a jaguar tonight?" Liliana asked.

"They are afraid of fire," Carolina said.

"And after we extinguish the fire?"

"Then we will be sleeping, and we will not be able to see them even if they are there, but don't be afraid."

"I am not afraid," Liliana said.

They put out the fire and settled into the tent. They were close, as close as they could be without touching, both of them making sure to give the other space. Carolina turned off the lantern.

"Why are we here?" Liliana asked.

"This is where I last saw William," Carolina said.

"What happened?"

"We had been searching for a Contra unit for days. They attacked a village near Santo Tomás, killing everyone, even the pigs and chickens. We weren't sure we were on the right track, but we kept going because El Justo said we were getting nearer, that he could smell them. It was just after dawn when we found them. We were camped not even a kilometer away; we smelled the fire burning, heard them clearing their throats, spitting. They were eating breakfast, the sleep still in their eyes, and we watched them for a few minutes before we attacked. El Justo made us wait. He said that watching them made him feel like God, and then he gave the order and we ran out from behind the trees and mowed them down. It was over in seconds. We took their weapons, kicked them to make sure they were dead. We ate what was left of their breakfast and put out the fire, and then we left.

"We walked for hours after that, heading deeper into the mountains because we knew there would be reprisals. William did not want to walk with us. He ran ahead, crashing over roots. He fell and got up, fell and got up, but then we could not see or hear him anymore. I wanted to run after him, run with him, but El Justo said that I needed to save my energy for fighting. He said that he would tire eventually and we would catch up with him, but we never did. Days went by. We sent scouts to all the villages between Juigalpa and Santo Tomás to look for him, but they came back shaking their heads. Then our unit was called to fight farther north on the Honduran border. We were detained there for months, making forays into Honduras, killing a few Contras here, a few there, but for every man we killed, they got ten of ours. We never had a chance, not with your country sticking its nose in our business."

Liliana waited for Carolina to continue, to get back to William, to his death, but instead she turned away, pulled the blanket up over her shoulders.

"But what happened?" Liliana said. "What happened to William?"

"I don't know," she whispered.

"You never found his body?"

"No."

"Then he could have survived. He could still be alive."

"He would not have abandoned me, abandoned us."

"But you don't know that for sure. You lied to us. You said he died during his first battle."

"It was his first battle. Would you have preferred to spend these years still hoping that he was alive, searching for him, waiting for him to return? Wouldn't that have been worse?"

"We could have done something, found out, at least, what happened. Didn't you want to know?"

"I knew that he was dead. That is what is important."

"You never wanted to know how he died?"

"We were fighting a war. I knew that if I allowed myself to think about William, to wonder where he was and why he abandoned us, I would not have been able to go on."

"Perhaps that would have been better."

"Perhaps," Carolina said, "but that is not what happened."

"Are you sure this was the place?" Liliana asked.

"I am sure," Carolina said, and Liliana began to tremble, thinking of the people Carolina and her brother had killed, thinking that they could be lying right now on the spot where the blood of those men seeped into the ground. She wanted to pull down the tent, run back down the mountain in the dark, stumble over roots, fall like William had fallen, but she didn't move, and Carolina lay still beside her while Liliana cried, for William and for Carolina who had fought and killed and it had not made a fucking difference. And for Irene, always for Irene.

Liliana awoke at dawn to the sound of birds singing, calling her to get up from this killing field. Carolina was not in the tent, so when Liliana stepped out into the day, she called for her, but no one answered, not even the birds, who were engaged in their own conversation. "Carolina," she called again. She walked over to where the horses had been tied up, and they were gone too. There was food, a pot of *gallo pinto* and tortillas and water, enough for a couple days, matches—no note. Liliana ate a few spoonfuls of *gallo pinto* directly from the pot. She would have preferred coffee, but *gallo pinto* was what there was, so she ate, and when she was full, she sat down on the ground and did not know what to do. For the first time since Irene had uttered those words, "I love him. I can't help it," she was calm. Her legs were weak from the calmness that had come over her, and she realized that she was still hungry, really hungry for the first time in months, so she ate more *gallo pinto* and drank more water, and she didn't care if Carolina had abandoned her and this was the only food she had. I will figure it out, she said each time she raised the spoon to her mouth. She left a few mouthfuls just in case, though it was so little she might as well have eaten everything.

How long, she wondered, could she go without food? How long had Bobby Sands lasted? William would know. He liked martyrs. On the wall above his desk he had hung pictures of Trotsky and Che, Malcolm X and Martin Luther King Jr., Joan of Arc, Jesus.

Bobby Sands was the last one he added. They argued about them once, the martyrs. "If they hadn't died, they would have become oppressors like all the others," Liliana said.

"We can't know that," William said.

"But we can imagine," Liliana said.

"Or we can imagine that they would have lived up to their ideals, that they would have been different," William said.

"We can imagine many things, but that doesn't make them true."

"You're just like our parents," William said. "All you believe in is survival. You don't believe that anything can change or get better."

But she did. Even though she refused to hang inspirational posters in her classroom, she believed what they said. She believed that education was a powerful weapon in fighting against injustice and ignorance. Perhaps, Liliana thought, she would die here in the mountains where William died. What would her death mean? Would it have more meaning than William's, have less?

The sun was high in the sky now and it was quiet, quieter than it had been at night with all those insects buzzing and animals scurrying in the bushes. She was awake and hungry again, though she had not moved from the camp. She wondered how long it would take before Santiago sent people out to look for her. Or perhaps he would just figure that she had moved on, left town without saying good-bye, and it made her sad to think that he would believe she would do such a thing. But Carolina would return. Liliana was sure of that. She was William's sister, after all. Carolina would not want any harm to come to her. But then why would she have taken both horses?

When night fell and Carolina did not come, Liliana was sure she would be back in the morning. She should have paid more attention to the path, she thought. But she hadn't, so the best strategy, she knew, was to stay where she was. It was one of the basic principles of survival that her father had learned at Birkenau: it is easier to shoot a stationary than a moving target, so, by the same token, it's easier to find a stationary lost person than one who wanders about looking for the way out. When he was in the camp, he never stopped moving. Even when they waited in line for food he jumped up and down. The guards used to laugh at him. "What, are you cold?" they would say, standing there in their warm winter coats, and he would laugh with them, jump even more vigorously. They called him The Kangaroo. Once, only once, when William was angry about some restriction their parents had imposed, he had stormed out of the house screaming, "I don't have to listen to a fucking kangaroo," and their mother had run after him, dragged him out of the elevator, and slapped him in the face, kept slapping him until their father came out to stop her. It was the only time she ever hit her children.

When everyone was back inside, sitting at the kitchen table, their father finally said, "I forgive you." He never spoke about it again. In the winter, when they complained about the cold, he never again said that in the camp he could even feel the cold in his eyes.

At least it's not cold here, she thought. She tried not to pay attention to her hunger. And there was plenty of water. She wondered whether, if it came to that, she would eat dirt or take her chance on roots and leaves. She wondered whether she would be fast enough to catch a lizard or how many insects she would have to eat in order not to starve, or at what point she would allow herself to eat carrion.

Carolina came in the early afternoon of the next day, when the sun was at its strongest. Liliana heard the muted thuds of the horses' hoofs in the distance, but she did not spring up, did not run down the path to meet her. She waited, sitting on the rock where she had been sitting since morning, watching the birds, taking a sip of water at seven minutes past every hour that went by. She was surprised how quickly the time had gone, how easy it was to do nothing. She had not eaten in thirty-six hours. She could have lasted so much longer, she was thinking.

Carolina dismounted, tied up the two horses, and poured water into a tin trough for them to drink. When they were drinking, she walked over to Liliana. "Did you see the jaguar?" she asked, sitting next to Liliana on the rock.

Liliana did not move over to give Carolina more room and did not turn to look at her. "Yes," she said.

"I knew he would come," Carolina said, pulling Liliana into an embrace. "Did he come close?" she whispered into Liliana's ear.

"Yes."

"How close? Did he let you touch him?"

"No," Liliana said, "but close enough so that I could feel his warmth," Liliana said.

"Twice he has allowed me to touch him, rest my hand on his head. Once, only once, he ate from my hand."

"Why did you leave me?" Liliana asked.

"He would not have come if we were here together," she said, looking off into the forest as if she saw him there still, watching them. "What did he say?"

"Say?"

"He didn't talk to you? He talks to me, not with words, with his eyes. He tells me he misses me."

Liliana began to tremble. "It's okay," Carolina said, putting her hand on her arm.

"No it's not," Liliana said, pulling away. "You left me in the mountains alone when you knew there were jaguars. I could have died."

"The jaguar is William. Don't you understand? William would never hurt you. He loved you. He misses you. He misses us all so much."

"You're crazy," Liliana said. "William is dead."

"If that's what you want to believe," Carolina said, "but I know what is true and what is not true."

"I didn't even see a jaguar. I lied. I don't know why, but I lied." Liliana felt a terrible strength rising in her, the same strength she felt when Irene and Stefan came to pick up some things not knowing that Liliana had quit her job and was home, lying on the living room floor, listening to Mahler, hoping it would make her so full of sadness and despair that she would not be able to stand it anymore and she would finally be able to get up off the floor, eat, go outside, walk. But they had barged in, though they did not think that was what they were doing, and Liliana insisted they stay even though they said they would come back another time, that it wasn't urgent, and Irene kept apologizing as if she hardly knew her, as if they were strangers. "No," she said. "You must have some tea," and so she made tea, and they sat at the dining room table, and Liliana could hardly keep herself from picking up a chair and smashing it over his head. She sat there through the whole tea-drinking torture imagining the sound of the chair smashing his skull. And now it was building up again, this anger, this desire to hurt. She picked up a rock, clenched her fist around it, but she turned away from Carolina and flung the rock as high and far as she could, watched it arc to the ground. She got up, then, and started walking toward the horses. "I want to go back," she said.


Though it had taken them six hours to get to the camp, they were back in Juigalpa in less than two hours. "If we had taken the more direct route, you might have tried to find the way back on your own," Carolina explained, but Liliana did not think that was an explanation. When they reached the stream, Carolina said, "You can stay at my house as long as you'd like. Now that William knows you're here, we can go to the mountain to visit him together. We are sisters now."

"We are not sisters," Liliana said, but as these cruel words left her lips, something let loose inside, and for the first time since Irene left her she didn't feel angry, not at Carolina for leaving her alone in the mountains, not at William for dying, not even at Irene, and so, because Carolina was so much more alone than she would ever be, Liliana said, "I'm sorry. I didn't mean it. We are sisters. We both loved him."

"So you believe me?"

Liliana shook her head. "I'm sorry," she said.

Carolina gave her horse a gentle kick and they started off toward town.

# CHAPTER 14

IN 1982, WHEN GUILLERMO'S SONS WERE OFF FIGHTING THE
Contras, when it was still possible to believe in the revolution, a foreigner came to stay in El Castillo. He got off the boat and walked
up the hill to the fortress. From there, according to the children
who followed him, he stood on the rampart and looked out at the
river for a long time, after which he came back down the hill and
stopped at the *pulpería* to ask where he could find lodging. He spoke
perfect Spanish. Guillermo and Marta sent him to Doña Rosita's.
"It is the only place."

The foreigner said that he only needed one place, and Federica,
their youngest, laughed because she thought the foreigner was making a joke, but the foreigner seemed puzzled by her response. He
stayed at the counter for a few moments longer, regarding Federica
as if she were about to say something, but in the end he turned and
headed toward the door, pausing to call out "thank you" before
stepping outside.

The foreigner stayed at Doña Rosita's place for five days without talking to anyone except Doña Rosita—at least that was what

people said. Doña Rosita said that he was an easy guest. He ate what she prepared and asked for nothing else. Every morning he paid for his room for the next night, but he would not tell her how long he would be staying. "It could be a long time" was all he said. For those first three days he kept to the same routine. He ate breakfast—*gallo pinto*, coffee, and a banana—at six. After breakfast he showered and was on the river by seven. All he took with him was water. Doña Rosita said that he did not argue about the price for renting her canoe. "I should have asked for more, but I didn't know he would be so accepting," she said. He always came back at dusk. In the evenings he ate whatever Doña Rosita put in front of him and he drank two Toñas. After dinner he sat on the veranda looking out at the dark river. He didn't smoke.

On the fourth day he did not go down to the river but went instead to the *pulpería*. "I would like to work," he told Guillermo. "You don't have to pay me."

"We don't need any help," Marta said.

"I can build shelves," he said.

"We have shelves," Marta said.

"I can build nicer ones."

"They do not need to be nice," Marta said, and the foreigner smiled.

"Very well," he said, but he looked so alone, standing there with his hands in his pockets, squinting.

"Actually, we do need some shelves for the storeroom," Guillermo said.

"Perhaps in the storeroom," Marta said, "in case the river floods."

She took a piece of *cajeta* out of the jar, wrapped it in paper, and handed it to him as if he were one of the poor barefoot children from the jungle who came to town on Sundays rather than a grown man, a foreigner with good boots and clean fingernails.

"I didn't think you'd agree," Guillermo said once the foreigner was gone.

"He seemed so lost," she said, and Guillermo knew that she was thinking about their sons. That night it was unusually hot, and Marta said, "I don't think I can bear this heat for one more night," so they slept outside on the veranda where it was cooler. It had been a long time since they had slept outdoors. Despite the heat it always seemed like too much of an effort, and they were always tired after a long day of work. They were naked on the veranda listening to the sound of the night, waiting to be touched, dragging out their longing until Marta said, "He seems like a nice boy," and she rested her hand on the inside of his thigh.

Afterward in the dark they said out loud what they would never have said if their sons had not been at war.

"Marco was always my favorite," Marta said.

"Why?" Guillermo asked.

"You love him more too," Marta said.

They both fell asleep thinking not of Marco or their daughters, Federica and Isabel, but of the other one, the one they did not love as much, knowing that if he were the one who died, they would never forgive themselves for this night.

They slept until morning without waking and were at the *pulpería* earlier than usual. When the foreigner arrived, they both walked to the door to greet him. "You are here," Marta said, and this time the foreigner smiled.

"I am a man of my word," he said.

The foreigner built the shelves, and the shelves were smooth and straight. It was a pleasure to run one's hand along their smoothness, and Marta said that she didn't know how they had managed without them, how they had kept track of their stock when everything was just lying around in boxes.

When the foreigner finished the shelves, he told Marta and Guillermo that he had no more money and could not pay Doña Rosita for another night's lodging.

"I will pay you enough to cover the room for tonight and the *lancha* to San Carlos," Guillermo said.

"But I don't want to leave," he said.

"There is nothing here," Guillermo said.

"But I have nowhere to go."

"Where is your home?" they asked, for they had not asked this before, had not spoken much during the time that he was building the shelves.

"I don't have a home," he said.

"But you have a place where you are from?" Guillermo said. They were sitting out on the veranda overlooking the river drinking beer.

"I suppose I did, but I don't anymore. It's a long story."

"Perhaps someday you will tell us," Guillermo said.

"Perhaps," he said.

"Perhaps you could at least tell us your name," Guillermo said.

"It's William, which is English for Guillermo."

"I too am Guillermo," Guillermo said, and they raised their beer bottles and drank to each other's health, and he was glad to share a name with this young man even though he knew it was not really the same name, just the name of a saint who had done something good a long time ago.

They drank more beer and it was late and they were hungry, so they invited William for dinner. After dinner, all of them, Marta and Guillermo, Isabel and Federica, accompanied William to Doña Rosita's place. "Here," Guillermo said, pressing a few bills into William's hand.

"Thank you," William said.

The next day William was waiting for them when they arrived at the store. "I want more work," he said.

"But there is nothing more to do."

"I can paint your house," he said.

The paint was peeling. It had been years.

"It's not good to let the wood get exposed to the elements," he continued.

"We haven't had time," Guillermo said.

"I was thinking that green would be nice, an avocado green."

"The house has always been blue," Guillermo said.

"Perhaps it is time for a change."

"No, it must be blue," Guillermo said, thinking that the Germans would not want the house to be any other color.

"Blue is also a good color," William said.

It was not long before William moved into the boys' room. "He can stay until they return," Marta said, and Guillermo agreed.

William painted their house blue, a deeper, more beautiful blue than before so that the house shone in the sun, glistened like a wet stone from the river, like the sea in poetry, not like the sea at the end of the river whose foam was brown with mud. When he finished painting the house, William wanted to build a chicken coop, but Guillermo said the chickens were happy running freely around the yard.

"But they need to be protected," William said.

"There is no danger," Guillermo said. "They have always been free, and nothing has ever attacked them."

"What about jaguars?"

"They do not come so close to town."

"What about when it rains?"

"They hide under the house."

"There must be something I can do," William said, and Guillermo said that he did not have to do anything.

"You are our guest," he said, but William did not want to be a guest.

"I am not on vacation," William said.

"Teach Federica English," Guillermo said. It was the only thing William could do that they could not do for themselves.

Upon Marta's insistence, though Federica was already seventeen and there were many girls even younger who already had children, William and Federica were never allowed to be in the house unsupervised. The lessons were to be held at the *pulpería* so that she could keep an eye on them. "We can't just leave her alone with him in the house," she said, though she was always complaining that Federica showed no interest in getting married.

To Guillermo's surprise, Federica agreed to the lessons, though she did not show any enthusiasm for the undertaking, nor did she study outside the allotted lesson time. "Don't you have to practice?" Guillermo asked, remembering how hard he had worked to parse out the words of the Germans' books.

"Practice what?"

"The words," he said.

"We practice during the lessons. That's what the lessons are for," she answered, and he left it at that, especially since William kept telling them what a good student she was, how quickly she learned.

"She hardly has an accent," he said, so Guillermo let them be and he did not ask them where they went every night when they thought he and Marta were asleep. Guillermo did not follow them, or call to them to ask where they were going. He did not tell Marta. Instead he lay awake next to her waiting for them to return, thinking of Pepa and the soft wetness of the jungle floor.

The first night they went out on the river together, William wanted to swim to the other side, and Federica laughed. "It's too dangerous, because of the caimans. No one ever does it."

"Never?" he asked.

"I don't think so."

"Then I will be the first," he said, and before she could stop him, he jumped into the river.

Of course nothing happened. He swam to the other bank and back to the canoe and climbed in, laughing, though she could tell he was glad to be finished with it.

"And you've never thought about it, not even when you were a kid?" he asked.

"I used to wade in and try to catch fish with my hands, but I never thought of swimming. I don't even know how to swim."

"But kids always do things that they're not supposed to do."

"We always understood the danger."

"Do it now," William said.

"Why?"

"Just to prove to yourself that you can do it, that you're not afraid."

"But I am afraid."

"That's why you have to do it," William said.

Federica jumped into the river. "What do I do?" she called to William.

"Just keep moving and keep your head above water," he said. She paddled her arms furiously and kicked her legs, and all sorts of slimy things touched her legs and belly, and she was coughing and sputtering, but she did not stop moving until William pulled her into the canoe. They paddled then for hours, upstream away from the rapids. She did not know how far, but Federica waited until William said that it was time to turn back, and they floated downstream and were back in their beds before dawn.

The next night she showed William how to see the caimans in the dark, scanning the shoreline with her flashlight, looking for their eyes that shone orange and strong in the night. They were out in full force, lining the riverbanks like soldiers. It was as if they were waiting for them, ready to slip into the river when they jumped in. "There aren't usually so many of them," Federica said.

"Maybe they called for reinforcements after we penetrated their territory." William laughed.

"Do you want to go in when you know they are waiting?" Federica asked.

"It was just as dangerous last night when we didn't see them."

"I know," Federica said, and they both jumped in.

In the next weeks he taught her how to float on her back just by moving her arms. "Just relax," he said, and he swam to the faraway shore while she stayed there, floating on her back in the shallow waters, the more dangerous waters, near the river's edge.

"Come get me," she whispered to the caimans. Once she thought she felt something hard touching her leg, but she lay still, holding her breath, and it went away.

"Eventually, if we keep taunting the river, something will happen," William said on the night that she was finally able to swim with him to the other side.

"Is that what you want?"

"I don't want anything to happen to you," William said.

"And to you?"

He turned around and started paddling toward the rapids. "Are you scared of the rapids?" he asked.

"No. I can run them blind. I know exactly where each rock is."

"They don't shift?"

"No."

"If they're not dangerous, why haven't we gone through them?"

"I thought you were looking for danger," Federica said, and William laughed.

"Still, it must be fun, exhilarating."

"It is during the rainy season, when the water is high, but not now."

"I want you to do it blind. Here," he said, taking off his T-shirt and throwing it to her. "Wrap it around your eyes."

Federica did not say that running the rapids blind was just a manner of speaking, like saying that you know something like the back of your hand even though people don't really know the backs of their hands. As a matter of fact, she thought, the back of her hand was one of the parts of her body she knew the least. But she knew the rapids, so she tied the T-shirt around her head, tight.

"Ready?" she said, and William said he was ready. "You must do exactly as I say," she said.

"I will," he said.

She took her time, listening to the rapids getting nearer and nearer until she could feel the spray on her. "Right," she called to William, "Paddle on the right. Left, hard, harder," she called, and she paddled furiously, though she really had no idea what she was doing or what lay ahead.

William was laughing again. "You did it," he said, and she tore the T-shirt from her eyes. William was standing up in the bow of the canoe.

"You did it," he said again, and she was trembling.

They couldn't paddle upstream through the rapids, so they disembarked along the shore and then carried the canoe down the main street of El Castillo, past the rapids to the dock on the other side.

They tied the canoe to the landing and headed back to the house, but when they got there William was not ready to go in. "I know I won't be able to sleep. Will you sit with me for a while?"

Federica sat down next to William on the veranda.

"I have barely been able to sleep since I left Juigalpa," William said.

"Wait," Federica said. She went inside and returned with a bottle of rum. "This will help you sleep."

"Maybe I don't want to sleep," William said.

Federica handed him the bottle, and he took a long swig and handed it back. She drank too, and they passed the bottle back and forth for a while. Finally, after the fourth or fifth swig, Federica asked, "Why were you in Juigalpa?" though she already knew the answer.

"I was fighting."

"Perhaps, then, the real question is why did you leave Juigalpa?"

"I'm not sure except that I know I don't want to fight. I thought I did. I thought that finally I had something real to fight for, something big, but it wasn't how I thought it would be, which is, I guess, what all soldiers realize once they're in it.

"When I was a kid, I was always getting into fights with the bullies. All it took was for someone to call another kid a fatty or pull a shy girl's hair, and I would be on top of the bully, pummeling him. Afterward, I always felt this calm, like when you've been swimming all day in the sun, and I would fall asleep as soon as I lay down, which I could never do otherwise. Ever since I was five or six, I had trouble sleeping. I could always hear my heart beating. It nearly drove me crazy. All this time I thought that I slept well on those nights because I had defended someone weak, because I had done something good, fought for justice, but now I know that it was the fight itself I needed. It was lying in bed afterward going over all of it in my head, the feel of my fists smashing bone and the boy's body giving into my weight and the begging for mercy and the crying."

William paused, took a long drink of rum, handed her the bottle. "Just a week after I joined the Sandinistas, we attacked a Contra unit. We attacked at dawn when they were eating breakfast. We just mowed them down, and it was over, and I didn't get to see their fear, to feel it. I wanted to hear them crying, begging us for forgiveness. I wanted them to realize that they were on the wrong side, but they were dead before they could even realize what hit them. Afterward, as we were heading back to our camp, I walked ahead of my comrades, fighting the urge to charge our leader, push him to the ground, punish him for what I had done, so I started to run, and I kept running even when I could no longer hear them calling to me. It took me three days to find my way out of the mountains and back to Juigalpa."

"Why did you come here?" Federica asked.

"My mother lived here during the war. They were refugees. Nicaragua was the only country that would take them in. If it weren't for this country, I wouldn't exist. Has your father ever said anything about them?"

"No, he never said anything about a family of foreigners living here. He just talked about the Germans, two men, who lived on the outskirts of town. My father did errands for them and they taught him how to read. Then they left, abandoned their house with everything in it when my father was working on the coffee *finca* in Costa Rica. When he came back my father fixed up the house, and that's where we live."

"The Germans," William said. "They gave my mother a book of poetry, Lorca. There was one that my mother says is the most beautiful poem in the world. We recited it on holidays instead of prayers, and when we were sick it helped us fall asleep."

"Recite it for me now," Federica said.

"*Verde que te quiero verde. Verde viento. Verdes ramas. El barco sobre la mar.*" William stopped.

"Keep going. It's beautiful."

"I can't. I wasn't going to come here, not after what I did. I didn't think I deserved to see it. Maybe if I had come here first, I would never have left, never have . . ." he paused. "I thought I could find some peace here." William picked up the bottle, put it to his lips, and blew over the opening, holding the note as long as possible, letting it seep into the night. It sounded, Federica thought, like emptiness.

"You know," Federica said, "it's not how you kill people but why that matters. It's war. They were part of an army, a whole system. They were defending the bullies. They were defending the people who have been beating us down for centuries."

He set the bottle back down, hard, as if he wanted to startle her, punish her, too, for what he had done. "What do you know?" he said. "You know only the river."

# CHAPTER 15

NOT LONG BEFORE DAWN, FEDERICA HEARD WILLIAM OPEN THE door to his quarters, heard him pause at the door to her room, but when she called to him, he did not respond, so she let him go. After she heard William leave without saying good-bye, not even to her parents who had taken him in, Federica fell asleep again, but with the first light, she awoke suddenly, feeling that something had happened, a temblor, perhaps. She walked through the house to see whether anything had fallen or was off-kilter, but everything was as it always was, so she began to light the fire in the stove. She took out the tortillas and put on the water for coffee. "You know only the river," he'd said, and she knew then that she could no longer stay in her house waiting for the Contras to cross the river, tending to customers at the *pulpería*, making the same small talk about the rain and the price of beans day in and day out, waiting to fall in love with someone who came in on the *lancha* from San Carlos or ever farther away than that, a salesperson perhaps like her mother or maybe even a foreigner. No, she could not stay. She had to find William and go with him wherever it was that he was going.

After breakfast, Federica went with her parents to the *pulpería*. She served the first customers while her parents replenished the shelves. When they were in the back, she took some money from the till, just enough to get her to San Carlos and to keep her from going hungry for a couple days. She put a note underneath one of the piles of bills. *If I told you I was leaving, I would never have had the courage to do it*, it said. Just before the mid-morning *lancha* was scheduled to leave, she said, "I'm going to bring Doña Rita her medicine."

"Try to get her to pay what she owes us for this month," her mother said as she always did when Federica set off to bring Doña Rita her medicine.

Federica was the last one to board the mid-morning *lancha*, so she got the worst seat, all the way in the back near the bathroom. She thought that once they got going, the smell of the river would overpower the stench of the bathroom, but it turned out the opposite was true. Twice she had to lean over the edge of the boat to vomit.

Federica was sure that William would be waiting in San Carlos, sitting at the dock when she got off the *lancha*. She was sure he would say, "I knew you would come," and she would go with him wherever it was that he was going. But when she got to San Carlos, he was not there. She asked at the ferry station, the bus station, in all the stores and restaurants, in the market and along the *malecón*. No one had seen a foreigner.

She spent a sleepless night at a cheap hotel. Outside, men were breaking bottles all night long. In the morning, when she left her room, there were men sleeping in the hallway, piled on top of one another like puppies. She returned the key to the woman at the desk who asked her whether she had slept well. She said that she had. "When I was your age I could sleep through anything, too," the woman said.

Federica went to the dock to buy a ticket back to El Castillo on the mid-morning *lancha*, but all the seats were taken. The next boat would not leave until two in the afternoon. "I guess you still haven't found your foreigner," the ticket man said, as if he understood everything when he understood nothing at all, and she realized then that she could not go back to El Castillo, where everyone would have something to say, something like there are other fish in the sea, and she would have to smile and ask them if there was anything else they needed or if they were sure they didn't want to take a look at the new dresses that had just come in, and the river would only remind her of William and everything that she did not understand. She looked up and saw the lake in front of her, saw the bigness of it, and wondered how it was possible that she had been to San Carlos so many times and never had any desire to cross the lake, to see what was on the other side. "How much is the cheapest ticket to Granada?" she asked. The man told her, and she counted out her money, pushing it through the space underneath the window.

"You'd better hurry," he said, stamping her ticket and passing it to her. "It leaves in five minutes."


When she arrived in Granada she went to a *pulpería* and asked after her mother's people because she did not want to spend the money she had left on lodgings. "Marta, the one who sold clothes?" the owner of the *pulpería* asked.

"Yes, the one who sold clothes."

"Her brother lives one block north of the police station," she said.

"And where is the police station?" Federica asked.

The woman told her, and Federica thanked her. On the way, she came upon the square, and, because she was in no rush, she went inside the cathedral and sat in a back pew. It was cool in the church and quiet. Perhaps, she thought, she would be able to think here, but a pigeon flew in and sat down right next to her, and she felt that if she did not keep completely still, the pigeon would jump on her, flapping its wings, defecating, though the bird, close as it was, was facing straight ahead toward the altar as if it were waiting for mass to start. Sitting there with the pigeon made her feel even more alone than she had felt on the ferry to Granada.

She remembered that birds' eyes are on the sides of their heads, which meant the bird was not looking at the altar but at her. "What do you want?" she said, turning to the bird, but the bird remained still, focused on her. She leaned over and looked into its eye, and still it did not move. "Go away," she said, her breath fluttering the down on the bird's neck. It did not turn or hop or move its wings, but she saw that it was trembling. She considered for a moment that it was hurt, but it had flown to its perch on the pew beside her with perfect grace.

She wondered then what she looked like to the pigeon. Was she blurry or clear, elongated or rounded or flat? Could it see the color of her hair, the pores on her face? Could birds smell? These were the sorts of question she used to ask her father and for which he always had an answer. She had never doubted him, but now that she was far away from him, she understood that he could not have possibly known the answers to all her questions. She slid to the far end of the pew and exited on that side. She turned to look at the bird before she left the cathedral, and it had not moved.

Outside the sun was hot and blaring like noise. She asked a woman selling cheap shoes like the shoes her mother sold at the *pulpería* where the police station was, and she followed her directions and came to the station, where she asked a young man which way was north, and then she was standing in front of the house of her uncle whose name she did not know.

The house was bigger and nicer than she expected. Though it

was by no means grand, it was freshly painted and the largest on the block. She realized she knew nothing about her mother's family or their position in the world. Still she always imagined that her mother's family was poor and that she had worked since she was a little girl selling cheap trinkets in the market, though she knew her mother could read and write and had been in school and that the nuns wanted her to be a teacher. Yet these two ideas of her mother never seemed, until now, to be in conflict with each other.

She knocked on the door. A girl of about seven wearing a blue and white school uniform with hair that reached the small of her back opened the door and did not say hello or smile. "I am looking for my uncle, Marta Jiménez's brother," Federica said.

The girl turned without speaking and walked back into the house, leaving the door open. After a while a young woman not much older than Federica came to the door. "Can I help you?" she asked.

"I am Marta's daughter. I'm looking for her brother, my uncle."

"We have not heard from her in a long time."

"El Castillo is far away," Federica said.

Her uncle, whose name was Pablo, was not home, but the woman, his wife Leticia, invited her inside. "He will be back for dinner," she said. The house was full of artificial flowers, boxes and boxes of them. In the living room were piles of colored paper. Unfinished flowers lay in various stages of completion in rows on the floor, like dead bodies, Federica thought. "At first it was just a hobby," Leticia explained, "but now I cannot stop."

Federica helped Leticia and her daughter, Consuelo, make flowers. She was given the task of wrapping paper around wire to make stems. "You have to wrap them tight, really tight," Consuelo explained, showing her how to do it. Finally, after about twenty stems, her cousin said, "This one is perfect," and Federica felt a sense of accomplishment that surprised her. After that she worked steadily, sitting on the floor with Leticia and her daughter, who both worked without taking a break or speaking, their tongues hanging limply from their mouths in concentration. Every hour or so Leticia assured Federica that her husband would be home soon, and when he was not home at nine, they ate dinner without him.

"Perhaps tomorrow we will teach you how to make the flowers themselves," Leticia said.

"I would like that," Federica said. "Do you sell them?"

"Sometimes I give them away to the church for Easter, for weddings and funerals, but Pablo doesn't let me sell them. He thinks that people would think he cannot provide for us if I am out peddling, as he calls it. Only peasants sell flowers, he says."

"But these are not real flowers," Federica said. "They are a form of art."

"It is something to do, something to pass the time."

When Federica's uncle finally came home, his wife acted as if they had not been waiting for him all day, as if he had come home exactly when he said he would. Only after she brought him his dinner and a beer did she introduce Federica, and he seemed exaggeratedly happy to meet her. "Bring my niece a beer," he said to his wife. "Sit," he said, indicating the chair opposite him at the table. "Have you come to fight?" he asked.

"To fight?" Federica said. "No."

Her uncle put down his fork, chewed his food for what seemed to Federica much longer than necessary. Finally he swallowed. "My child is too young," he said. "How old are you?"

"Seventeen."

"Seventeen is old enough, and you look strong. Your mother was strong. Once she wrestled down a dog that was attacking me. It was a big dog, too, bigger than me at the time, and she just threw him down. She knew exactly how to grab him, but she didn't know what to do once he was down, so she just kept him in a stronghold while he barked and growled and tried to get away until the neighbor came out and shot him. Is she still strong like that?"

"I suppose," Federica said. She knew that her mother could lift two sacks of rice onto her shoulders at the same time. Even the market women could only manage one. Yet she had never thought of this as remarkable.

"And are you strong like her?"

"Yes," Federica said. She did not say that her mother did not want her to be this way. She wanted a daughter who dreamed of her wedding day. She wanted a daughter who didn't go out with her father at night into the jungle looking for jaguars.

"We are making progress. With the help of the United States, we will be rid of those fucking communists soon."

Federica did not really know much about communists, but she knew from her brothers and William that the United States was trying to destroy the revolution. Why she did not really understand, but she knew it had something to do with the fact that America was rich and Nicaragua was poor, though she did not understand why if a country was rich and had everything it needed, it would want to destroy a country that was poor and had so little. "And you, are you fighting?" Federica asked.

"Look," he said, lifting up his shirt. "We were eating breakfast. The bullet went right through my left lung. Look," he said again, though she was still looking. He traced the scar that ran from his collarbone to his belly with his forefinger. "Cowards," he said, picking up his fork again, his shirt still rolled up under his chin. "They thought I was dead, so they just left me there. If they had killed my horse, I would have died out there in the mountains. Poor horse would have died of hunger if I hadn't survived," he said, putting his fork down again without taking another bite.

"Where was it?"

"What?"

"Where you were wounded?"

"In the mountains near Juigalpa," he said. She wondered whether it was a bullet from William's gun that had pierced her uncle's lungs.

"Wouldn't you have done the same?" she asked.

"What do you mean?"

"If you had come across them, if they had been eating breakfast, wouldn't you have ambushed them?"

Pablo pushed his plate away and pulled down his shirt. "You will make a good soldier," he said.

She wanted to leave, go back to the ferry, back to San Carlos, back to El Castillo, but it was late, and she was tired, so she did not say that she would never fight for the Americans. Never. She smiled, and Pablo patted her on the back when she got up from the table, and she smiled again and thanked him.

Leticia insisted she sleep in Consuelo's bed. "She likes to sleep on the floor. She's afraid of falling out of her bed," she said, so Federica agreed.

"Don't mind the boxes," Leticia said when they came to her room. "It's just the flowers." Except for the bed and a small walkway from the bed to the door, the room was completely filled with boxes.

"When I was your age, I was afraid of falling out of my bed too," Federica said to her cousin when they turned off the lights.

"I'm not afraid. I just tell my mother that so that she lets me sleep on the floor."

"Why do you like to sleep on the floor? Isn't it uncomfortable?"

"Yes," her cousin said.

"And why do you want to be uncomfortable?"

"Because when I am a soldier I will have to sleep on the ground. I'm practicing."

"But you're too young to fight."

"Soon I will be old enough," she said. "You're lucky. You are old enough now."

"But I don't want to fight."

"Coward," her cousin said, and she turned to face the wall.

In the room next door she heard her uncle grunting and the bed springs squeaking. She lay awake for a long time thinking of her brothers sleeping on the ground, missing their beds.

Not long after she fell asleep, she woke up suddenly. It was dark in the room, but she was sure someone was watching her from the doorway, so she sat up and looked straight at the doorway, where she knew her uncle was standing, and after a while she heard footsteps in the hall, and then she heard him close the door to his room, and the bed springs whined as he settled into his bed, and then it was completely silent. There were no insects calling to each other, no river rushing over rocks, no monkeys screeching, no wind rustling the leaves of trees. Her cousin made no sound at all.

Shortly after Federica had fallen asleep again, her uncle woke her up. "Get dressed; you have a big day ahead of you," he said, as if she were a child and it was her first day of school. He waited until she had gotten out of bed and pulled on her pants before leaving the room. "Breakfast is served, so hurry," he said before shutting the door.

Her cousin was already up and dressed in her blue and white school uniform. She sat on her bed watching Federica get ready. "Do you like making flowers?" Federica asked.

"Yes," the girl said, looking down so that Federica could not see her eyes.

"Why?"

"Because they are beautiful," she said.

"If you become a soldier, you will see many ugly things."

"Then I will think of the flowers," the girl said.

"Do you really want to be a soldier?"

"Of course I do. It is my responsibility to help protect our country from the communists."

"And what is bad about communists?"

"Everything. They are the devil."

"I don't believe in the devil," Federica said.

The girl laughed. "You'd better hurry. My father is waiting," she said.

Federica and her uncle walked for about twenty minutes until they came to a blue and white colonial house at least three times the size of her uncle's house. A soldier with a sub-machine gun stood guard at the gate. "This is Colonel Vargas's house. His family has lived in this house for three hundred years. Before that it was a convent," he said.

"It's very nice," Federica said because she did not know what else to say.

"I bet you've never been in a house this big."

"No, I haven't."

"The fucking communists tried to take it away from him. They knocked on the door early in the morning, but he and his sons were ready for them. They sent the maid to open the door and invite them in. She led them to the living room, had them sit down, brought them coffee. Then, just as they were lifting the coffee cups to their lips, he and his sons took them by storm, *dac, dac, dac, dac, dac, dac, dac,*" her uncle said, pantomiming how they had swept the room with machine gun fire. "When the coffee cups fell from the traitors' hands, they didn't break. That's how plush the rug was. After that the communists left him alone."

They continued toward the lake. When they got to the lake, her uncle paused again, and they stood looking out at it together. "There are sharks in this lake," her uncle said.

"Once my father caught a shark in the river," she said. "They come up the river from the Caribbean."

"That is not possible. Sharks cannot swim upriver."

"Then how did they get into the lake?"

"They have always been here, like the other fish," her uncle said. "Did you eat the shark?"

"No, my father threw it back in."

"Were you there with him?"

"No."

"Then how do you know he was telling the truth?"

"My father is not a liar," Federica said.

"Everyone is a liar," her uncle said.

They headed back toward the plaza again, down a smaller street, then up the hill to the market, where there was a truck waiting. Girls were sitting in the back of the truck on bags of produce, not talking. The driver was leaning against the truck smoking a cigarette. "She's a strong girl," her uncle told him, and the driver looked her up and down and nodded.

"Good-bye," her uncle said as soon as she was settled in the truck.

"Good-bye," she whispered, but, given the girls' silence, she felt as if she were screaming. Later, once it was too late to turn back, she wondered what would have happened if she had refused to get into the truck, but at the time she was simply relieved to be rid of her uncle and his house full of flowers, so she did not think of protesting.

It was not until they were out of town and on the road that she thought of asking where they were going.

"To León," the girl sitting next to her said.

"What will we do there?"

"We will find out when we get there," the girl said.

Federica looked down. The girls all had the hands and feet of people who worked in the fields, callused and strong, the nails broken and cut short.

"Shh," another girl said.

"They told us not to talk to each other," the girl next to her whispered.

"Why?" Federica asked, but the girl just shrugged.

After that there was no more talking. When the road got worse, the driver swerved left and right to avoid the worst potholes, throwing them against each other. They righted themselves and waited for the next bump. They stopped only once. The driver got out, came around to the back of the truck, and counted them. There were fourteen, the same number as when they started. "Good," he said, and they continued on. Some of the girls had brought tortillas, and the ones who had food shared with the ones who didn't. Federica was not hungry, but she accepted the tortillas and ate.

When the sun was at its hottest, they stopped in a small village, where they were met by two soldiers with machine guns, who helped them out of the truck. "I can do it myself," Federica said. The soldier turned away and spat as she jumped off the truck.

They followed the soldiers through the village to a house, where they were told they would spend the night. One of the soldiers led Federica and the girls to a room that contained only a bed. They stood there for a moment, not knowing what to do. "Lie down," he said, and they lay on the floor around the bed. The soldier laughed and lay down on the bed, put his hands behind his head and his knees up, grinding his dirty boots into the white sheet before getting up and leaving them on their own.

At some point when it was dark, an old woman brought them tortillas and beans and water, and they ate sitting cross-legged on the floor. They did not lean on the bed, though that would have been more comfortable, nor did they look at the boot prints that the soldier left. After they had eaten and the old woman collected their plates, they were led by another soldier, one at a time, to the latrine outside. Then they were told again to sleep, and Federica lay awake for a long time listening to the soldiers talking in the other room. She tried not to let herself think of William or of how it felt to lie on her back in the river. She wondered whether he regretted leaving without saying good-bye and whether he remembered what he said to her. "What do you know? You know only the river," she whispered. But now I know this, she thought, and she closed her eyes.

The roosters woke her just before dawn, and she was surprised to have slept at all. Around her the girls began to stir. Again they were led to the latrine. Again the old woman brought them tortillas and beans and water. Then they were divided into two groups and told to sit with their group on opposite sides of the bed. "Stand in order of height," a soldier ordered, and the girls scrambled into order. Federica was the tallest in her group. "You," he said, pointing to Federica and to the tallest girl in the other group. "Come," he said, and she and the other tall girl followed him into the front room. "You will be the leaders," he said. "It is the most dangerous position and an honor."

The other girl looked down, but Federica did not.

"Look up," the soldier said without a trace of gruffness, as if he were an artist painting her portrait. The girl looked up. "That's better," he said.

He left them and went outside, returning a few minutes later with another soldier, older than the two who had been guarding them. Along each smooth forearm ran a thick vein. Like a river, Federica thought.

"What are you looking at?" he asked.

"The veins in your arms," Federica said without averting her eyes.

He looked down at his arms as if he had never seen them before. "Ha," he said without smiling. "You are observant. That will serve you well. Come," he said, and they followed him outside to two trucks that were filled with baskets of food—bananas, mangoes, avocadoes, cabbages, cheese, and unplucked dead chickens. Federica was told to climb into the first truck, the other girl into the second. "Look inside the basket with the chickens," the soldier said. Federica knelt down and put her hands into the basket, pushing the chickens to the side. Federica knew what was inside, could feel the hot smoothness of the barrels.

"Take them out," the soldier commanded, so she pulled the chickens out first, setting them carefully on the truck bed. Two guns and ammunition. "Are you strong enough to carry them?" he asked, and Federica nodded. She put them back in the basket and heaved it onto her head. "Walk," he said, and she began walking down the road. "That's enough. Come back," he said, and she turned around and returned to the truck.

When the other girl had done the same, he told them to look inside the other baskets. Some contained weapons and others contained only produce. They had to memorize what was in each basket and were given a test. Federica got all the questions right. The other girl did not, and the soldier made her take everything out of all the baskets and then put everything back. He tested her again—with a gun to her head. She was sure he would have pulled the trigger if the girl had not answered the questions correctly, but she got them all right, so he put the gun back in its holster, took out a cigarette, tapped the end of it on the face of his watch, lit it, inhaled deeply. "This is the plan," he said. "One of the groups will be dropped off at the southern end of the city and the other at the northern end. Each girl will carry a basket and walk into the city with them."

"What if the other girls ask why the baskets are so heavy? What if they ask why they are carrying baskets into the city?" Federica asked.

"They will not ask. They are used to doing as they are told," the soldier said.

Federica and the other girl had to memorize a map as well. This time they both were able to answer all the questions about the map the first time around. "Good," the soldier said, but Federica could tell that he was disappointed, that he would have liked to hold the gun to their heads.

There was a warehouse near the marketplace. People would be there to receive them. These people would open the warehouse, and they would bring their baskets inside, and that would be it. It was easy, the soldier said.

"And then what?" Federica asked. "How will the girls get back to Granada?"

"That is not my problem," the soldier said.

Federica wanted to embrace the other girl before she got into her truck, but the girl jumped in before she could reach her, so she waved to her instead, and the girl waved back, smiling meekly.

Federica waited until her team was on the truck before climbing in. "Good luck," the soldier said.

Federica sat on the tailgate of the truck, facing her group and the baskets and the guns that were in the baskets. When the road became more rutted, the truck did not slow down. Federica had to hold on to the truck so that she would not be thrown off. "It's dangerous up there. Come sit with us," one of the older girls suggested, but Federica stayed where she was. When they got to their destination, Federica's arms were twitching from holding on so tightly. They kept twitching as she walked with the basket of dead chickens on her head, twitching like a dying fish that had just been dumped from the net onto the dock.

They walked three abreast, taking up the road. The soldier had ordered them to converse and laugh as they walked so they would seem like ordinary market girls, but when Federica tried to get the others to talk, asking them whether they had boyfriends, they merely shook their heads or nodded, so Federica began to sing a silly song she had sung in school about a frog who fell in love with a fly. The other girls knew it and sang along, and when they came to the third verse, they did not remember all the words, so they made them up, each verse more absurd than the one before it so that by the end of the song they were laughing, and people who passed them smiled and some of them waved. After the song about the frog and the fly they sang "*Las mañanitas.*" They passed a group of young men painting a sign on the side of a school building: *PATRIA LIBRE O MORIR.* "Hey," the young men called. "Whose birthday is it?"

"Mine," Federica said.

The young men clambered down from the scaffolding and followed them. "Let me take your basket," one of the young men said, coming up to Federica and reaching for it.

They had been given strict orders to talk to no one. Federica pulled away from him, walking faster, looking straight ahead, but the young man was not so easily defeated. He reached for the basket again.

"I can manage myself," Federica said.

"You should not have to work on your birthday," the young man said.

"I do not have that luxury," Federica answered.

"Where are you going?" he asked.

"To the market."

"I will come with you, and when you have sold all your chickens we will go out dancing."

"I don't like to dance," Federica said.

"I don't believe you," he said, grabbing her around the waist, spinning her around so that she had to hold on tight to her basket with the dead chickens and the guns beneath them. They spun around, and the other girls stopped and clapped, and they started "*Las mañanitas*" again from the beginning. She let herself be pulled by the young man, let his arms hold her, and she thought of William and how they had gone down the rapids together with their eyes closed. "What's your name?" she asked.

"Felipe," he said. He smelled of paint and sweat and she kissed him, plunged her tongue into his mouth that smelled of cigarettes and something sweet. "Mangoes," she said.

"What?"

"You taste like mangoes," she said.

The girls stopped singing. Federica put her basket down, and the other girls did the same. They watched Federica and Felipe looking at each other. They watched Federica pull him close and whisper in his ear.

She pulled away and pushed him hard so that he almost fell, but he regained his balance and took her hand again, and they danced. "Sing," she said to the girls, and they began to sing again, louder than before, and he spun her around and around the basket of dead chickens until the young man's friends called for him to return to work.

"I will be waiting for you," he said to Federica as she took up her basket and began walking again. The other girls followed, keeping up with her, though the sun was hotter now. They were hungry and thirsty, and the chickens were beginning to rot.

They reached the warehouse sooner than Federica expected. The door to the warehouse opened as soon as they reached it, and Federica walked inside first, telling the girls to wait, though that had not been part of the instructions. As soon as she stepped inside, music began to play. It was cool inside and very dark, except for a few dots of light that came in through the cracks in the roof. She could tell by the way the music filled the room that the space was large and empty. The music got louder, and she could sense someone approaching. Though she could hear no footsteps, no rustling or breathing, she knew from the smell of cigarettes and sweat that it was a soldier. He put his hand on her shoulder, and she did not flinch. He turned on a flashlight, shone it directly into her eyes, but she didn't close them.

"Where are the others?" he asked.

"They are waiting outside."

"Tell them to come in," he said, turning off the flashlight, making her find her way back to the door in the darkness. "Quiet," she told the girls when she opened the door, though they were not making a sound. As soon as they were all inside, the music stopped.

"Close the door," the soldier said.

She did.

"Put down your baskets."

They did.

"Go."

They did.

Once outside the girls did not know what to do. "We will go where you are going," they said.

"I am not going anywhere," Federica said, but they followed her anyway, so she headed back to the school because she had to take them somewhere and because she did not want to be alone with them. When they arrived the girls ran up to greet Felipe as if he had been waiting for them, not Federica, and he hugged each one as if they were his children.

They spent the night in the school. As soon as the other girls were asleep, Felipe took Federica to meet his commander, a man they called El Justo. He lived with other commanders in the house that used to belong to a colonel in Somoza's army. This colonel had been a painter, and the walls of his house were covered with watercolors of the colonial buildings of León. They were led into the living room where El Justo was sitting on a blue velvet couch, and he asked if she liked the paintings.

Federica went up to the watercolors to get a closer look, to take them in. The buildings seemed as if they were fading away, receding, as if the colonel had tried to erase them.

"They look like ghosts," she said.

"Ha," El Justo said. "Do you believe in ghosts?"

"No," Federica said.

"Sometimes when I can't sleep I can almost hear him walking around, coughing. He was a chain-smoker. They say he smoked eighty cigarettes a day. He liked to put out his cigarettes on his victims." He paused, taking up a package of cigarettes. "Do you mind if I smoke?"

"No," Federica said.

"Actually, I don't smoke. These were his." He threw the pack of cigarettes across the room. "It's a nasty habit. It makes people weak, and we cannot afford to be weak, can we?"

"No," Federica said.

"I thought we would agree. I want you to join us when we attack a warehouse. We have received information that the enemy just received a shipment of weapons."

Federica looked at Felipe. He nodded. "I do not know how to fight," Federica said.

"You will learn," El Justo said. He walked over to her and took her hands, squeezed them hard enough for her to feel his strength, but there was also something gentle in his grip, a softness. His eyelashes were long and thick and his breath smelled nutty, like the freshly roasted cashews they sold at the *pulpería*.

"You are beautiful," he said. "And strong." If he had not said that she was strong, perhaps she would have walked away, gone back to El Castillo, to the sacks of rice and tin cans and the ringing of the cash register, but he said she was strong, and so she learned how to fight, as did the other girls, because they did not know how to get back to where they had come from.

The next night they all fought valiantly at the warehouse, and after the battle, they drank to the girls who had died, to their sacrifice, to the revolution and to the weapons that they had wrested from the hands of the enemy. They toasted Federica, their leader, and she and Felipe danced, and when it was time to sleep, they went together to one of the classrooms and she let Felipe take off her clothes and kiss her. She let him push her onto the floor, and when he was inside her, when he whispered in her ear, "You are a hero," she thought of the men who died in the warehouse, the men they killed, and she thought of William. Where are you now, she thought as she felt something release inside her, and she held on to Felipe, held on to him like he was a canoe going over the rapids.

Federica and the other girls, except for the three who died, were sent up north with El Justo to the border with Honduras where the heaviest fighting was. They fought bravely there as they had fought in León, and they became known as El Justo's women, though he never talked to them, but one evening, after a four-day battle that ended with the enemy's retreat back over the border into Honduras, El Justo called Federica into his tent.

He was sitting at a table upon which stood a bottle of rum and his revolver. "Sit down," he said, pointing to the chair across from him.

El Justo poured two glasses and set one in front of her. "Drink," he said, and she drank it all in one shot as she had learned to do since she had entered into this new world, though it had only been a week since she had been a soldier, since she had learned to kill. El Justo emptied his glass as well and set it back down on the table.

"They say that a foreigner, an American, passed through your village," he said.

Federica did not reply.

El Justo picked up the revolver, held it in the palm of his hand as if it were an offering rather than a weapon. Federica did not understand, so she did nothing, just sat there waiting for El Justo to speak.

"William," he said, switching the revolver to his left hand and raising it as he had done before.

"William," Federica said.

"You know him?"

"Yes."

"Where is he?" he asked, lowering his left hand, resting it on his thigh.

"I don't know."

"The others say you know."

"They are wrong."

"Where did you see him last?"

"In El Castillo."

"What was he doing in El Castillo?"

"I don't know."

"He was your lover?"

"No."

"And where did he go from there, from El Castillo?"

"I don't know."

"If you hear from him, you will tell me," El Justo said.

Federica did not answer.

El Justo walked over to Federica and stood behind her, lifted his arm, pointed the gun at the back of her head. She didn't feel it, but she knew it was there.

El Justo laughed.

"Go," he said.

After that he was always watching her. He watched her while she ate, while she cleaned her gun. He watched her when she came out of the bushes after going to the bathroom—even when she went in the middle of the night. It was as if he knew the rhythm of her bodily functions. He never said anything to her again, nor did she speak to him, and she did not tell Felipe that El Justo was watching her. She did not want him to think that she needed protection or that she was afraid, and after a while she got used to his presence as one got used to the rain.

The Contra forces pushed back over the border. There were so many more of them this time, armed with newer and more powerful American weapons. Near Ocotal, Federica's unit was ambushed. Four of El Justo's women died there—and Felipe. After that they were almost always on the move. Sometimes they did not even set up camp but stood all night long in the darkness, clutching their weapons, waiting to be attacked. On those long nights Federica focused on not thinking of Felipe, on not remembering the sound of his voice or his smell and how sometimes she awakened in the night and heard him crying.

Soon after Felipe died, they ran out of provisions and were ordered to go to Estelí, where, they were informed, they would be trained by Russian military personnel to use the most advanced Soviet weapons. It took them a week to walk to Estelí. They stayed clear of the villages, for they could not be sure of them anymore, now that the Contras had taken over. They survived on what they could hunt, which was not much, a parrot the first day, rodents and lizards after that. Federica did not want to eat the parrot, but El Justo insisted. "If one of us is hungry, we are all hungry," he said. He pulled the meat off the bird himself and distributed it equally among all of them, and because she did not want to call attention to herself, she ate her piece of the parrot, ate the bones too. On the fourth day, one of the men almost caught a wild boar, but it escaped. At night it was difficult to sleep because of the hunger.

The first night they were in Estelí, they slept in the house of a wealthy landowner who was living in Miami, working as a gardener, El Justo said. The women that were left took turns taking baths, and the men sat on the veranda on the cane furniture drinking. When the women were clean they came out and sat on the men's laps, the cane furniture creaking with their weight. Federica did not sit in a man's lap. She went to bed early and lay awake listening to their laughter.

In the morning no one came to pick them up, so they ate what was left of dinner and waited. Finally, in the late afternoon, Federica and a couple of the other girls went into town to find El Justo. At the local Sandinista headquarters, the soldiers on duty laughed when they mentioned the Russians. El Justo, they were told, had been called to Managua. "What about us?" Federica asked. "What should we do?"

"Go home," they said. "It will soon be over."

They returned to the rich man's house. After three days, when there was no more food or rum, all of El Justo's men and women walked together into town. In the plaza an old women gave them avocadoes and bananas and said, "*Qué viva la revolución*," and they thanked her and walked away with the avocadoes and bananas and sat on the benches facing the cathedral to eat. They were still hungry, but they did not complain, for they had been hungrier in the mountains, hungrier on their walk to Estelí when they did not catch the wild boar. Federica left them on the benches, the sun in their faces, the boys licking papaya juice from the girls' chins. "Where are you going?" they called after her.

# CHAPTER 16

FEDERICA HAD A HANGOVER. SHE HAD NOT MEANT TO DRINK SO much or stay out so late, but her parents were always telling her to get out more, so she had given in, and then one drink led to another, and she found she was enjoying herself.

No one thought, least of all herself, that she would stay in El Castillo for more than a few months, but it had been three months since she had been released from the hospital and returned to El Castillo, almost a year since the plane accident, which had occurred on January 10, 2007, the day of Daniel Ortega's inauguration. In fact, she had been watching his inauguration speech while making the final preparations for the flight to Greytown, where she was to pick up the next tour group. Though she had learned from her own experiences with war and revolution not to have much faith in politics, she felt a tinge of optimism on the day she fell out of the sky, an optimism that was soon to be squelched by pain and the tedious routine of recovery.

She had been sure when she returned to El Castillo that she would get tired of walking up and down the same paths, past the same houses, the same chickens and pigs. She thought she would get tired of seeing the same vultures sitting on the same rocks along the river. Her father had been the most skeptical of all.

"The river was never enough for you," Guillermo said when she told him she was staying.

"There is more here than the river. You are here," she said.

"Yes, I am here," he replied, as if he too was surprised to still be in El Castillo.

Federica's back hurt. It always hurt. The pain was the first thing she noticed when she woke up in the morning, the last thing she felt before she fell asleep at night. The doctors told her some days would be better than others, that perhaps at some point she would not feel the pain at all, but she no longer believed that. In the beginning, when she was still recovering from the accident, she monitored the fluctuations of her pain carefully, taking consolation in the good days and forcing herself not to harp on the bad ones, but now all she knew was that the pain was always there, a dull reminder of the life she could no longer live, though it could have been so much worse. She could be dead or sitting in a wheelchair unable to move anything, not even a toe, which was why she got out of bed, did her exercises even though she didn't think they made a difference. It was like saying a prayer just in case something out there was listening, which she knew there wasn't.

This morning the exercises seemed to diminish her headache, which was now more like the memory of a headache rather than a headache itself, and she felt almost sorry that it was gone, that it was not still there to remind her of the good cheer of the night before.

"Here," her father said, handing her a cup of coffee when she emerged from her quarters in the back of the house.

When she was on her second cup, she asked her father whether she could help him with anything, which is what she asked him every morning. Of course she knew that he didn't need her help and that sometimes he even made up things for her to do. It was like when he used to take her and her siblings into the jungle at night to look for the jaguar. He had them convinced they were helping him, that he was the one who wanted to find the jaguar, but when they got older they began to see that he invented the game for them.

Once when they were playing the jaguar game, they spent the entire night in the jungle, waiting. "This is the night," her father said. "I can feel it." He cut down giant leaves and lay them on the ground for them to sleep on. "I will wake you when he comes," he said, but Federica could not sleep.

"Do you think that the jaguar is watching us?" she whispered to her father after she was sure her brothers and sister were sleeping.

"Yes," he said.

"I have to see it," she whispered.

"I know," he said, and she felt that he understood she wanted to see the jaguar more than she ever wanted anything before, and that this wanting was as frightening as it was beautiful, like the jaguar itself.

In the morning when they arrived home, her mother was furious. "You never think about me," she yelled at all of them, and she flung plates at her father, and they crashed to the floor. She left them for a week, went on the ferry across the lake to her people in Granada.

After they spent the night in the jungle, Federica's brothers and sister did not want to go into the jungle to wait for the jaguar, so she and her father went by themselves, leaving them at home in their comfortable beds. On the night before her mother returned, Federica had seen a form, a shadow in the bushes. "There," she whispered.

"That's him," her father whispered back, and she was sure it was looking at her, but in the morning, when the sun was up and the world was exposed and she looked at herself in the mirror, looked right into her own eyes, she could not be sure she had seen a jaguar.

"Remember that night we saw the jaguar? When Mamá left us?" she asked her father now as she helped him carry the bucket of slop for the pigs.

"I remember," he said.

"Did you really see him? Did I really see him?"

Her father emptied his bucket, and the pigs came running, grunting. "You'd think they were starving. You'd think I never fed them," he said.

"I'm serious," Federica said.

"If you believe you saw him, then you did," her father said.

"That is not the way things work."

"It is the way things work in the jungle," her father said. "There are things we will never see, and things that we think we see but do not."

After her mother returned from being with her people in Granada, she did not speak to their father for two weeks except to talk about the business of "Dónde Don Solano," which is what everyone in El Castillo still called the *pulpería*. At the dinner table no one spoke, not even Federica's younger sister, Isabel. Finally, on the fourteenth day, their mother announced that their father would no longer take them into the jungle at night to look for jaguars. So Federica started going out alone. Sometimes she went to the river, took the canoe out onto the water. At first she always paddled upstream to avoid the rapids, but one night she went in the other direction and she did not stop. The rapids pulled her down, and she kept paddling, and the water enveloped her, and she did not resist. When it was over, when she was on the other side of danger, she looked up at the stars and at the darkness along the banks of the river.

"I am alive," she said. "I am alive," she screamed into the night.

"Why did Mamá get so angry about us going to look for the jaguar?" Federica now asked her father as they headed back toward the house.

"Because she was afraid that something had happened to us, and the one thing she hates more than waste and laziness is fear. You see, she wasn't really angry with us. She was angry at herself for being afraid."

"But you used to go by yourself. You used to sneak out of the house in the middle of the night. We all knew you did. Mamá was always in a bad mood the next day and snapped at us about the most insignificant things."

"I did?" her father said, which is what he always said when he did not want to talk about the past. "You know, your mother is getting worse. She's started telling people when they are going to die. Yesterday it was Julia's little girl. You know Julia. She's married to Rolando, the *palanga* driver. 'Your daughter's day is April 12, 2050,' she told Julia, and then she said she was sorry that she wouldn't live a long life. Isabel doesn't know what to do with her anymore, but if Isabel doesn't take her to the *pulpería*, she cries until I take her, or she talks and talks about that stupid canal. I can't get her to understand that it is not going to run through the river, that the route is north of here through the jungle, that she won't be able to see it even if they do build it, even if that Chinese guy is crazy enough to go in with Daniel and all of them, despite the fact that there already is a perfectly good canal in Panama."

"But everyone knows it's the Alzheimer's. They don't believe her, do they?"

Her father shrugged. "You know how people are," he said. "They prefer to believe in miracles than to believe in facts."

"I'll stop by today to help Isabel," Federica said. Her sister had come back to El Castillo from Miami just a little over a year ago when their mother started forgetting things.

"That would be nice."

"You still haven't told me," Federica said.

"The jaguar?" Her father stopped walking.

"Yes," Federica said. "Come, sit down. You're tired," she said, pointing to the bench underneath the mango tree.

"I'm not tired," he said, and he remained standing. "It was just a way to be alone, to think."

"Think about what?" Federica asked.

"Just things, like the ocean and trains and snow and all the places in the world I would never see."

"You could see things. You could go to visit Juan Carlos in New York. You could go in the winter when it snows."

"It would never be as beautiful or mysterious as it is in my imagination. It's the thinking that I like, knowing that there are all these places that I will never see, all these people I will never know that carry on without me or my thoughts, like the jaguar."

"But you have seen a jaguar."

"The point is not to see it but to look for it, to imagine it watching us, so close that it could take us."

"That's what it feels like in those moments before you pull the string on the parachute. You feel how close you are to death, and at the same time you believe that you can fly, that you are invincible, immortal even."

Her father smiled, but Federica knew that it was not for what she said but for something else, something far away. "Come, it's getting too hot to be outside," he said.

When they were inside, her father sat down at the kitchen table, took up a knife, and began peeling a mango, concentrating on the task, breathing heavily like a child when he is focused intensely on cutting in a straight line.

"So then you really didn't need us to help you find a jaguar," she said. "You just wanted us to know what it felt like to search for one."

"Is that what I said, that I needed your help?"

"Yes, but once we were grown up, we used to laugh about it, about how you had made us feel so important."

Her father laughed. "Here," he said, holding out the plate of cut mango.

"Do you think she will recognize me today?" Federica asked.

"Probably not," he said.


Federica did not head directly to the *pulpería*. Instead she walked up to the fortress, which is what she did every morning after helping her father with the animals. The gate was still locked since the ticket office did not open until ten, so she climbed over the wall. When she was a child there was no locked gate, no ticket office. There were no signs prohibiting climbing on the ramparts. There were no tourists, no hotels, no restaurants, no jungle tours. The fortress belonged to the children during the day and to lovers at night, though sometimes children would lie on their bellies on the ramparts, looking down at unsuspecting lovers who believed they had the night to themselves, that not even the monkeys were watching, not even the stars. Why they believed this Federica could never understand, for hadn't they been children, too? Hadn't they watched young lovers with thrilling horror from the crumbling ramparts? But now she understood that forgetting can be an act of will—a protection against the pull of nostalgia that, like gravity, can send you crashing to the ground—for since the accident, this had been her life, this willful forgetting of her life as a pilot, this erasure of her beloved Cessna and the view from on high, of the bigness of the world. She never understood why her passengers so often focused on how small things looked from a plane, why they saw the river as an insignificant ribbon rather than marveled at its length. It was, she supposed, a question of perspective, but she preferred to delight in the vastness—the never-ending sky, the uncountable number of trees, the reach of rivers, the untouchable clouds—than bemoan her own insignificance. Thus, though her days were an exercise in forgetting the thrill of flying and focusing on the details of her circumscribed life, every morning she came to the highest point of El Castillo. Did she do this to hold on to the memory of what she had lost or to appreciate the beauty in her newly limited world? Perhaps, she thought, it was a little bit of both.

Was it possible, then, that her mother's loss of memory was also an act of will? Perhaps she was tired of being the practical one, the one who could not sleep unless every *córdoba* in the ledger was accounted for, who did all the bargaining because her father didn't care enough about the bottom line to get a good deal, the one who kept them safe from ruin and tried to convince them of the dangers of the river and jungle, even though Federica and her brothers scoffed at her warnings and did not believe her cautionary tales like the one about the three brothers, Pablo, Pedro, and Paco, who fell into the river and were devoured by the caimans. "No one would name their children Pablo, Pedro, and Paco," Federica and her brothers always said when their mother tried to tell them about how the boys' mother had died from grief.

"What about the twins Juan and Juana?" Isabel, the only one who heeded their mother's warnings, would counter.

But her earnest argument just made them laugh more, and as soon as they had the chance, they would run off to the river to look for caimans sunning themselves on the rocks along the riverbank. When they were feeling especially brave, they would lean over as far as they could and touch them.

Perhaps, Federica thought as she looked down at the river, her mother was tired of worrying about caimans and jaguars and plane crashes and war. Maybe it was easier for her to erase everyone she loved from her memory than to keep living with her fear of losing them. Maybe it was finally time for her mother to dream.

Federica eased herself down from the ramparts. "Careful," she said out loud, talking herself through it. "Left foot first, now the right." She stood for a moment against the wall before moving away and standing on her own. "That wasn't so bad," she said. She took a step, then another. Today was going to be a good day. Perhaps she would go to the bar again in the evening.

Federica's mother was sitting on the porch. She was looking up at the rain, watching it fall from the sky. "It's raining," she said to her mother. "You should come inside before it gets too strong."

"I know it's raining," her mother said. "Come sit down." Federica sat next to her mother. "Do you want me to tell you?" her mother asked.

"Tell me what?"

"I'm sure Isabel has mentioned it. She's furious about it, but we can't be afraid. It makes it worse if you're afraid."

"Actually, Father told me."

Her mother looked at her, confused. "Father?" she said wistfully.

"Do you know who I am?" Federica asked.

"It is not necessary to know who you are in order to know your day."

"Is it soon?" Federica asked.

"It's neither soon nor a long time from now."

"I see," Federica said.

"You don't want to know the exact date?" her mother asked.

"No," Federica said.

"July 15, 2022."

"I said I didn't want to know," Federica said, and her mother leaned her head back, opened her mouth, and let the rain pour in. "It tastes like silver."

"Silver is tasteless," Federica said, but her mother just smiled.

Federica's mother turned to the river. "There was a time when important people came down this river on ships as big as the fancy houses of the rich. They had parties on the ships and musicians played and you could hear the music from far away, and women wore beautiful necklaces made of pearls and diamonds. Look at it now, decrepit and empty like an old woman's womb, but Daniel has plans. This time he'll build a canal, and then imagine the business we'll have."

"There already is a canal, in Panama," Federica said. "And what about the fish and the jungle and the birds? A canal would destroy it all."

"You and your father," her mother said. "You don't believe in progress."

"Will it be completed before I die?" Federica asked.

"Yes," her mother said, taking her hand and gripping it hard, as if the completion of the canal were Federica's dying wish, not hers.

Federica went inside to talk with Isabel, who was sitting at the counter watching one of her shows. "So when are you going to die?" Federica said by way of a greeting.

"It's not funny," Isabel said, and she put the television on mute, though she did not turn her eyes away from the screen. "We're going to lose customers."

"Papá says that she cries all day if she stays home."

"It's as if she's doing it on purpose, as if she wants everything to fall apart just because she's falling apart."

"My date is July 15, 2022. I have only a few more years to live."

"Don't be ridiculous," Isabel said.

"What if she's right, though? What if she knows?"

"Since when did you believe in anything?" Isabel said.

"I believe in a lot of things, just not the same things that you believe in."

"Tell me one thing that you believe."

"I believe in the river."

"That is not something one has to believe in. It's just there. You can see it. We can all see it."

"Who are you?" her mother called from the doorway. "Who are you?"

"It's Federica," Isabel said.

"And I am Marta, but what does that mean?"

"Federica, your daughter," Isabel said.

"I thought she fell out of a plane and died."

"She did fall out of a plane, but she did not die," Isabel said.

"That is not possible," their mother said, and she went back outside to sit in her chair.

Federica walked out of the store and was already a ways down the road when her mother called out to her, "Come back, my daughter. The rain has stopped." So Federica turned back, and her mother told her to pull up a chair. "Sit for a while," she said, and they sat without talking until her mother gave her permission to leave. "You can go now, but next time bring an umbrella," she said, and Federica got up, put the chair back against the wall where it had been, and walked out into the rain, which was coming down harder now than before.

# CHAPTER 17

WHEN FEDERICA LEFT JUIGALPA, LEFT THE WAR, SHE WALKED TO the main road that went north to Managua and south toward the river, toward home. She did not know how far south the road went, but she figured she would walk until the road ended and then she would ask how to continue, how to keep going south until she came to San Carlos, to where the river ended or began, depending on how you looked at it, depending on where you were from or where you were going. Perhaps, she thought, a car or a truck would stop along the way. She did not think about how far away she was from San Carlos, or of the war that lay behind her. It was as if she were drifting on the river, letting the current take her, and she was lying on the floor of the canoe, looking up at the stars, feeling the darkness around her.

When night fell, she slept in the bushes that lined the road. At dawn it was raining, and she was surprised that nothing had woken her up, not her hunger or mosquitoes, or the muddy ground beneath her. She could do nothing about the hunger, but she assuaged her thirst by licking water off the thick leaves on the bushes that surrounded her, and then she made her way back to the road.

On the second night she stopped in a village, where she found shelter at the house of an old couple who had just learned how to read and write. They showed her their notebooks filled with the words they practiced. There were three pages dedicated to the word *pájaro*. "Do you like birds?" Federica asked, and the couple said that of course they liked birds, except for vultures.

"How do you write *vulture*?" the man asked.

She told them, and the old woman took up her pencil and wrote it in her notebook. "Is it correct?" she asked Federica.

"Yes," Federica said.

"Write it in yours now," the woman said to her husband, and he took her notebook and copied the word carefully into his own, showing it first to his wife and then to Federica.

After dinner they took Federica to meet the young women who had come from Managua to teach them. One of the women was a foreigner from New York like William. "Have there been other foreigners?" Federica asked the young women.

"There was a Spanish priest who stayed for a while, but other than that just us. We will be moving on soon to the indigenous villages farther south."

"If you see a foreigner named William, tell him that I am alive," Federica said.

"We will," the young women said.

In the morning the old couple gave her water and a dozen tortillas to take with her for the rest of the journey. "Can we write to you?" the woman asked before she left, and they asked her to write down her address for them.

"Of course, and I will write to you," Federica said, and the woman began to cry.

"We had three children," the man explained. "They died of yellow fever, one after the other in the same order they were born. We thought the youngest was going to live. The doctors were hopeful.

The doctors were from a foreign place, a man and a woman, a couple. Imagine that, a woman doctor. 'Make her drink water,' they said, and we did. Her fever broke and she sat up in bed and drank soup, but then she asked for her brothers, and we did not answer, so she knew. In the middle of the night, we called for the doctors, and they came. They sat with her for the rest of the night. The woman sang a song in her language that we did not understand, and then our daughter died, and the doctors cried. Can you believe it? The doctors cried."

"I am so sorry," Federica said.

The old woman got up and went to the kitchen. Her husband followed. Federica could hear them whispering, and she did not know whether she should leave or wait until they returned. She waited for thirty minutes, and they were still talking, so she tore a page from the man's notebook and wrote her address on it along with a few words of thanks, and she left their house. The sun was already hot, but she had water now and the tortillas, and as she walked she imagined the couple finding her note, reading it out loud, sounding out each word, and she wanted to believe that this act of reading would comfort them. She wanted to believe that it was worth killing and dying so that this old couple could learn to read and write.

"You must not keep count of the number of men you kill. You must never think of them or try to remember their faces," El Justo told them the night before their first battle.

"Why?" she asked.

"Trust me," El Justo answered, and she obeyed. The attacks happened so quickly that it was impossible to know how badly the men were wounded, whether they would rise again or become food for the vultures.

The day grew hotter, as it always did. When she was hungry she ate a tortilla and when she was thirsty she drank water, but now that she was away from the fighting, she could not help thinking that the old woman could tell she had killed by looking at her. She started walking faster, wanting to put distance between herself and the old couple, but she felt something pulling her back to their village. "William," she said out loud, and she was sure that they were lying for him, had made a promise to keep his presence there a secret.

She turned around and began to run, stumbling over rocks in the road, slipping on mud. Her clothes became caked in mud, her hands and knees bled, but she did not stop, not to drink or eat, until she came to the village.

The old couple took her in again and washed her clothes and gave her food to eat and their bed to sleep in. She stayed with them for three weeks. Every morning she asked about William, whether they were sure he had not been there, and they always said they were sure. They never showed impatience or annoyance with her, nor did the villagers, for she questioned them all. Every night just before she fell asleep, she promised herself not to bother them about William anymore, but by morning her resolve had weakened. She was convinced that this time they would tell her something different. It was like when she used to wait in the jungle with her father for the jaguar.

When the teachers from Managua left for the jungle, they agreed to take her with them as far as San Carlos, but when they came to San Carlos and she stood at the dock where the lake meets the river, she knew that she could not go back to El Castillo to sit in the *pulpería*, to wait for William, to not think of the men she had killed, so she continued on with the teachers to where the Rama lived.

For the next few months Federica lived with the teachers from Managua in the jungle. They taught the Rama to read and built a school and a clinic. When the clinic was finished, two Canadians arrived with fifty cases of rum and a crate of yellow fever vaccines.

They gave every man a bottle for each member of his family that agreed to be vaccinated. Every morning there were more people waiting outside the clinic. At night the men drank and sang and then when the rum ran out, they smashed the bottles and went home to their women. In the morning the women cleaned up the mess.

Federica did not ask the Canadians or the Rama about William. The urgency she felt on the road was gone. She concentrated instead on teaching and tried not to hate the Canadians. She talked to them about their methods, but they called her naïve. "We tried explaining the vaccines to them the first time, and they just laughed," the Canadians said.

"What did you tell them?"

"We told them that the vaccine would protect them, that no one in their village would ever die from yellow fever again."

"And what did they say?"

"They laughed."

"So now you are killing them with rum," Federica said.

Every night the Canadians and the teachers sat on the clinic steps drinking rum, though they never smashed bottles or sang.

Federica did not join them. After she finished her duties for the day, she walked in the jungle. She did not think of the future or the past. She lived for the letters of the alphabet and for tortillas and beans and sleep. When the teachers were called back to Managua, she asked again whether she could go with them, and they agreed. They took the slow *palanga* to Greytown, where there was an airstrip. From there they took a Cessna 337 to Managua.

There were six seats on the plane and fifteen passengers on board—eleven soldiers, the three teachers, and Federica. The soldiers insisted that the women take the seats. "Can the plane take all this weight?" the teachers asked, and the pilot, a Russian with red hair, laughed. "Lenin will protect us," he said. Federica did not know who Lenin was.

The plane took off and the teachers began to cry, holding on to each other and to her, but Federica was not afraid. She could see the river below her, and she felt her stomach sink and her ears pop, and she wanted to stay in the air forever. "Isn't this wonderful?" she said, and the teachers cried harder. The plane banked and dipped and soared higher, then dropped abruptly. One of the soldiers started praying, and the other soldiers and the teachers joined him. The pilot started singing something in Russian. The plane dipped again, and she understood that he was doing it on purpose. "Again," she called to him, and down they went, then up again, higher than they had been before.

When they landed in Managua, the teachers and soldiers could not get off the plane fast enough. They ran toward the terminal as if they were being pursued by a wild animal. Federica did not run. She waited next to the plane while the pilot checked the instruments and gathered his bags.

"Isn't there anyplace in this country where it isn't hot?" he said, when he stepped off the metal stairway.

"No," Federica said.

"Of course not. Did you enjoy the ride?"

"Yes," Federica said.

"Was it your first time?"

"Yes."

"When they told me I was being sent to Cuba, I couldn't believe my luck. I had longed for the heat, for beaches and all that, but now the only way I can fall asleep is to imagine the snow."

"I would like to see the snow," Federica said, though she had never thought about snow before. She imagined the old woman writing *snow* into her notebook, holding the pencil hard, mouthing the letters.

"It's not enough to see it. You have to feel it, smell it, even though it doesn't smell at all."

"How can you smell it if it doesn't smell?"

"You smell the coldness."

"What does it smell like?"

"Like the opposite of hot," he said.

"Ah," she said, breathing in deeply.

"Are you hungry?" he asked.

"I'm starving," she said, realizing only then that she had not eaten since morning.

They took a taxi into town, and the pilot, Sergei, took her to his favorite restaurant in Managua. He ordered enough food for six people, and Federica ate more than she had ever eaten in her life.

"I want to learn how to fly," Federica said.

"To flying," Sergei said, raising his glass.

She went with him to a dirty hotel. The bed creaked, and the fan with its blades caked with dust spun like a man crying out into the night for salvation, but Sergei was gentle and talked with words that she did not understand and afterward he held her. They were dripping in sweat and he said, "Think of snow," and she did.

The next day Sergei and Federica returned to Greytown. The plane was packed with weapons and ammunition to fight against the insurgents hiding across the river in Costa Rica. "Are you sure you want to come?" he asked.

"Yes," Federica said, and Sergei kissed her.

"Watch, but don't ask any questions," he said, when they were settled into the cockpit. She reached out to touch the control yoke in front of her. "Don't touch anything," he said. She pulled her hands away.

"Do you have a pen and paper so that I can take notes?" she asked.

"Just watch. Never take your eyes off the instruments. Never."

She watched in the same way her father taught her to watch the river, noting every rock in the falls, every rock along the shore where the caimans slept. She could feel the plane struggling to lift itself, feel Sergei's muscles relax as the boats on the lake grew smaller and smaller. She looked where Sergei looked, followed his eyes. He did not speak to her until they were on the ground again, the plane shaking still from the effort. "Show me what you saw," he said, and she put her hand on the yoke and repeated every one of his movements.

After that she always flew with Sergei on his runs from Managua to the border. Sometimes on the way back to Managua they flew over El Castillo. From the crumbling ramparts of the fortress flew the red and black Sandinista flag. When she sat at the controls with Sergei at her side and looked down on the river she did not think of William. She did not wonder whether he might hear her plane flying overhead.

# CHAPTER 18

SANTIAGO WAS NOT HOME WHEN LILIANA GOT BACK TO HIS house, so she took a shower and, because she began to sweat again as soon as she started to get dressed, she lay down on the bed under the fan naked. No matter how hot it was, how still and thick the air, Irene could never fall asleep without something covering her. As if a sheet could ever protect anyone from anything. Even mosquitoes could bite through a sheet. But she did not want to lie on a bed naked thinking about Irene, not after making it all the way through her shower without thinking about her, without thinking about any-thing, so she concentrated on the rhythm of the fan and the breeze on her body. It was as if she were swimming, letting the waves lead her, letting the water wash over her, and she fell asleep, and dreamt not of Irene or William or jaguars or dogs, but of water.

In the morning Liliana went with Santiago to check on the twin calves. El Justo was standing at the gate when they arrived as if he had been expecting them, though Santiago had not called ahead to let him know they were coming. "Welcome, my friends," he said.

It was cooler at El Justo's ranch than in Juigalpa, and the air smelled of lumber.

"How are the calves?" Santiago asked as soon as they were inside the gate.

"They had to separate them yesterday. The female would have killed her brother had they been kept together. My men wanted to finish her off, make a feast out of her while she is still tender, but that would not have been fair."

"Can I see her?" Liliana asked.

The calf was pawing the dirt, flicking her tail against the barbed wire fence. Drops of blood fell from her tail onto the dirt.

"You should put her out of her misery," Santiago said.

"How do you know she's miserable?" El Justo asked. "Maybe she feels strong and hopeful that one day she will find a way out of her captivity. What do you think?" he asked, turning to Liliana.

"I think she's frightened and angry and doesn't know what she wants."

"Perhaps she is happy. Perhaps she likes digging up the dirt. Maybe it gives her a sense of accomplishment."

"Has she eaten since you separated them?" Santiago asked.

"Yes," El Justo said. "She eats enough for two."

"That is a good sign," Santiago said.

"A good sign of what?" El Justo asked.

"A sign that she is not miserable, that she wants to live."

"You see," El Justo said, putting his hand on Liliana's shoulder. "We must trust the doctor, don't you think?"

Liliana went to the fence and put her hand through the wire, holding it out for the calf to sniff the way she used to do with Guadalajara. "*Ven, vaquita*," she whispered, but the calf just kept pawing the earth. Liliana called again, "*Ven, vaquita*." Still no response. She walked over to the gate, opened it. No one stopped her. She felt El Justo's eyes on her, watching. "Come," she said in English, forcefully, like a mother talking to a recalcitrant child. The calf looked up, saw the open gate, and ran, head down like a bull. Once outside, she did not know what to do. She ran around in circles and then stopped, falling to the ground. El Justo raised his pistol.

"No!" Liliana called, and he lowered it.

Santiago ran to the calf, crouched down to her level, held her head in his arms. She was shaking. He spoke to her softly so that they could not hear what he was saying, but after a while the calf stood up, and Santiago led her back to the pen. She went willingly, and after he had closed the gate, leaving her alone, she began to paw the dirt again.

"Well, that's that," El Justo said. He began walking back toward the house. Liliana lingered, watching the calf. She gripped the fence hard, as if she were the one inside.

After a few moments, Santiago pulled gently on her arm, and she followed him back to the house where El Justo was waiting for them on the veranda.

"Rum?" El Justo asked when they were settled.

"I am disappointed too," El Justo said, after they had emptied their glasses.

"Disappointed?" Liliana said, though she knew exactly what he meant.

"You expected her to charge."

"Perhaps," Liliana said.

"If you are going to keep her, I should bind her tail so that it doesn't get infected," Santiago said.

"I will send some men to help you hold her down," El Justo said, taking out his phone. Within seconds, five men appeared, and Santiago went with them to bind the calf's tail.

"So," he said, turning to Liliana and pouring more rum.

"I want to know about my brother."

"William," El Justo said. He leaned forward. "I knew the moment I saw you, even though you don't look at all like him. There's something I cannot put my finger on."

"I want to know how he died."

"That is something we will never know," El Justo said. "Sometimes, when I can't sleep, when I can hear the animals groaning and pacing in their pens, when my back hurts more than usual, I feel that he is still alive. It is as if he were in the room with me, sitting on the bed, telling me everything that has passed since we saw each other."

"So you believe he is still alive?"

"No, I am not saying that at all. I am saying that memories are like a wound gushing blood. Sometimes you cannot stop the flow. But, tell me, why have you come now after all these years? If you are looking for answers, you certainly won't find them here. We don't even ask questions anymore."

"Is that why you are so rich, because there are no more questions?"

"Ha," El Justo said. "A question for which there is no answer."

"So there are still questions," Liliana said, emptying her glass.

"They are not real questions," El Justo said.

"Will you kill the calf?" Liliana asked. "Is that a real question?"

"It is a question but not an important one."

"It's important to the calf."

"The calf will kill herself," he said. "There will come a time when she will get tired of struggling."

"And if she doesn't?"

"Then maybe I will get tired of watching her struggle."

"And then you will kill her?"

"No, then I will not look at her anymore."

"What happened to William? Is that a real question?"

"It is and it isn't, but, in either case, I do not know the answer."

"Carolina said you know."

"Carolina says lots of things, most of which make no sense at all."

Liliana reached for the bottle to pour herself more rum.

"Please, let me," El Justo said, taking the bottle from her.

She let him fill her glass to the top. "Did you like William?" she asked after he had set the bottle down.

"A strange question," El Justo said.

"A simple question," Liliana said.

"There is no such thing as a simple question, but if you are such a fan of questions, tell me, why have you waited all these years to find out what happened to your brother?"

"I wanted to come when we first got the news, but my parents," she paused, "they couldn't face knowing how he died. They were afraid they would find out that he had killed."

"And you? Were you afraid?"

"I don't know what I felt. My father lost two children in the Holocaust, so I always felt that my sadness wasn't real, that his was the only real sadness."

"But you're here now."

"Yes," Liliana said, taking a drink, thinking not of William but of her father on his last birthday, using all his strength, all his concentration to hold his glass up high. "*L'chaim*," he said, and the glass slipped from his grip, but she caught it just before it hit the table.

"What did Carolina tell you happened to William?"

"She told me that William ran off into the woods after an ambush. She said your unit killed them all before they even knew what hit them."

"Did she tell you that about a week after he disappeared, we were attacked in just the same way? Only five of us survived. Afterward, when Carolina and I were lifting up one of our dead comrades, carrying him to the hole we had dug to bury him, we saw William. He was watching us from behind the trees, watching us throw the body into the grave, and then he was gone."

"Are you saying that he betrayed you to the Contras?"

"I am saying that it is possible."

"If he had, he wouldn't have let you see him."

"Perhaps, but it is something we will never know. Carolina couldn't stand the doubt. That's what destroyed her. First, she started tearing out her hair, but she said that birds came at night and plucked it out. Birds sleep at night, we told her. Not all birds, she said, not all birds. Then one night she tried to kill me. I woke up and she was kneeling next to me, pointing a gun at my head. I could feel the heat coming from her body, the anger. She pushed the gun hard into my temple. Her hand was steady, her breathing even. I was sure she was going to pull the trigger, but she just collapsed and lay curled up on the ground shaking. That is when she left us to look for William, and when she didn't find him, she went back to Juigalpa to her parents' house, which is where she still lives, though her parents died long ago."

"She told me she has children," Liliana said.

"Lies," El Justo said.

"Why should I believe you?"

"You can believe me or you can believe her. It is your choice," El Justo said, raising his glass. "*Salud.*"

"And if you are both lying?"

"That is another possibility." El Justo leaned back in his chair.

"Why is there a mausoleum in his honor if he was a traitor?"

"Carolina's idea. They were always looking for an opportunity to stir up revolutionary fervor. Even now they bring out the old men to quote Rubén Darío and Carlos Fonseca. They bring out the *bandas* and the children dressed in their school uniforms as if there were still soldiers fighting in the mountains, as if the goddamn president of America was still staying up late into the night consulting with his generals about what to do about little Nicaragua. And while all of us sing revolutionary songs, Daniel and his capitalist buddies will get rich. So what does it matter, in the end, whether William was fighting for them or for us?"

El Justo stood up, put his fist in the air. "*Solamente con el fuego guer-rillero podremos romper las cadenas de esclavos*," he proclaimed.

"But you are rich," Liliana said.

"And so we have come back to where we started, with neither a question nor an answer," he said.

"But what do you think, deep down, about William?" Liliana asked.

"We are all traitors in one way or another," El Justo said.

"If we are all traitors, then the word has no meaning," Liliana said.

"Exactly," El Justo said.

Liliana clutched her empty glass. She could feel her pulse bashing up against the hard glass. She squeezed even harder, willing the glass to shatter. She wanted it so badly that she could feel the shards cutting into her palm. She stood up, tipping to one side, then righting herself. She set the glass back down on the table. El Justo shifted in his chair, crossed his legs, made himself comfortable. She turned and walked toward the pens.


El Justo watched Liliana from his chair. It was obvious she was focusing all her effort on walking straight, on not stumbling. "Be careful," he said, but she was too far away to hear. He leaned back and closed his eyes. Perhaps, El Justo thought, it was time to move to Miami, leave everything behind, the cars, the house, the animals. If he moved to Miami, he could work as a taxi driver or a gardener or sell ice cream on the beach, push one of those little carts around, ringing a bell. Then he wouldn't have to think about justice ever again.

When he was young he believed in justice so much that he arrested his own father, tied his hands, shoved him into the back of a truck, drove him to the prison, turned him over. He believed in justice so much that he did not cry when his father was executed, lined up against a wall with the other members of the *guardia* that did Somoza's dirty work. Once he believed that it was possible to bring his father and all the other men who were like his father to their knees, but he understood now that there was no army big enough, no revolution passionate enough to do away with men like his father or the men who created the men like his father, the men who sat on their verandas laughing at it all. And what, William would have asked, is the difference between you and the men who are laughing?

"The difference is that I am not laughing," El Justo said.

"But look at your fleet of SUVs, your cows, your bulls, this house, the pool, the gate, the men protecting your gate. What is the difference?"

"The difference is that I don't want all these things."

"But how are we to know that?"

And that was the question. How was anyone to know that? How was he to know it? It was at times like these, when he had drunk too much rum, that he missed William the most.

The night he met William, El Justo and his unit were drinking in a bar in Juigalpa where they had been drinking every night for a week, making plans, cursing the Americans, listening to a man play the guitar and sing. On that night, their last night, they tried to convince the musician to come with them to the mountains to fight. "I do not like silence," he said. He wished them luck and got up to leave, but El Justo put his gun to the man's head.

"Sing," he said. So the man sang, and he did not tremble at all even though El Justo did not lower the gun. When the song was finished, El Justo let him leave. "We are fighting for you," he said.

"If that is what you believe, I cannot convince you otherwise," the man said, and he walked out of the bar.

The men ordered more beer, and they were silent, each thinking about what lay ahead of them in the mountains where they were heading the following day. A young man, a foreigner, entered the bar and sat down at a table in the corner toward the back. He did not look like the idealistic foreigners who came to Nicaragua armed with vaccines and literacy primers. He looked more like a boxer, alert, muscular, beardless. The waiter went to the foreigner's table. The foreigner ordered, and shortly after that the waiter returned with a beer, and the foreigner took a book out of his back pocket and began reading, mouthing the words.

When the young man finished his beer, he put the book back into his backpack and got up, leaving money for his drink on the table, but when he was almost at the door, he stopped, turned around, and approached their table. "I want to fight," he said. "My name is William."

Once they were in the mountains, El Justo asked William what made him pause on his way out of the bar.

"Because you called to me."

"But I didn't say anything," El Justo said.

William smiled and breathed in deeply. "It smells like rain."

"Yes," El Justo said.

"Why do they call you El Justo?"

"I wish they didn't," El Justo said.

"That was not my question."

"I just felt a drop. Should we go inside the tent?"

"I like it," William said, leaning back, letting the rain fall on his face. "And you haven't answered my question."

"I brought my own father to justice."

"You are a lawyer?"

"I was, and for a short time, before we had to fight, I was a judge. Now I am a soldier."

"What was his crime?"

"Torture."

"Did you love him?" William asked.

"Don't you love me even a little bit?" his father had once asked, when he was given the chance to speak at his trial, just before El Justo pronounced the verdict.

"No," El Justo had said.

"Yes," El Justo told William. "If I had not loved him, I would not have been able to pronounce the death sentence. I wouldn't have been angry enough. My father was one of Somoza's guards, high up. He had a uniform with medals. I went to a high school especially for sons of the military elite, and it was only there that I learned about what he did, what they all did. One of the boys brought in a photograph, a Polaroid his father had given him of a man with a sack over his head, his feet and hands bleeding. He passed it around at lunch and all the boys laughed. I laughed, too, but in the next class I couldn't get the image out of my head. I ran out into the hall and vomited. No one suspected that it had anything to do with the photograph. They called home and my mother sent a car to get me. I stayed home for three days until I no longer saw the photograph every time I closed my eyes. My parents thought it was the stomach flu. The first evening I was sick, my father came into my room still in his uniform to check on me. That was the first time I noticed that his fingernails were chewed down to the cuticles.

"'What's wrong with your nails?' I asked him.

"'Nothing,' he said, putting his hands under his thighs. 'A silly habit I've had since childhood.'

"Before I went back to school, I told my mother about the

photograph. 'Is that what he does?' I asked, but she did not answer. She just started crying. That night I allowed myself to think of my mother underneath my father, begging him to push harder, to hurt her like he hurt his victims, and I hated her for loving him, hated her more than I ever could hate him."

"But you can't forgive him, either, right?"

"No."

"That is the hardest part, not the love or the hate, but not being able to forgive. My father had another family before us. They all died in Birkenau. You know about Birkenau."

El Justo nodded.

"His wife, his son, his daughter. He didn't even try to escape. He registered them all, packed their suitcases, arrived early at the train station in order to get a good seat. He lifted his children onto the train. He never could forgive himself for that."

"He told you that?"

"When my sister or I did something naughty, he would punish us by forcing us to look at his weakness. He made us listen to the story of how he lifted his children onto the train. When he finished, he would tell us that we had to be good for them, for their memory, but what he was really telling us was that if we allowed ourselves to be weak, to do something without thinking about the conse-quences, we would end up like him. I tried to block it out, the same slow telling of the story, the somberness of it, but each time he told us, I saw everything, his tweed suit, the hat, heard him say, '*Opla*, there you go,' like he said when he lifted me up onto his shoulders in the park."

"After I saw those photos," El Justo said, "I used to stand in the doorway to my parents' bedroom and watch them sleep. One night I took a pin with me. I wanted to plunge it into the raw flesh where his fingernails had been. I wanted to feel the pin go in deep, hear my father's pain fill the night, but, of course, I couldn't do it."

"But you brought him in, killed him in the end."

"Yes."

"Do you regret it?"

"No. Do you know what my father said after I pronounced the sentence?"

"Yes," William said.

"Tell me, then," El Justo said, not knowing whether he wanted William to be right or wrong, so he answered himself before William had the chance. "'I will always love you.' That's what he said."

"I know," William said, but El Justo would never know whether he had known or not, just like he would never know what would have happened if he had reached out right then and touched William.

"When I was ten years old," William began, "my father came into my room in the middle of the night. He sat on my bed and put his hand on my forehead as if he were checking for a fever. I pretended that I was sleeping. I kept my eyes closed and counted. When I got to 637, my father started crying. I should have opened my eyes then, wrapped my arms around him, but I didn't. I just kept counting, and after a while he removed his hand from my forehead and said, 'I'm sorry.'

"The next morning my father woke me up as he always did, saying, 'Wake up, my son. You have great things to accomplish today,' and I got up as I always did, and we all ate breakfast together as we always did, but when it was time to clear off the table, which was my job, I felt a terrible anger welling up inside me. I picked up my plate and I was about to throw it at the dining room wall, but my mother looked at me as if she knew what I was thinking, so I brought the plate to the kitchen. That day in school I got into my first fight. There was a girl the other girls made fun of. She was fat, and during recess two pretty girls smeared peanut butter all over her desk and wrote *FATTY* in it with their fingers. I came inside to get my baseball mitt, and they called me over, laughing, to show me what they had done, and something came over me like with the plate, but this time I did not try to control myself. I pushed one of the girls to the floor, the leader, the prettier one, and kicked her. She screamed and I kicked her again. She begged me to stop, so I kicked her again. I kicked her three times before the teacher came and pulled me away."

William took out a cigarette, lit a match, let it burn until the flame was almost touching his finger before he leaned in.

"I tried to explain to the principal why I had done it, that I was trying to protect that girl, the fat one, but all he kept saying was that a man should never ever hit a woman. 'What if a woman is leading your children to the gas chamber?' I asked, and he didn't have an answer.

"That night when I said the same thing to my father, he said that the circumstances were different, that the fat girl was not being led to the gas chamber, that she wouldn't have died if she had seen the peanut butter smeared on her desk. 'I am so disappointed in you,' my father said. Then he got up and went into the living room and put on Mahler's Fifth Symphony. While he sat there in the dark listening to it, I felt the anger rising in me again, and I knew that what I was feeling was the anger that my father could not allow himself to feel, and I felt strong."

"I wish I could feel that anger," El Justo said.

"You don't feel it when you are fighting?"

"No," El Justo said.

"Then how do you do it?"

"Do what?" El Justo asked.

"Kill?"

"I do it for the revolution, for justice," El Justo said.

"And how many have you killed?"

"I don't know. I don't count."

"But you must count."

"Why?"

"Because otherwise you will forget the gravity of it, of your revolution, of death. Promise me you will count them from now on."

"I promise," El Justo said, and he almost did it then, almost put his hand on William's thigh, but Carolina appeared and ruined everything. "There you are. What are you two doing out here in the dark? The mosquitoes must be eating you alive," she said, putting her arms around William from behind.

"Just talking," William said.

"Come," Carolina said, pulling him up from the rock upon which he had been sitting.

"Good night," William called over his shoulder.

He felt it then, the anger that William had talked about, but what could he do, run after William, push him to the ground, kick him until he cried for help?

The day after, El Justo was counting the ammunition, and Carolina and William emerged from William's tent together. They stood for a moment, breathing in the air. William said something that El Justo could not make out, and Carolina laughed, and William pulled her close. El Justo lifted his pistol, aimed it at Carolina first, then William. They were kissing, oblivious to his presence, to the danger they were in, but then Carolina must have sensed something, for she pulled away from William and turned abruptly toward El Justo. He lowered his gun. "Are you crazy?" she yelled, but she did not run away. El Justo laughed, but he was trembling.


When Liliana reached the pen, Santiago was lying inside holding the calf in his arms, rocking it, his head tucked into the calf's belly. She stood on the other side of the fence, waiting for him to see her, but he did not sense her presence, and she began to feel that it was wrong to watch him. It was like watching someone sleep. It gave her a power that she did not want to have, so she stepped inside the pen.

Santiago opened his eyes, but he kept a firm grip on the calf, who was trying now to break free. "Liliana, it's not safe," he said, using all his force to keep the calf down, but she kept walking toward him. The calf strained, and lurched forward, but Santiago still held on. "Run!" he said, and she ran toward the gate, but she tripped and fell. She smelled the cow, smelled her strength. She could feel the earth beneath her, trembling. It was as if a herd of horses were approaching, but there were no horses, just the calf kicking and flailing and Santiago holding on to it.

"Get up," he said, but she couldn't get up. The sky was spinning and the sun was hot, and her mouth was dry and sour. She turned to the ground and vomited.

"Get up," Santiago yelled again. "I can't hold her anymore."

Liliana covered her head with her arms the way she had learned to do for earthquake drills in San Francisco, and the sound of hoofs grew louder. She closed her eyes hard. There was a shot, and she felt a heavy weight upon her, and then all she heard was her own breathing.

Santiago and El Justo pulled the calf off Liliana. She could smell the rum on El Justo's breath, and she was afraid to open her eyes, to see the calf dead in the dirt. They brought her water, and she drank, and Santiago and El Justo slid a board under her, and two of El Justo's men carried her back to the house.

The injuries were minor, bruises mainly and some scratches that Santiago cleaned and bandaged. He was sure there were no broken ribs. "Does this hurt?" he asked, pressing lightly first on her left then her right side.

"Just a little bit," Liliana said.

"If they were fractures you would be squealing with pain," he said. "You were lucky."

"And the calf?"

"El Justo is a good marksman," Santiago said.

She punched her ribs on both sides as hard as she could, but all she felt was a dull ache. She lifted her arms to punch them again, but Santiago grabbed her, and she did not struggle. "We would have had to put her down eventually," Santiago said, letting her arms fall.

El Justo came to the doorway, but he did not come into the room. "Is she okay?" he asked.

"She'll be fine in the morning," Santiago said.

Two women came with a basin of hot water. They washed her, one taking the left side, the other the right. When they finished washing the front of her body, they turned her on her side and washed her back, her buttocks. They lifted her from the bed, wrapped her in a sheet, and led her out of the room, down the hall to another room where there was a clean bed waiting.

She woke once in the night, thirsty and cold. She drank the glass of water that Santiago had left by her bedside. She got up to turn off the fan. The floor was cold like a floor in a country where there was winter. She found the light, looked up, and there was no fan, just coldness that flowed from a vent in the ceiling. She tried to open the window, but there was no latch. Only then did she realize that she was naked. She raised her fist and struck the window with all her strength, struck it again and again until there was a gaping hole and the hot air came into the room, bringing the sound of rain, and she reached out as far as she could into the night, letting the rain wash away the blood.

There was a knock on the door, and when she did not answer, El Justo came in, took the sheet from the bed, covered her, and they stood at the window looking out. "I'm sorry," Liliana said. "I don't know what I was thinking, going into the pen like that."

"She wasn't meant for this world," El Justo said.

He picked the glass out of her new wounds with tweezers, washed and bandaged them, and put her back to bed. "Sleep now," he said. She closed her eyes, and he leaned over to push her hair from her face. "There," he said.

# CHAPTER 19

WHEN, AFTER SIX MONTHS, SERGEI WAS CALLED BACK TO THE Soviet Union, he arranged for Federica to join a group of Nicaraguan engineering students who were going to the Soviet Union for training in high-level industrial equipment mechanics in preparation for the industrialization of their country. He promised that he would visit her. He showed her on the map where he lived in Kharkov and where she would be, in L'viv. "It is only one thousand kilometers away," he assured her. "By plane it is nothing," he said, but she understood that it was a great distance.

Once she was living with Sergei in Managua, she had sent word to her parents that she was well, apologizing for running off, for worrying them. She did not tell them about her time in the mountains, about the killing. She received a reply from her father. "We are just relieved to know that you are alive," he wrote. "Will you be coming home soon?" he asked. She replied that she would come when she had a chance. She was learning to fly, she explained. "That must take a long time," her father wrote. He always ended his letters with the same line, "Your mother sends her love."

Before leaving for the Soviet Union, she finally went to visit them, but she did not write to let them know she was coming. On the way there she imagined her mother jumping up from her stool behind the counter, running to the door to embrace her. She imagined her father dropping the box he was carrying, but when she arrived, he was out on a delivery and her mother did not rush to embrace her.

"Do you know what it is like to wake up every morning for 273 days not knowing whether your daughter is alive or dead?" she said.

"I'm sorry," Federica said.

"I counted them, the days," her mother said.

"I didn't plan to stay away so long, but one thing led to another. I was fighting. It was impossible to send word."

"You could have found a way," her mother said.

"I'm here now," Federica said.

"But you will leave again," her mother said, going back to her bookkeeping.

That night she sat on the veranda with her father, listening to the sound of the falls and the insects. "I am going far away," she told him.

He waited for her to continue, looking toward the jungle as if he were waiting for someone to appear.

"They are sending people to the Soviet Union," she said. "We will have factories here soon, and I will learn how to run them."

"What will the factories produce?"

"All the things we need, like cars and planes and ships and refrigerators."

"You will see snow," he said.

"Yes," Federica said.

"I think it will be beautiful," he said. "What if you never return?"

"I will return," she said. "They will need me here, for the factories," she said.

"Will they build them here, on the river?"

"They will be everywhere," she said.

"Will that be a good thing?"

"Yes," Federica said, but she was not sure at all.

The snow was, indeed, beautiful. She had not imagined the silence, but that was the most beautiful part, especially since her life was filled with the churning of machinery, the constant clacking and clanking and clanging that stayed with her even when she was no longer in the factory. She hated the machines, the noise, the grease, the largeness of them, but she understood them better than the others did. She could lay her hand on a machine and know that it was too hot or put her ear to its belly and feel that there was something wrong. They called her Dr. Federica.

She lived with the other Nicaraguans in an apartment near the factory. They were always cold. At night they huddled together, all six of them on the floor in front of the coal stove, covered with the six blankets they had been allotted, drinking vodka until they were able to sleep. In the mornings when the coal had turned to ash, they could see their breaths. Sergei did not visit. When it snowed they went out into the night, and they ran through the snow. Those were the best times.

In addition to technical training they attended Russian and Marxism-Leninism classes. The classes were held right after they finished their work at the factory, when they were tired and hungry and cold because they were always cold. The Marxism-Leninism teacher was a woman who had learned Spanish in Cuba, where she had been sent as a young woman to fight in the Cuban Revolution. She had, she told them on the first day of class, killed thirty-one capitalists. She asked them how many people they had killed, and the engineering students bowed their heads, for they had not killed anyone. "Seventeen," Federica said.

"A true hero of the revolution," the Marxism-Leninism teacher said, and Federica hated her after that, but the woman was always smiling at her, standing as close as she possibly could without touching her. She started inviting Federica to her apartment. "I have Cuban records," she whispered.

Federica declined many times, but in the end she ran out of excuses, so she went to the Marxism-Leninism teacher's apartment. The apartment was thick with furniture. There were three sofas and eight armchairs and side tables upon which sat heavy lamps. The walls were covered with paintings. Despite the abundance of lamps, when Federica arrived on a Sunday afternoon, the apartment was gloomy, as if it were already dusk. In the dim light all Federica could discern about the paintings was that they were mostly portraits. And the apartment was warm, the warmest place she had been since she arrived.

The Marxism-Leninism teacher was wearing a cream-colored sleeveless evening dress and white ankle boots. She served Federica tea and showed her how to hold the sugar cube between her teeth and let the tea pass through it. The teacher had three gold teeth. Federica sat on the sofa, her legs crossed, holding the sugar between her teeth. Because she was wearing her usual armor against the cold—two shirts and two wool sweaters—which she never took off, except to bathe once a week, she began to sweat, and the sweat dripped down her face and through the gulley between her breasts. Still, she sat there politely, sipping tea, and when the teacher came out with a plate piled high with pastries, she ate three.

The teacher put on a Cuban record and began swaying, then dancing. "Do you like mambo?" she asked.

Before she could answer, the teacher pulled her up from the couch, leading her through the maze of armchairs and sofas and tables. When the song was over, the teacher swung Federica around and they fell together onto the sofa. "Marvelous," the teacher said, laughing, and Federica thanked her for the dance, which made the teacher laugh even more. When she finally stopped laughing, she sprang up from the couch and mamboed out of the living room. Federica was in the middle of pulling off the first layer of sweaters when the teacher returned with a bottle of vodka and two shot glasses. "Let me help you," she said, setting the bottle and glasses down, then pulling the sweater over Federica's head and flinging it onto the couch. "How many layers do you have? Lift your arms," she said.

"I can manage, thank you," Federica said, stepping away from her, but as soon as she began to lift the sweater, the teacher grabbed it and jerked it up over her head.

"There," the teacher said. "Shall we have some vodka?"

She filled the two shot glasses and handed one to Federica. "Cheers," she said, and she drank hers all at once, so Federica drank hers in one gulp, hoping that the alcohol would soothe her stomach, which was in revolt from the sugar and the heat. The record came to an end, and the teacher ran to the record player, plucking the needle up and setting it back down at the beginning.

Federica was still sweating. "Here," the teacher said, taking a handkerchief from inside her bra and handing it to Federica.

"Thank you," Federica said. "I'll be fine."

"It's clean," the teacher said, so Federica could not refuse. The handkerchief smelled of perfume, of roses. She dabbed her face and handed it back to the teacher. The smell made her stomach, which was just starting to calm down, begin churning again. They drank another shot of vodka and immediately after that another. The teacher leaned back and closed her eyes. Federica could feel the weight of the teacher pushing down on the cushion so that she had to hold on in order not to let herself slip down the incline into her fleshy body. She tried to imagine her when she was young, in uniform, fighting in Cuba. She tried to imagine her running, the muscles on her calves taught and strong.

"I thought you would like it warm, like in your country," the teacher said.

"I do like it. Thank you," Federica said, but she felt as if she were locked in a box. She wondered if this was what it felt like to be in a coffin underground, to be dead, but she knew that being dead meant one didn't feel anything at all. She laughed though it wasn't funny. Perhaps, she thought, the vodka was going to her head.

The teacher laughed too. Then she stopped abruptly, realizing, perhaps, that she did not know what she was laughing about, and Federica suddenly felt sorry for the teacher, for her dance dress and the folds of flesh. They sat there, the teacher with her eyes closed, tapping the rhythm of the music on her thigh, Federica with her eyes open, looking straight ahead at the portraits whose faces she could not see. The teacher's breath smelled like vomit, and she wondered why she had not noticed this before even though she had been sitting next to her all this time. She turned away toward the window. It was snowing. She wondered what her own breath smelled like.

When the record came to an end, the teacher got up and lifted the needle onto its cradle. She returned to where Federica was sitting. "Thank you for coming," she said without sitting down again, so Federica got up from the couch.

"Thank you for having me," she said.

The teacher brought Federica her sweaters and coat and when she was bundled up, she said, "You won't tell anyone that you have been here. Not even the Nicaraguans."

"Of course not," Federica said.

"I know that I can trust you. You have a great future ahead of you," she said, shaking her hand as if they had just made a deal.

*

Two days after this strange evening, Federica sat in her usual seat in the second row of the Marxism-Leninism class with her homework out and ready to be collected. When the teacher came into the room, she stood up with everyone else and greeted her as usual. The teacher showed her neither more nor less attention than before her visit, and Federica showed neither more nor less eagerness to learn than usual, and this was how things continued for many weeks. Still, Federica knew that the teacher was watching her, testing her somehow, but she did not know what she was being tested about. All she knew was that the Marxism-Leninism teacher was watching her in a different way than she was watching the other students.

The next week, Federica was awakened in the middle of the night by the sound of one of her roommates crying. When she went to the girl to offer her comfort, the girl turned away and whispered, "Please don't tell anyone."

"I won't," Federica said, sitting down beside her on the bed.

"Go away," the girl said, turning toward the wall.

For three days the girl would not talk to Federica. Federica wanted to reassure her again, but she knew that would only make her roommate more nervous. On the fourth day, the girl was called into the Marxism-Leninism teacher's office, and that evening the Marxism-Leninism teacher asked the girl to come to the front of the room. She walked slowly down the aisle to the front. When she reached the front of the classroom, she took a piece of paper from her pocket, unfolded it, and began to read. "I have been weak and selfish and stupid. Without the Soviet Union I am nothing, my people are nothing," she said. She thanked Marx and Lenin and the Marxism-Leninism teacher for showing her the truth.

After that, even on the coldest nights, they slept in their own beds wondering, no doubt, who was the traitor among them, though all of them had, in fact, betrayed the crying girl by participating in her shame. After that they did not go out and dance in the snow. They prepared meals in silence and ate alone, sitting on their beds.

As a child, Federica preferred the company of the river to that of other children. In school she kept to herself, and because she caused no trouble and was polite to everyone and good at her lessons, neither her teachers nor the other children paid her much attention. Only her mother seemed to worry about her lack of companionship. "It is not natural," she would say.

"What is natural?" her father would ask, and her mother would get annoyed and throw up her hands.

"You and your ideas," she would say.

This was not natural, Federica thought as she lay in bed listening to the other girls breathing, and though she had always been comfortable being alone, she now felt loneliness for the first time, and she understood that loneliness was more powerful than fear. The warmer it got, the more blossoms appeared on the trees, the sweeter the breeze, the stronger the sun, the more she longed for snow so that it could cover her loneliness, cover the eyes of the young men lying on the jungle floor, their bodies limp like dolls that seemed to be watching her now, too, like everyone else.

In the spring the Marxism-Leninism teacher asked her to tea again. "It is important," she said, and Federica knew that in the end she would run out of excuses, so she accepted.

This time the apartment was filled with flowers. There were vases on all the tables filled with daffodils and tulips, but there was no mambo, no music at all, no vodka. This time they sat at a table, the teacher across from her, her hands on her thighs. Federica sat in the same way, as straight as possible, her back up against the chair the way they had been taught to sit in school.

"You have proven to be trustworthy," the teacher said.

Federica waited for her to continue.

"You like airplanes," the teacher continued.

"Yes."

"Why?"

"I just do," Federica answered.

"That is not an explanation. There is a reason for everything."

"There are many reasons, but I cannot put them into words," Federica said, knowing that if she put her feelings into words, she would lose the little piece of herself she still had left, and she realized that her loneliness was part of this, part of what was left of herself, so she clung to it. The teacher waited, staring at the center of her neck, and Federica could feel a coldness where the teacher's eyes were fixed.

After about five minutes during which neither of them moved, the teacher said, "You have been chosen for a very important mission. When you return, you will be rewarded. Pack your things and be ready in an hour. A car will come for you. It will be waiting outside your building. Do not tell anyone." She stood up and led Federica to the door.

"I have no choice?"

"No."

Federica did as she was told, packed a bag, and went down to meet the waiting car, not because she was afraid to resist but because it did not matter to her whether she stayed or went somewhere else.

The trip took ten hours, during which the driver said nothing and smoked one cigarette after another. They stopped only once so that she could go to the bathroom behind some trees. "Is it much farther?" she asked when she was back in the car, but the driver did not answer. By the time they arrived at their destination, it was nighttime. The driver pulled up to a dark house, and they waited in the car for almost an hour before two men came out of the house. "Welcome to the ancient city of Kamianets-Podilskyi," one of the men said. The driver got out and he and the men moved far enough away from the car so that she could not even hear their voices, though she would not have understood what they were saying anyway. She rarely could catch more than a few words when people spoke in Ukrainian, despite the fact that she was the best student in the Russian class and was often given praise for her pronunciation and for the compositions they were assigned to write about the glory of the revolution and the struggles of the proletariat.

The driver returned and she was told to get out of the car. The two men with whom the driver had consulted led her—each grasping her upper arm—into the house, where she was given soup and bread, which she ate while they watched. Every once in a while one of them said something, and the other one laughed. When she finished eating, they brought her to a room with a bed made up with fresh sheets smelling of the outdoors, a sink, and a pitcher of water. She did not want to ask them about a bathroom, so when she was alone in the room, she urinated into the sink.

She lay in bed for a while, feeling the presence of the men outside her door, wondering whether she should be afraid, but fatigue overcame her, so she slept, and when she awoke it was morning, and there were birds chirping outside her window. She could smell bread baking. She got up and went to the window, from which she could see a gorge and a river directly below and beyond that a fortress, not the ruins of a fortress like the one that watched over El Castillo, but a commanding edifice with walls and towers and ramparts. Beyond that was the endless green of the steppe. She tried the latch and it was not locked, so she leaned out the window as far as she could, letting the sun warm her face. I could jump into the river, she thought, when someone knocked on the door.


There was an airfield on the steppe beyond the fortress where she learned to do tricks in the air. Aerobatics they called it. They were

training for an international competition that was to be held in
Czechoslovakia in July. They practiced every day, even Sundays,
and the later it stayed light the later they practiced. When they
were finished for the day, a car came and drove them all back to
the military base on the outskirts of town where they lived together
in special barracks.

Her favorite maneuver was called the Cuban 8. She was fond
of it not out of loyalty to her continent but because the eight, if she
stretched it out enough, looked like the symbol of infinity. Once she
had mastered the maneuvers on her own she became the sixth and
final member of a team. She found that the hardest part was trust-
ing the other pilots. They flew so close that if any one of them mis-
calculated, there would not be enough time to avoid a crash. From
high up, the fortress, which had protected the town of Kamianets-
Podilskyi (and, according to her flying instructor, Europe itself)
since the fourteenth century, seemed almost as insignificant as the
ruins of El Castillo.

The five other pilots were in the Soviet air force. They had medals from the war in Afghanistan. Federica did not know where Afghanistan was, so they showed her on a map. Although she was
constantly reminding them that she was from Nicaragua, they insisted on calling her La Cubana. At first it annoyed her, but then
she understood that it was not because they were belittling her
country but because she loved the Cuban 8.

Before they moved into the barracks, they each had to sign a
paper saying they would not drink until the night of the banquet
that was to be held in their honor before they took off for the competition. They also understood that if anything happened between
Federica and any of them, they would all be considered enemies of
the revolution. In the evenings after dinner, they sat outside and
listened to the leader of the pilots, the one who flew at the head of
the V, play the violin. When he got tired of performing, they played

cards and the other pilots taught her songs from their childhoods. They didn't talk much, and she wondered whether they talked more when she was not there, or whether they were too exhausted from concentrating all day on staying aloft for conversation.

Five days before the competition, the Marxism-Leninism teacher came to visit. She spent the day with them at the airfield, watching them go through their routines, taking photos. At the end of the day the workers at the airfield presented her with a huge bouquet of roses, and more photographs were taken of her with the roses and of the team with her and with the roses. "Are they treating you well?" the Marxism-Leninism teacher asked Federica when the other pilots were off taking a cigarette break.

"Yes," Federica said. "How are my friends, my roommates?"

"They are well," the teacher answered.

"Will they be going back to Nicaragua soon?"

"This I do not know," she said.

That night there was a banquet in the pilots' honor, held in the main yard of the fortress. It was the first time Federica had been inside its walls. Many toasts were made to flying and to the team, and they all drank too much vodka, and Federica danced with the mayor and other important people in uniforms heavy with medals, and with the pilots, though they were careful not to hold on to each other too tightly. When the band stopped playing, she and the pilots climbed up to the ramparts and looked out into the darkness through the holes where the canons had once been positioned. She imagined what it must have been like to be there alone at night looking out onto the steppe, listening for the sound of horses.

"Come," the pilots said, pulling her to her feet. "Drink." And she drank from the bottle they had brought with them. When the bottle was empty, the violinist flung it out into the night and they heard it shattering on the rocks below.

At the end of the evening, the Marxism-Leninism teacher kissed

Federica on the cheeks three times. "When you come back I will make you important," she said, and Federica turned and walked away. "Good-bye," the teacher called after her, but Federica did not turn around. In the morning when she woke, before she opened her eyes, the first thing that came into her consciousness was the smell of the Marxism-Leninism teacher's perfume, and for a moment she thought when she opened her eyes, the woman would be there by her bed, watching her, but it was only her perfume.

That day they did not practice. Federica wanted to go up by herself, but the pilots wouldn't let her. It was bad luck, they said. Everyone knew that. It was like the groom seeing his bride on their wedding day, they said, and they went back to bed to sleep off their hangovers. She spent the day walking. She walked to the town and sat in the square and watched people walking by, and she wondered why she had never thought of coming to town before. She wondered whether someone was keeping an eye on her as she sat in the square, and she amused herself by trying to figure out which of the people she was watching was, in turn, watching her. Was it the young man who smiled at her or the old woman who scowled? She stood up and walked toward the bridge that led to the fortress. She was sure she could hear footsteps behind her, but she didn't dare turn around. She stopped in the middle of the bridge and looked at the gorge below. If she tried to jump, someone would stop her, and then she would know who was following her, she thought, but she didn't want to jump. She wanted to fly.

In her excitement, she did not sleep that night, yet when they left the barracks at five in the morning, she felt rested and calm.

"How did you sleep?" the other pilots asked her.

"Like a baby," she said.

The Marxism-Leninism teacher was at the airfield to bid them farewell. "We are counting on you," she said. She kissed them three times and gave each a box of chocolates. "Your favorite," she whispered to Federica, though she had never eaten chocolate in the teacher's presence before. "The instructions are inside."

"Thank you," Federica said.

"Make us proud."

"I will," Federica said.

A band played, though the Marxism-Leninism teacher and their flight instructors were the only people there to see them off. Once they were settled in their planes, the other pilots waved, so Federica waved also, and their instructors and the mechanics and the Marxism-Leninism teacher waved back.

After that it was just the sky. She wished that she could be in the lead so that there was nothing but the open sky in front of her, and she wondered whether the other pilots felt the same, whether they were secretly envious of the leader or whether they preferred the security of being led. In the seat next to her sat the box of chocolates. She opened them up. They smelled like the Marxism-Leninism teacher, like perfume and morning breath, and it was as if she were still there with her, sitting on her lap, between her and the controls, and Federica could not swallow or breathe, and she felt the plane slipping, falling from its place in the V, but she pulled it back up again and kept her eyes on the plane in front of her.

They came in fourth in the competition. Again, there was a banquet with dancing, but they received nothing, not even a certificate, and Federica did not dance. The banquet went on for hours, the speeches, the toasts, the duck. She had never eaten duck before. When they were finally allowed to leave, it was dawn. Back in her room, the box of chocolates was still sitting on the dresser, the instructions that the teacher had spoken of still unread. She stood in the middle of the room staring at the box, postponing the inevitable—to do whatever it was that the Marxism-Leninism teacher demanded of her—which, she understood now, had been her sole purpose from the beginning. She opened the box and lifted the tray. Underneath it was a gold bracelet with stones, diamonds, she imagined. It looked old, as if it had been passed on from generation to generation. The clasp was tricky, but she managed to get it on. She walked to the window, looked down at the street below. A bus stopped in front of the hotel and people got off and on. She lifted her hand, waved. "Look," she said, holding the bracelet up to the window, but, of course, no one looked up. No one knew that she was there, wearing the bracelet, feeling its weight on her wrist. She went back to the dresser, took off the bracelet, set it back in the box, and she felt as if she had been relieved of a great burden, like she used to feel when she unslung the machine gun from her shoulder and leaned it against a tree.

She read the instructions: *Put the box and its contents on the pillow on the bed when you leave. The chocolates are for you. They are of the highest quality.* She chose one of the chocolates, lifted it from its place in the tray and smelled it, but instead of putting it in her mouth, she threw it into the wastepaper basket. She threw the other chocolates away also, dropping them into the wastepaper basket one at a time.

On the flight back she wore the bracelet. It rained and there was lightning all around. The other pilots dove and swerved, trying to avoid the lightning, but she kept a straight course, for it was impossible to predict where the lighting would strike and she was tired of aerobatics. It was only once she was out of the storm that she realized the gravity of the crime she had committed, and she considered fleeing, leaving the flock of planes, heading west again or north, but that, she knew, would just make it easy for them. They would not even have to report the accident. So she kept going, following the other planes, though she did not feel anymore that she was following.

At the airfield, there was no one there to meet them, so they stood in the rain and waited until a car finally appeared. They got into the car, and the car took them to the bus station in Kamianets-Podilskyi. "Where should we go?" they asked the driver.

"Go home," the driver said.

"How?" Federica asked, but the driver didn't answer, and the other pilots were already in line buying tickets.

She returned to L'viv though it was not her home, to the apartment where she had lived when it was winter. "Where were you?" her roommates asked.

"It's a long story," she said, and they did not ask any more questions.

She went back to working at the factory. The Marxism-Leninism teacher was gone and there were no more classes. She had been arrested, Federica was told. "What did she do?" she asked.

"She betrayed the revolution," they said, pronouncing the words extra carefully, separating them from each other as if it were her hearing or poor language skills that were the cause of her lack of understanding.

About a week after she returned to L'viv, she was called into the factory manager's office. A man wearing a uniform whom she had never seen before asked her questions about the Marxism-Leninism teacher. Before he began the interrogation, he told her that he knew all the answers to the questions he was going to ask her so it would be unwise not to tell the truth. "Do you understand?" he asked, and she nodded.

"Good," he said, lighting a cigarette, leaning forward and blowing the smoke into her face.

She did not flinch.

"Do you smoke?" he asked.

"No."

The telephone rang, but he didn't answer. It rang thirty-two times. She counted while he smoked.

He asked whether she knew the Marxism-Leninism teacher and whether she had ever been to her apartment. She said she had. He asked what she had done at the apartment, and she told him what had happened on both occasions. He asked her why they lost the competition in Czechoslovakia, and she said that it was because the other teams were better. That was the only time he smiled. She answered every question he asked truthfully and with details, except for the last question. "Did she give you anything to take on the plane before you left for Czechoslovakia?" he asked.

"No," she said.

The telephone rang again. This time it rang forty-seven times. During the ringing, Federica looked straight ahead, right into the man's eyes. On ring nineteen he looked away, tapped another cigarette out of the pack that lay on the desk, lit it, and blew the smoke toward the ceiling.

"Well, that will be all," he said when the ringing stopped. "For now," he added. He stood up and opened the door for her, and she walked back onto the factory floor.

After her interrogation, Federica waited for something worse to happen. She lay awake at night, the bracelet under her pillow, waiting for a knock on the door. She could feel it pulsing like a heart, and she hated the bracelet, hated all the women who had worn it and the jeweler who had conceived it. In the darkest hour of the night, she always resolved to destroy it in the morning, but when dawn came, she clung to it as if it were part of her, like her liver or her lungs. In the mornings, she always understood that up until the moment she had decided to take the bracelet, she had allowed herself to be carried along, without will, without feeling, neither love nor hate nor fear nor joy, like a leaf on the river, like silt, but it was the bracelet that had set her free, had given her the opportunity to disobey, and she would not let them take that from her. She thought of the Marxism-Leninism teacher lying on the floor of a cold cell dreaming of Cuba, and she no longer hated her.

A few days after her interrogation, she knocked on the manager's door during her lunch break, and when no one answered, she walked in and sat in the chair where the man in the uniform had sat. She crossed her legs and waited. On the desk was a pack of cigarettes and a lighter and she considered taking one, lighting it just to prove she was not afraid, but she had never smoked a cigarette before and this was not a time to begin. Instead she put the pack in her pocket. She left the lighter where it was, though she knew that would make the absence of the cigarettes even more obvious.

After about ten minutes the manager came in. "Did we have an appointment?" he asked.

"No," Federica said, though she understood that the manger's question was not a question at all. "I'm sorry to interrupt, but if you have just a few moments."

The manager nodded, looked at the spot where the cigarettes had been, shook his head, opened the middle drawer of the desk, then the other drawers, then, when he did not find the cigarettes, he looked up. "Yes?"

"I would like to apply for permission to return to Nicaragua."

"Apply?"

"Well, I am not sure what the process is."

"You must go to Moscow, to the Nicaraguan Embassy."

"Thank you," Federica said, taking the pack of cigarettes out of her pocket. "Cigarette?" she said, holding it out to him.

"Thank you," the manager said, taking a cigarette, lighting it, breathing in deeply. "I thought you didn't smoke."

"I don't," Federica said, giving him the pack.

*

On the train to Moscow, she threw the bracelet out the window. She did it in the middle of the day with all the people in the compartment watching, though she made sure they didn't see what it was she was throwing. Once she was free of the bracelet, she knew she had done the right thing, that if she had allowed herself to cling to the bracelet, to believe it would save her, she would never get out alive.

When she returned to her seat, she pulled up her sleeve just to be sure the bracelet was gone. It was, but there was still a mark, almost a perfect circle left from the clasp crossing the vein just below the heel of her palm. She lifted her arm, enjoying the lightness. To the woman sitting across from her this gesture must have looked like waving because she smiled and then turned her face to the window.

# CHAPTER 20

Marta, who was sitting at the counter adding up a long column of numbers, did not look up when Liliana entered the *pulpería*.

"Hello," Liliana said, approaching Marta, who held up her hand to keep Liliana from saying anything more during her calculations.

Liliana waited. She gathered a few bags of cashews and a bottle of water and set them down on the counter. Marta's hand went up again, so Liliana continued to wait. When Marta was finished she looked up at Liliana and threw the pencil across the room.

Liliana moved the items she wanted to purchase closer to Marta. "That's it," she said.

"My daughter will be back in a few minutes," Marta said. "She doesn't let me handle the money."

"Actually," Liliana began.

"Actually," Marta repeated. "What was I saying?"

"You were saying that your daughter would be back shortly."

"Which one?"

"I don't know. You were the one who mentioned it."

"There are two. One of them fell out of an airplane and the other one didn't," Marta said. She opened a drawer and began rummaging around in it. "What on earth did I do with that pencil?"

"You threw it over there," Liliana said. She went and picked up the pencil and brought it back to Marta, who was still looking through the drawer.

"How much do I owe you?" Marta asked.

"Nothing," Liliana said, setting the pencil on the counter.

"Here," Marta said, pulling a handful of candies from her pocket.

"Thank you," Liliana said.

"You're welcome. So that's taken care of," Marta said. She picked the pencil up and threw it across the room again. "Don't you like candy?"

"Of course I do," Liliana said, unwrapping one of them and putting it in her mouth.

"Can I have one?"

"Of course. Which one do you want?" Liliana asked, putting the candies down on the counter in front of Marta.

"I don't want any of them," Marta said, pushing the candies away. "They're for you in exchange for the pencil. I told you that."

"Thank you," Liliana said.

"Well," Marta said. "Will you be staying here long?"

"Perhaps," Liliana said.

"My daughter, the one who fell out of the plane, does nature tours. Do you like nature?"

"Yes," Liliana said.

"Why?"

"Why not?"

"I suppose you're right," Marta said. "I suppose there's something to like about everything, even birds."

"You don't like birds?"

"No, I hate birds."

"Why?"

"Because they fly," Marta said, folding her arms across her chest.

The bell rang and a woman hurried in.

"It's the one who didn't fall out of the plane," Marta whispered.

"I hope you haven't been waiting long," the woman said to Liliana.

"Not at all."

"Would you like to purchase these items?" the woman asked.

"Of course she would," Marta said. "Isn't it obvious?"

The woman took the items and started putting them in a bag. "Eighty-five *córdobas*."

"Actually, I'm looking for a woman called Federica," Liliana said, counting out her money and handing it over. "Perhaps you know her," Liliana said.

"That's my sister," the woman said.

"The one who fell out of the plane," Marta said.

"I'm so sorry," Liliana said.

"She's not dead."

"July 15, 2022," Marta said.

"Stop it, Mother, please."

"One must face the truth. Isn't that right?" Marta said, turning to Liliana.

"One must," Liliana answered.

"You see," Marta said.

"Did you find one of her brochures about the nature tours at the Hotel Gran Lago in San Carlos?" Federica's sister asked.

"Yes," Liliana lied. It was El Justo who told her that the only answers might be found in El Castillo. "Ask for a woman named Federica," he told her. "She is your last hope."

"If Federica tells you that she knows where the jaguars are, don't believe her. There have been no jaguars here for decades," Marta said.

"My sister's night tours are especially popular. The river is beautiful at night. She will show you where the caimans are. Their eyes glow orange in the dark," Federica's sister said.

"You have never been on the river at night," Marta said to her daughter. "You were always afraid of the river."

"Where in town are you staying?" Marta's daughter asked, ignoring her mother's comment.

"I haven't found a place yet," Liliana said.

"May I recommend Hotel Luna del Río. It is both economical and clean. Here is their card. Tell them Isabel at the *pulpería* sent you. Federica doesn't have a phone, but Martín at the hotel will send his son with a message."

"Thank you for your help," Liliana said.

"I hope you enjoy your stay," Isabel said.

"Remember about the jaguars," Marta called after her as she headed for the door.

"I will," Liliana said, waving.


After checking in at the hotel, Liliana climbed the hill to the fortress. In her imagination the fortress had always been gigantic, like an entire walled city, but perched and crumbling on the hilltop it was not even as impressive as the abandoned buildings she used to see from the elevated train in the Bronx. At least with those she could imagine people living in them. She thought that if she got up close to the fortress, climbed on its crumbled walls, she might feel the grandeur of it, but when she was at the top, she understood that it was the river, not the fortress, that dominated.

She walked back to town and to the end of the main road, past the *pulpería* and the dock where the *lanchas* stopped. Then she turned around and walked to the other end. She walked back up the hill, past the fortress to what used to be the bullring but was now just an empty lot filled with weeds. She passed the soccer field, after which the path ended. Beyond there was only jungle. She tried walking into the jungle, but the mud grew increasingly thick and deep, so after falling once, she turned around. On the path that led back to the main road she met a girl of about seven or eight carrying two chickens. She held them by the feet, one in each hand, struggling to keep them high enough so their heads did not drag along the ground. "What happened to you?" she asked Liliana.

"I fell."

"Do you need help?"

"No, but thank you," Liliana said.

The chickens squirmed and the girl leaned over and whispered to them, first to the one on the left, then the one on the right, and they calmed down.

"What did you tell them?" Liliana asked.

"I told them that we are almost home," the girl said. "You are bleeding." She pointed to Liliana's leg.

"It's nothing," Liliana said.

"Make sure to wash it thoroughly," the girl said.

"I will."

"If you don't, it could get infected."

"I know."

The chickens were fussing again, and this time the girl yanked them up high, and they fluttered their wings and clucked. "I'd better get going," she said.

"Yes," Liliana said. As she made her way to the main road, she could feel the mud working its way into the scratches the calf had made.

When she got to the hotel she took a bath, and the water turned red from the mud. She could feel each cut the calf had made, each line, as if they were words carved into her flesh, as if they were part of her, but there was no pain, so she lingered, letting the water caress her wounds so that by the time she got out of the bath it was already getting dark. She left the hotel, turned right, and walked to the end of the road. She walked up to the fortress and back down, up and back down, like a lion pacing in its cage, she thought, like a jaguar. When she got tired of pacing, she returned to the hotel and sat on the balcony looking out onto the dark river, listening to the rapids, eating cashews. At some point Martín, the owner of the hotel, sat down opposite her.

"Am I the only guest?" she asked.

"There are not many visitors during the rainy season."

"Do you know a woman named Federica? I would like to book a night tour. I have been told that those are the best."

"It depends what you want to see," Martín said. "If you are interested in birds, that is not the best choice."

"I'm not really interested in birds."

"Many foreigners are. They keep records of all the birds they have ever seen. They write them down in notebooks. They are very devoted to birds."

"I want to go on the river at night. The woman at the *pulpería* told me that it's beautiful at night."

"The river is always beautiful," Martín said. "It's twenty-five dollars per person, but the minimum number of people for the night tour is four."

"Perhaps she will give me a deal since it's the rainy season and I imagine she doesn't have many customers."

"If it rains, she will not take you."

"I will discuss the price with her when she comes to pick me up, if it doesn't rain, of course."

"She doesn't like to talk about money. I take care of that end."

"Well then perhaps you can give me a deal?"

"I am sorry," Martín said, looking down as if he were a child who had done something wrong.

"Of course," Liliana said. "I will pay for four."

"Will you pay now?"

"Of course," Liliana said, taking out her wallet, handing over five twenties.

That night when Federica came to pick her up for the night tour, it was raining, but she said that it was just a drizzle, so they could give it a try if Liliana wanted. If it started raining harder, they would have to turn back, she said, and Liliana agreed. They walked in silence to the dock. Federica walked ahead carrying the paddles and a backpack. Liliana wanted to help, at least with the paddles, but Federica refused her offer. When they got to the canoe, Federica held it for her, and in her effort to appear as sprightly as possible, Liliana almost tipped over getting in and had to right herself by grabbing the gunwale. "Here," she said, handing her a life jacket.

"I'm a good swimmer," Liliana said, trying to get out of wearing it.

"I could lose my license if you don't use it."

Liliana put on the life jacket. "What about you?"

"Oh, they don't care about us, just the tourists."

Once they were on the river it started raining harder, but Federica said that it wasn't hard enough to turn back unless Liliana was afraid.

"I like the rain," Liliana said.

"I don't have rain ponchos," Federica said.

"I don't mind getting wet," Liliana said.

"You're not cold?"

"Cold?" Liliana laughed.

Federica did not reply.

"I met your mother at the *pulpería*," Liliana said. "She said you fell out of an airplane."

"Did she tell you when you were going to die? According to her I have only until 2022."

"Now I understand. She told me 2022 also."

Federica laughed. "A coincidence."

"Your mother said you know where the jaguars are," Liliana said.

"My mother has lost her mind," Federica said.

Federica paddled toward the middle of the river. When they reached it, Federica set the paddle on the floor of the canoe and stood up. She turned on the flashlight, directed it toward the riverbank. Slowly she moved the light along the shore. "There," she said, keeping the light focused on one spot. "Can you see it?"

Liliana looked, but all she saw was a splotch of light on the riverbank. "Yes," she said.

Federica sat down again and began to paddle toward the shore. When she was just a few feet from the bank, she stopped paddling. "There," she whispered, pointing again with the light.

Liliana still couldn't see anything. "Yes," she said again.

"You're lying," Federica said.

Liliana began to cry. Federica turned the flashlight off, and they sat there in the canoe, the rain falling on them, Federica in the stern, Liliana in the bow. "Are you okay?" Federica said.

"I'm sorry," Liliana said.

"A lot of people lie," Federica said. She turned the flashlight on again. "Look, can you see it now, the eyes? It's a big one." She began paddling softly toward the shore, toward the eyes. She stood up, so smoothly that the canoe did not move, and then she swooped down and picked the caiman up. She held it high over her head and then flung it into the water. Liliana heard the splash, heard it swimming away frantically.

"Do you ever think about how afraid it must be getting scooped up like that?" Liliana said.

"It's what the tourists want to see."

"How do you know?"

"They always tip me more when I do."

"Well, I didn't want to see it," Liliana said.

"Do you want to go back?" Federica asked, pushing away from the shore.

"No, it's okay. I'm sorry," Liliana said. "Everything makes me cry lately."

"Do you want to go down the falls? It always makes me feel better."

Liliana nodded, and Federica turned the canoe downstream. It was raining harder now. "Are you ready?" Federica asked when they reached the top of the falls.

"Yes," Liliana said.

"Here." Federica handed her a paddle. "When I say 'right,' paddle on the right side as hard and you can, and when I say 'left,' paddle hard on the left. Don't stop until I tell you to. Are you ready?"

"Yes," Liliana said, gripping the paddle, leaning forward.

Liliana could feel the pull of the water, and then they were in it, and there was water all around, "Move with the canoe, don't fight it." "Left, faster, right."

"You did great," Federica said when the water was calm and dark around them.

"I want to go back," Liliana said.

"You said you wanted to do it."

"I did, but now I have had enough."

"Very well," Federica said, paddling toward the shore.

When Liliana was standing on the dock, her legs were weak, shaking like after sex, and she thought she would have to sit down, but she managed to keep standing and to hand Federica a twenty-dollar bill.

"No," Federica said.

"Why? You said that tourists tip more when you pick up a caiman, and that's what you did, so I should pay you for it."

"But you didn't enjoy the tour."

"I didn't say that."

"I can feel it."

"Like you could feel I was lying?"

"Yes."

"Take it," Liliana said, holding the money out again. "I'm not angry, really."

Federica took the money, put it in her pocket. "Thank you."

"Your mother said that you fell out of a plane. Is that true?"

"Actually, I jumped out, when we were just about to crash."

"Were you afraid?"

"I didn't have time to be afraid."

They walked together up the embankment to the road. Liliana tried again to help Federica carry the paddles and the life vest. "You are my guest," Federica said, and Liliana did not argue, though she did not feel like a guest at all. At the road they parted, Federica going one way, Liliana the other. "You know how to get back?" Federica asked.

"Of course. There is only one road."

Liliana started running. She ran past the hotel to the end of the road and back to the other end, back and forth and back and forth. She longed for the hill that she climbed each day from the BART station to her house. She wanted to run up that hill and back down to the other side. She wanted to run for hours to the ocean, to the bay, up more hills, but she was stuck on this one road and the paths that led to a fortress that was not what she had imagined it would be and to the jungle thick with mud, and she thought of what her mother said that the difference between people who live in El Castillo and Manhattan is, that people in El Castillo know that the world outside their tiny patch of earth is enormous and full of things they do not understand or even know exist, but New Yorkers think that their tiny island contains within it all that there is to know.

Liliana returned to the hotel, but despite all the running, she was not tired, not even after she had showered and drunk rum with Martín on the balcony. She lay in bed, the fan whirring above her, wide awake. After about an hour, she was more awake than when she first lay down, so she got dressed and went to the reception area to look through the books that other guests had left behind. She had long since finished the one book she brought with her, a Spanish novel about the depressing childhood of a Moroccan girl growing up in Barcelona, and had not read anything except the newspaper since then. She had, in fact, never gone this long without a book, but there wasn't anything among the books that interested Liliana, just bestsellers, something in Finnish, Harry Potter, a book about meditation. She read the first page of each, decided on the Finnish one, and began reading it out loud. After getting through the first chapter, the only word she recognized was *Helsinki*, but she took it up to her room, staying up until dawn reading the Finnish book out loud, understanding nothing, yet just the act of reading gave her a strange sense of accomplishment, as if she had spent the entire night studying for an exam.

After breakfast, which she devoured in minutes, realizing only when Martín brought it out how hungry she was, she asked Martín to contact Federica to see whether she was available for a day tour. Birds and monkeys were the best animals to see during the daytime, Federica explained when she came to the hotel to discuss the details, and Liliana said that birds and monkeys would be great.

"I didn't mean to scare you last night. I've never done that before," Federica said.

"Done what?"

"Taken a customer down the falls at night."

"It was fun," Liliana said. "I've been down scarier rivers in California," she added, though this was not true. She had gone rafting only once, in Utah with her students, but the river there was tame, so tame that the kids were disappointed.

"Still, I shouldn't have. I guess I miss my life before the accident.

I was a guide for extreme adventure tours. We jumped out of planes, with parachutes of course, but parachuting into the jungle is not the same as parachuting onto flat land."

"What happened exactly when you fell out of the plane?"

"Something went wrong with the engine. I always did all my own maintenance, but something went wrong, and by the time I made sure everyone else had jumped it was too late for me. There wasn't time to pull the cord."

"Did everyone else survive?"

"They walked away without a scratch."

"And you?"

"I was in the hospital for six months. They thought I wouldn't walk again. I have to be so careful all the time, and I hate it. I haven't been free of the pain since the accident, not until last night, not since going down the falls."

"Do you feel it now?"

"Yes," Federica said, "but somehow, after last night, I feel that I won't have it forever, that one day it will be gone."

"Why did you jump out of planes?" Liliana asked.

"I liked the moment when you hit the ground, when you know that you're safe."

"But why put yourself in danger in the first place?"

"We are always in danger," Federica said. They had reached the path that led into the jungle. "We have to be quiet now," Federica said. They walked in silence, and all Liliana heard was the sucking sound of the mud as she lifted her feet. "There," Federica whispered, pointing to a tree. Liliana looked up but all she saw were leaves. Federica handed her the binoculars, angling them so they pointed to the right place. "Do you see them now?"

This time she did see them, six parrots perched on a branch. "They're beautiful," she said, and as if her words were a command, they flew away.

They walked deeper into the jungle. Federica pointed out a termite nest the size of a car, and they saw more birds and monkeys.
They came to the place where Federica had been seeing sloths for
the past few weeks. They circled around the area for a while, keeping their eyes peeled on the trees, but there was nothing. "Sorry,"
Federica said, and Liliana said that it wasn't her fault, that one
can't expect wild animals to be there when one wants them to be.

"I didn't come to see animals, anyway," Liliana said. She took
in a deep breath, held it, exhaled. "I came to find out if anyone
here knows anything about my brother. He died fighting the Contras twenty-five years ago. I know he was here."

"William," Federica said as if this were an answer.

"So you knew him?"

"Yes, he lived here with my family for about a month. He helped
my father build shelves for the *pulpería*. He left without saying good-
bye," Federica said, leaning over to brush off a log. "Come sit
down," she said. They sat side by side.

"He didn't tell you where he was going?"

"No," she said.

"We got a letter. He's been dead all these years. I just wanted
to know what happened. The letter was from his girlfriend, Carolina. Do you know about her? I went to see her in Juigalpa, but
she's crazy. She told us he died in battle, but now she thinks that
he's alive, that he turned into a jaguar. She believes that the jaguar
comes to her and lays his head on her lap." Liliana paused, and
when Federica did not respond, she said, "Did William tell you
that our mother lived here for three years when she was young?
They were refugees during the Second World War. My grandparents were doctors, so when the United States wouldn't give them
visas, they got jobs with the Nicaraguan government and were sent
here to help control yellow fever."

"Not until the night before he left. Before that whenever I asked him where he was from he said we are all from Africa, but I didn't understand what he meant by that until years later. But that night he told me, only me. He made me promise never to tell anyone, and I never did. Never." Federica turned to face Liliana. "You don't look like him at all, but there is something about the way you stand, a little tipped to the side like you're looking around the corner. And your voice—you sound just like him."

"He looks more like my father, and I look like my mother, but people always knew we were related. When we were kids when we answered the phone, even my grandparents couldn't tell us apart."

"I went after him," Federica said. "I left the same day on a later boat, but I never found him, and then I ended up in the war, too. He told me that I couldn't understand him, that I knew nothing, only the river. I wanted so much to feel what he felt. I wanted to feel his suffering. I thought that we could share it."

"That sounds to me like love," Liliana said.

They sat, listening to the buzzing of insects rising to a crescendo, then subsiding to silence, then building up again. "I don't know what love is," Federica said, "but I know what it's like to kill and I know that there's no going back afterward. You just have to keep moving. It's like flying. If you're not moving forward, you're falling, and when you hit the ground you break into pieces."

"I don't know what love is either," Liliana said. "I thought I did, but," she paused, looked up at the trees. "So was it a good or bad thing, that you followed him?"

"It was my life," Federica said, "but I still miss him, even after all these years, especially now that I'm back here. Sometimes in the morning when I'm still half-asleep I can almost hear him talking with my father out on the veranda, but then I come to, and I realize it's just my father talking to the pigs, telling them how lazy they are."

"I miss him, too," Liliana said, taking Federica's hand, and they sat there together and cried.

# CHAPTER 21

GUILLERMO HAD NOT SLEPT WELL. MARTA HAD BEEN UP ALL night talking about moving to San Miguelito, convinced it was going to be another Panama City, only more beautiful and more prosperous once the canal that he said was never going to be built was finished. He had woken up in the middle of the night to the sounds of her packing, found her sitting on the floor in the kitchen surrounded by newspapers and their dishes and pots and pans. She asked him to go to the *pulpería* to get boxes right then in the middle of the night. "If we delay any longer other people will get there first," she insisted when he suggested they wait until morning, so he took the horse and went to the store because he was wide awake by then anyway and being out in the night was preferable to arguing with her about boxes. When he returned with the boxes the dishes were back on the shelves, the newspapers discarded, and Marta was in bed sleeping, so he sat out on the veranda until morning. When Federica got up, they made breakfast, and he told her about the boxes and they laughed about the canal that would never be built.

"Where did you go last night?" Marta asked, when he woke her for breakfast.

"I went to get the boxes," Guillermo said.

"In the middle of the night?"

"Yes," Guillermo said, "in the middle of the night."

Marta was silent after that, turning her attention to her breakfast, which she consumed showing neither pleasure nor distaste.

Federica and Guillermo talked while Marta ate. Martín's son had come by first thing to tell Federica that the American wanted to hire her again. Whether Marta was listening or understood what they were discussing they did not know. "I'm taking that same American out again today," Federica said.

"Don't forget to show her the termite nest. It's been a long time since I've seen one so big," Guillermo said.

When she went off to meet the American and Isabel picked Marta up to take her to the *pulpería*, Guillermo was finally alone. This is what he had been waiting for, but he couldn't find a way to sink into his solitude. He tended to the animals, teasing them as he always did: "Never worked a day in your lives. Bunch of fatsos is all you are." They sidled up to him, the pigs rooting into his legs with their snouts, the chickens pecking him fondly, all of them clucking and grunting like a choir of old men. He knocked the ripe mangoes down from the tree, catching them in his shirt as they fell. He checked the corn, though there was nothing to do with it but let it grow.

At noon he ate an avocado. He thought he would sit for a while on the veranda and then walk over to the *pulpería*, but he fell asleep. He was still sleeping, dreaming about something that he would not remember, when Federica put her hand on his shoulder and said, "Papá, you have a visitor." He opened his eyes and there, in front of him, was Pepa, though he knew this was not possible, that if Pepa were alive, she was old like him. Was this apparition before him a sign that he would soon be like Marta, believe in canals that did not exist and in powers he did not have? Yet, he thought, if he knew this woman standing in front of him was not Pepa, then perhaps he was still Guillermo, the Guillermo who had fathered four children, none of whom had succumbed to yellow fever or war or the river.

Once Federica and the woman who looked like Pepa sat down on the bench across from him, he could see the difference between them, though it was not in the features or stature or even in the eyes. It was in the way this woman sat, stiff and uncomfortable. Pepa was never stiff; strong, but not stiff. Pepa sat as if she were about to be served a wonderful meal. This woman sat as if she knew she were about to be punched in the stomach.

"This is Liliana," Federica said, and they greeted each other.

"How do you like our river?" Guillermo asked when Federica went into the house to get refreshments. Liliana said that it was beautiful and peaceful.

"Did you see any sloths today?" he asked, and Liliana said they had not, but that she still enjoyed the day.

"We saw all kinds of birds," she said, "and a termite hive and monkeys, of course."

"That hive is getting bigger every day. I haven't seen such a big one in a long time."

"Does that mean something, when they get so big?"

"I suppose it means something," Guillermo said, not quite understanding the question.

"I mean are they bigger when it rains more or less, for some environmental reason?"

"There is a reason for everything, but we don't always know what it is," Guillermo said.

"Yes," Liliana said, laughing. "It was a silly question."

"No, not at all. Federica can look it up later, on the computer.

Everything is on the computer now." He thought that it was the kind of question Pepa would have asked.

Federica returned with papaya shakes and cashews. "From the garden," she said.

Liliana thanked her, took a handful of cashews, a sip of juice. "My favorite nut," she said.

Before he went to work on the coffee plantation, he and Pepa gathered the cashews for the Germans. It was one of the tasks given to them so they could make some money, and, of course, they paid them way too much, especially since Guillermo and Pepa ate so many as they went along, and the Germans gave them half the crop to sell to Don Solano at the *pulpería*. The Germans would be happy to know that the trees still bore fruit, that he still picked the cashews himself and sold them at the *pulpería*. He looked at the woman who was not Pepa, smiled, then lowered his gaze.

If Pepa were here she would look him straight in the eye. She would say that it was not interesting to talk about nuts. Liliana put a cashew in her mouth.

"You are Pepa's daughter," he said.

He thought his words would come in a torrent then, cover the entire world with memory. He could feel them lining up behind his lips, clamoring to be released, but he did not say anything more.

Pepa's daughter was looking at him, waiting. He wanted to close his eyes, sleep. He was so tired. Finally she spoke: "Did you know her?"

Did he know her? That was always the question.

"She was the doctors' daughter, no?"

Liliana nodded. "Yes, the doctors' daughter."

"She had a brother, Karl, I think his name was."

"That's right."

"And how is she, the doctors' daughter? Is she well?" he asked, gripping the arm of the bench, for he knew it was possible she was not well, that she was dead, had been dead for years.

"Yes, she's fine, still working," Pepa's daughter said, and then he could no longer understand what she was saying. It all sounded like nonsense to him, like another language, or not even a language at all except there were words he recognized floating around him—train, cold, fan, stairs. Stop, he wanted to tell her, but the words kept coming.

Finally the noise stopped, and Federica and Pepa's daughter were looking at him, and he knew they were waiting for him to respond, so he smiled again, and Pepa's daughter smiled, and it was the kind of smile that people reserved for old men.

"I am glad she is well. Please, tell her Guillermo says hello and that I am glad she is doing well."

"I will, of course," Liliana said. "I wanted to ask you about my brother, William. He spent some time here during the revolution."

"William," Guillermo said.

"You remember, Papá," Federica said.

"Of course I remember. We were all so fond of him." How could he not have seen Pepa in William, he thought, heard her in his voice, and why had he stayed here all that time and said nothing? "He didn't look like your mother," he said finally.

"He looked more like my father, though he was much taller, bigger. He used to joke that he was adopted, but he was so much like my mother." She paused. "My father was a small man." She added, "in stature."

Guillermo tried to imagine him, a small man in a suit and hat like in the movies. He imagined Pepa standing next to this small man, her husband, the father of her children. She was looking up at him, her husband, this small man, but he could not tell whether she was happy.

She stayed for dinner, Pepa's daughter, and Marta asked her all sorts of personal questions like whether she had children or was married, and she answered them graciously, explaining that she had no children, that she had just broken up with her partner of many years, a woman. When Marta asked her what exactly two women did in bed because she never understood it, Federica apologized profusely. "I don't even know how she thinks of such things," Federica said, and Guillermo stood up to get more beer so that he would not have to think about Pepa's daughter naked, so that he would not think of Pepa naked.

When he returned with the beer, Marta was asleep at the table. "I'm sorry, my wife is not well," he said. He crouched down and whispered into Marta's ear, "Wake up, Martita. It's time for bed," and she turned to him and smiled without opening her eyes. "Come," he said, and she stood up and began walking toward the bedroom, holding her hands out like a child pretending to be blind. When they reached the bedroom, she stood in the center of the room and took off her dress and found her way to the bed, still pretending to be blind. She lay down on top of the sheets. "Turn on the fan," she said.

He wanted to cover her with a sheet. "You'll be cold," he said, but she shook her head. "Look at me," she said, and he did. "Are you looking?" she asked.

"Yes."

"How do I know you are not lying?"

"You can open your eyes," he said, and she laughed as if he had just told her she could fly.

He lay down next to Marta, his wife, and he took her hand, squeezed it. "Open your eyes," he said.

"They are open," she said, but they weren't.

\*

Liliana was left at the table with Federica. Why, she thought, had she expected that everything would be revealed to her just because she wanted it, because she was ready, because she had finally made this journey to the river? How was she different from the tourists who expected the sloths to be hanging in plain sight just for them to photograph? How would she tell her mother the truth about William, the only truth she found—that he had killed?

"Thank you," she said, getting up from the table. "Thank you for everything."

"I will walk you back," Federica said. "The path is dark."

Liliana followed Federica, on the narrow, overgrown path. At some points the vegetation was so thick Federica had to hold the branches back so Liliana could pass through. When they came to the main road, they were able to walk side by side, and they walked like this without speaking until they came to the hotel, where they stopped to look down at the river. It seemed still in the darkness, but they could hear the rapids and knew there was no stillness there, that the river was always moving on its relentless path to the sea.

"William loved the river," Federica said. "The first time I went over the rapids in the dark was with him. He dared me to do it with my eyes closed, and I did. And we swam in the river. We swam all the way to the other side. I didn't know how to swim, but I jumped in, and he taught me how to float on my back. He made me realize how afraid I was, but with him I felt safe even though he was leading me to danger. I can't explain it exactly."

"I used to feel that way, too, like nothing bad could happen when William was around." She paused. "I want to swim in the river."

"It's too dangerous. The caimans."

"But you and William did it and lived to tell the tale."

"That is because we were young and stupid. At the time he wanted to believe that the river could wash away what he had done, purify him somehow, but it couldn't because the river is only the river."

"I still want to swim in it. I want to feel what he felt."

"Now I think he wanted the caimans to get him. I think he wished for that."

"Come," Liliana said, and they made their way around the side of the hotel to the muddy path that led to the river. A pig grunted as they passed, and its smell took over the night.

"I can't come with you," Federica said.

"I know," Liliana said. "I know."


At first all she smelled was the pig. She kept her head up so as not to swallow the contaminated water.

She swam faster, kicking so hard that she wondered whether she would even know if something touched her. She wondered whether Federica would be able to see if something got her, pulled her down into the dark river. It was best not to think at all. Just swim, she said to herself, just swim, so she swam in rhythm to the Sabbath poem, *verde que te quiero verde*, and it was as if the words were the river. How many times she repeated the poem, she did not know, but when the smell of the pig returned she knew she was close to the shore.

# PART III

# GUILLERMO

GUILLERMO NEVER HAD ANY DESIRE TO SEE THE WORLD FROM above, but now that Federica is flying again, he accompanies her on flights from time to time because he knows it makes her happy. Marta, however, refuses to join them. "Flying is for birds," she said.

"But don't you want to see it?" he asked.

"See what?"

"Everything."

"No matter how high you climb, you can only see a small piece of what there is to see," Marta said.

"But you can see more than you can see from the ground," he argued.

"I can see everything I need to see with my eyes closed," Marta said.

Before he knew what it was like to fly, he thought it would be quiet high up above the world, but once he was in the sky it was as if he were inside a giant hive of buzzing bees and, at the same time, as if the hive were inside him, as if he had swallowed it so that the buzzing was both outside and within. As they climbed higher and he saw the river spreading out beneath him, the din of the engine and the constant shaking turned into a type of silence, a silence of noise and movement, like being in the rapids, inside the belly of the river.

When they were over the lake—halfway across, when all he could see was water—he understood, finally, after all these years, what Pepa meant when she told him it was only when she was completely surrounded by water, when all she could see was water, that she finally could breathe, that she could look out at the horizon and know her life was still ahead of her.

It surprised him how quickly day turned to night over the lake. It was as if the world existed and then the next moment it did not, as if it were all extinguished, the past and the present, the water, the sky, the clouds, but he was still there, watching the end of everything, the roar of the plane in his ears and his daughter at the helm, steering them, keeping them aloft, alive. It was beautiful, he thought, this darkness, and he wanted to enter into it, swim in it as if it were water, but it was not water, and he did not know whether the lake was still beneath them, or whether they had crossed to the other side, but it didn't matter because in the darkness there was no difference between water and land, between sky and earth.

# PEPA

**IT IS A COMFORT TO HAVE LILIANA NEAR, TO WAKE UP IN THE** morning knowing she is in the next room, knowing she will be there at the end. It is even a comfort to drink the homeopathic teas and antioxidant-rich shakes Liliana prepares for her, though they both know they will have no effect. There was a time when she would have been annoyed by these efforts, but she no longer has the energy to be annoyed by things that are not really important. If it makes Liliana feel useful, then there is no harm in it.

Pepa worried that when she told Liliana about the tumor, Liliana would insist she see a specialist, get second opinions and chemo and all of it, but Liliana accepted her mother's decision without argument and petitioned only for the teas and shakes. When Liliana returned from Nicaragua, they made tea every night after dinner and drank it sitting side by side on the sofa, while Liliana told her what she learned on her journey, but Liliana did not talk about the battle, the first and only battle. She was waiting, Pepa knew, for her to pose the question. Waiting until she was ready. On the fourth night, Liliana showed Pepa the photographs—the mausoleum that did not contain William's body, crazy Carolina, the horses, El Justo, and Santiago, who had been so kind to Liliana, like a brother, the ugly church of Juigalpa, the musicians, El Castillo from the *lancha*, El Castillo from the fortress, the *pulpería*, the Germans' house that no longer contained books, the birds and trees, the rapids, monkeys, and chickens, and Federica, who once had fallen out of a plane, Federica who had loved William, who looked for him but could not find him.

And Guillermo. Guillermo on the veranda. Guillermo at the table. Guillermo on the sofa with his wife.

"They look nice," Pepa said, and Liliana said that they were, though the wife was not right in her mind anymore.

"And the husband?"

"The husband seems much younger than his years," Liliana said, and that was a great comfort.

"Remember when I used to tell you how I woke up that night and knew there was something outside, and how I crept out into the garden?"

"The time you saw the jaguar?" Liliana said.

"I never saw it. There were times when I would go outside in the middle of the night and stare into the trees, and I tried to convince myself that I saw its eyes shining in the moonlight, but I know that I never did. It was just something I wanted. I guess I thought that if a jaguar allowed me to see him, it would mean he felt a kinship, that he recognized something in me, a wildness or courage, whatever that is, I don't know, something that made me different from others." She set her teacup on the table and turned to Liliana. "I am ready to see it now," Pepa said, her lips trembling. "I am ready to know."

"It was an ambush," Liliana began. "William and his unit attacked the Contras when they were eating breakfast. They didn't even have time to grab their weapons."

"Continue," Pepa said, looking straight into Liliana's eyes. "How many?"

Liliana did not look away. "Remember what Papá always said. 'Whether it's one or six million, it's always too many.'"

"If they didn't have time to grab their weapons, then . . ."

"But he didn't stay to kill again. He abandoned his unit, ran so fast they couldn't keep up with him."

Pepa could see him now, running, his muscles straining, his eyes on fire. She could hear his heart pounding. "Keep going," she said. "Tell me again about his time in El Castillo. Tell me about how he swam in the river. What color was it that he painted the house?"

"Blue," Liliana said.

"Why didn't he stay? One month is not enough time."

"He thought he could find some peace, but he couldn't."

"So little time," Pepa said. "Tell me again about the caimans at night."

"Their eyes are all you can see."

Pepa closed her eyes. "I can see them there where that rock juts out into the river."

"Yes," Liliana said. "And there's another one looking right at us."

"Yes, I see it. Can you hear the rapids up ahead?"

"I can hear them," Liliana said, moving closer to her mother, resting her head on her shoulder.


On the good days, Pepa takes a taxi to the store. The customers do not ask her where she has been, but she knows from their heartfelt smiles and earnest appreciation that they understand she is not well. In the afternoons she gets tired, so she lies down on the couch in the office in the back of the store. Sometimes she sleeps. When she is feeling particularly strong, she unpacks boxes, breathing in the humid smell of new books.

When she does not go to the store, she sits in the armchair by the window that looks out over the Hudson and rereads sections of her favorite books, drifting off into sleep more often now than before. When Liliana comes home from work, they eat dinner, which is always *gallo pinto* with avocado. It is the only food that doesn't make Pepa ill.

Liliana is teaching again, at a charter school in the Bronx. Her students are refugees from all the violent places of the earth. They have crossed seas on rubber dinghies and entire deserts on foot, ridden on the tops of trains, swum across rivers. Many of them did not know before they entered her class that the earth and the planets revolve around the sun, so in her world history class, Liliana starts with the big bang. She worries she will not teach them enough. Her students are worried, too, about a little sister they left behind, about their grandparents, who raised them, who sold their wedding rings to pay for the journey here, to the winter, to apartment buildings where the elevators never work and the stairwells smell like urine, so they can learn about the big bang. In Liliana's advanced English class they are writing poems.

At night, when she cannot sleep, Pepa lets herself remember. It is Saturday morning at the bookstore. Outside it is raining. The first customer has yet to come in, and Pepa is standing in the doorway to the storage room, watching William and Liliana playing in the canoe they constructed out of boxes. They are paddling the air with brooms. "Keep in time, keep in time," William calls from the stern.

"I am," Liliana replies, leaning into each stroke.

"Switch," William says, and they switch sides without missing a beat. "It's raining," William says.

Liliana tilts her head up to the sky and opens her mouth. She looks so small, Pepa thinks, like a baby bird waiting to be fed.

"Keep paddling. We're almost at the rapids," William says.

"I'm ready," Liliana assures him. "I'm ready."

When the pain intensifies, Pepa thinks of the pills the doctor gave her for the pain. She is saving them for when she is ready. She likes to think of them as stones. When she swallows all of them at once, she will become so heavy that she will sink to the bottom of the river.

# WILLIAM

BY THE TIME THE *LANCHA* BACKED AWAY FROM THE DOCK AT EL
Castillo, William no longer felt the overwhelming desire to flee
but rather he had no will at all—he could not remember getting
up from the bed, or walking out of Guillermo's house, or getting
on the boat and choosing the seat in the front row. He did not
even know whether the *lancha* was going west to San Carlos and
the lake or east to the Caribbean, though the man who sold him
his ticket must have asked him where he was going. The ticket
gave no clue. On it only the date and the price were written. He
focused on getting his bearings as the *lancha* turned to the east and
headed downriver toward the sea. He felt a sense of relief then,
that he was not going back to San Carlos, that he was heading,
instead, into unfamiliar territory. He allowed himself to lean back
against his seat, close his eyes. Perhaps now he would be able to
sleep, but after just a few moments, he opened his eyes in a panic,
sure he had left behind something precious in El Castillo, but this
fear soon gave way to a new sense of relief when he remembered
he did not own anything precious and had certainly not brought

anything valuable with him. He had, in fact, never felt any attachment to objects.

When he was a child he did not beg for toys, not even a bicycle. Every year when his grandparents asked him what he wanted for his birthday, he made something up so that they could have the pleasure of giving him a present, but he ended up giving all his gifts away to the neighborhood children or to Liliana. He had even given away the Lorca, left it with Carolina at the camp. He would have given it away sooner, but he didn't want to hurt his mother's feelings. She had made such an occasion of presenting it to him. Still, he could not shake the feeling that something was missing, something important.

He put his hand in the water, could see the water flowing over it, but he could not feel it, and he realized he could not feel the hard bench beneath him or the wind on his face. He put his hand on his face and felt nothing. He turned around to look at his fellow passengers. The *lancha* was quite full, and he could see the people around him talking, but he could hear nothing.

He turned to the man sitting next to him and asked where he was going. He knew he had asked this question because the man turned to him and was clearly answering, but William could not hear him speaking. William asked whether he was going home or setting forth on a journey. The man answered, and William smiled, and they talked like this for a while until the man seemed to realize William had no idea what he was saying. The man politely shook his hand, grabbed his bags, and got up to find another place to sit.

William watched him settle into a new seat far in the back near the bathrooms, and it saddened him to think that a fellow passenger preferred the familiar stench of human waste to the discomfort of speaking with him, but he felt no anger toward the man for making this decision. Across the aisle a woman spread out a giant *nacatamal* on her lap and began eating. He remembered that he had not eaten since noon the day before, but he was not hungry. Still, he knew he should eat, so he took out a bag of cashews. He put one nut in his mouth. He tasted nothing, not even the salt. Still, he ate twelve nuts, one at a time.

Since sight was now his only sense, William focused on the scenery, watching the herons and vultures drying out along the shore. As the sun rose in the sky, the world came into sharp focus, and he found that he could see vines hanging from the trees lining the shore and the blues and reds and yellows of parrots deep inside the cover of leaves. He saw monkeys swinging from branches and the pink snouts of pigs drinking at the river.

When they were young Liliana loved to ask him questions that had no good answers. "If you had to choose between being blind or deaf, what would you choose?" was one of her favorites, and every time she brought it up, though they enjoyed discussing the pros and cons of each, neither was able to make a decision. Yet he was not troubled by the absence of sound. Perhaps this was what he needed, for it was so much easier to shut one's eyes than one's ears.

When they arrived in Greytown, the final destination, William was sleeping. He slept through the entire disembarkation process, and when everyone had gotten off and the bags of rice and beans and cornmeal and the bananas had all been unloaded, he was still sleeping. The driver's assistant tried to wake him. At first he put his hand gently on William's shoulder, but he did not stir. He shook him, then, not too hard, but hard enough, and he did not wake up. The assistant backed away from him, frightened. "I think he might be dead," he told the driver.

"But his eyes are closed. If he were dead his eyes would be open."

"Not if you die in your sleep."

The driver shook his head and went to deal with William himself. "*Despiertese cabrón, pinche extrajero,*" he said several times, raising his voice with each attempt, shaking him hard so that the assistant thought he might fall over, but William did not stir.

In the end they agreed he was drunk. They did not discuss the fact that they did not smell alcohol on his breath, for that would have made things more complicated, and they were too tired after twenty-seven hours on the river for complications. So they carried him off the boat, the driver taking his legs, the assistant his arms, and left him in the shade under a tree behind the ticket office, placing him on his side with his backpack under his head so that he wouldn't choke on his own vomit, which is what had happened to the assistant's cousin. "He'll be okay," the driver said as they parted ways, each heading home to his own much-needed sleep.

"I know," the assistant said, but after he was home and had eaten a generous helping of fish stew and made love to his wife, after she had pulled down the shades to keep out the bright afternoon sun so that he could rest, he could not sleep. He worried about thieves and mosquitoes and rain, so he left the comfort of his bed and walked back to where they had left the foreigner, but he was gone. Rather than return home, he walked to the center of town, where he asked in all the shops and both bars and the hotel that rarely had guests whether anyone had seen a foreigner, a tall young man with hair so short one could not determine the color, but no one had.


William awoke from his slumber to the buzzing of mosquitoes. He raised his hand and slapped a mosquito between his palms. "Got you," he said out loud, though he did not open his eyes to see whether this, in fact, was true. His voice sounded only vaguely familiar, as if it were the voice of someone he had not spoken to in years. He lay still, keeping his eyes closed, fearing that if he opened his eyes—now that he had his senses back and could hear again, now that he felt his skin burning from what seemed like hundreds of mosquito bites and he could smell rotting fruit and rain—the sight of the world would be more than he could bear. He stood up and slung his backpack over his shoulders without opening his eyes. He put his arms out in front of him as children do when they play at being blind, took a step forward, then another until he felt the sun on him, strong like a searchlight. He walked until his outstretched arms hit a wall. He could feel the heat of the sun coming off the wall. The air was still as ice. He ran his hands along the wall. There was a sign, a poster on the wall. It had just recently been put up. He could still smell the paste. It smelled, he thought, like bread.

From not too far away he heard someone calling, "*¿Extranjero, dónde estás?*" He opened his eyes. *PATRIA LIBRE O MORIR* the poster said, and the words were like gunshots, like punches, and he jumped up, pulled himself over the wall, letting himself fall to the ground on the other side. "*Extranjero,*" the man called again, and William waited, holding his breath, listening for footsteps, but he did not move, not until dawn gave way to night. Only then did he leave his hiding place.

He kept close to the wall, following it away from the river until he came to the corner. He thought of continuing on along the wall, but he knew if he kept following the perimeter he would end up where he had begun, so he climbed over to the other side. There he found a dirt path that crossed a clearing. When he came to the other side of the clearing, he kept going into the trees. At first he stumbled over roots and slipped in the mud. He fell several times, once hitting his knee on a rock, but after a while his eyes adjusted to the dark and he found that he could discern the individual leaves on trees and see the roots on the ground below. He continued walking, weaving around the trees with no particular direction, sometimes circling back to where he had been before so that he felt, when at dawn he lay down on the ground to sleep, as if he were home.

*

The assistant left before dawn to go back on the river. For the next week he asked every passenger that got on the *lancha* whether they had seen or heard of the foreigner, but no one had. Finally, the driver put an end to his inquiries. "People are complaining," he said, though the assistant was sure this was not true, that the driver was just tired of feeling guilty for having abandoned him. "Forget about him, *pinche extranjero*," the driver said, so the assistant stopped talking about the foreigner.

Still, there were times when he felt the foreigner's presence just before he fell asleep at night or in the moments between sleep and wakefulness in the morning. Sometimes he sensed that he was peering in through the window when he made love to his wife, and he was sure that his wife felt it too, for on those nights she loved him as she had loved him in the beginning when they still talked about leaving Greytown and danced until dawn on Saturday nights and stayed in bed all day Sunday. Sometimes when he could not sleep, he snuck out into the night to look for him, and so it continued even after the Americans attacked and everyone fled to the jungle, even after the Americans had all gone home, even after they built a new town where they had taken refuge and let the jungle take over Greytown.

William awoke to a late-afternoon rain. He lay on the ground listening to the rain falling on the thick leaves. He opened his mouth and drank, letting the water in, letting it feed him. When the rain stopped and the sound of insects replaced the sound of water, he fell asleep again until hunger awakened him. He ate the last of the cashews, but still he was hungry, so he got up and began walking toward where he sensed the town must be. He came to the clearing but he realized that he did not want to leave the cover of the trees, so he turned back, walking even farther into the jungle than he had gone the night before, walking until he was tired enough to sleep, remembering what his father had told him about hunger: "At first sleep is an escape, but when you get close to death, sleep becomes more frightening than pain." But he was not afraid, so he slept, and when he woke up he was hungry and he imagined his father lying on the bunk in Birkenau, praying for food just to keep from falling asleep, for his father knew that prayers were futile, more futile even than death.

One night, just before liberation, when his father was trying to stay awake so that he would not sink into eternal sleep, he caught a rat as it was scurrying across his emaciated belly, squeezed it to death, and ate it raw, including the bones.

"What did it taste like?" William asked.

"Like life," his father said.

William got up without making a sound and crept to the cover of a tree. He crouched down and waited. Above him the monkeys were skirmishing, and the constant din of insects was like a buzzing in his head, and the mosquitoes would not leave him be, and his stomach was on fire with emptiness, but he waited, and sweat poured down his face, stinging his eyes, but he did not move. He waited until he could no longer feel his feet or legs, until the monkeys went to bed, until he was sure he would give in to sleep, but then he heard it, a rustling in the trees. It emerged from the shadows, stopped for a moment to sniff the ground. William held his breath. The jaguar came closer, still unaware of his presence. Then it froze—its eyes, a bright gold, held his gaze. He felt the muscles in his calves and thighs tighten like a bow, and it was so quiet he could hear the blood running through his veins like the river running toward the rapids, getting faster as it approached the fall.

# *Acknowledgments*

This book has a long history that begins with the stories my grandparents and mother told me about their years as refugees, first in Panama and then in Bolivia. These stories inspired not only my writing but my life: from a very young age I learned that what might seem on the surface a foreign, incomprehensible world can be where we find safety and, even, for a moment, peace. So thank you to my family for their stories and to Bolivia for providing refuge when no other country would.

When I was teaching at City Arts and Tech High School in San Francisco, my colleagues Suzanne Motley, Ana Sanz Levia, Tom Skjervheim, and I organized a trip with students to Nicaragua. There I found a country of storytellers, where history is very much part of the present, a place where middle-aged men gone soft in the belly lift up their shirts to show you their battle wounds and you can meet a Soviet-trained pilot cum taxi driver who lived through three cold Bulgarian winters. For this experience, thank you, Suzanne, Ana, Tom, and all the students who traveled with us. A special acknowledgment goes to Suzanne Motley for returning with me to Nicaragua in 2015 to explore the Río San Juan. Without that trip, this book would not exist.

Thank you, again and always, to the wonderful Counterpoint Press, to Dan Smetanka, for his vision, his sense of humor, and brilliant editing, to Dan López, Lena Moses-Schmidt, Wah-Ming Chang, Katie Boland, Megan Fishmann, Jennifer Kovitz, Miyako Singer, and Hope Levy. Thank you, of course, to my agent, Esmond Harmsworth, who helped me get this book into shape and who was the first of the "gate-keepers" to believe in my writing.

I would also like to thank my sister Catherine Raeff for reading this book in its early stages, for her encouragement, and for remembering with me the stories and experiences of our childhood.

I would never have written this book, never have written even one line without my muse, my fellow-traipser-around-the-world, Lori Ostlund, my wife. And finally, thank you to Juztice, who has brought a new kind of love into our lives.

**ANNE RAEFF**'s short story collection, *The Jungle Around Us,* won the 2015 Flannery O'Connor Award for Short Fiction, was a finalist for the California Book Award, and was named one of the 100 Best Books of 2016 by the *San Francisco Chronicle.* Her novel *Winter Kept Us Warm* was awarded the California Book Award's Silver Medal in Fiction, was a finalist for the Simpson Literary Prize, and was a finalist for the Northern California Book Award. Her stories and essays have appeared in *New England Review, ZYZZYVA,* and *Guernica,* among other places. She is a proud high school teacher and lives in San Francisco. Find out more at anneraeff.com.